# TANGLE OF THORNES

Eva Thorne Book One

Lorel Clayton

Tangle of Thornes/ Lorel Clayton. — 2019 Ed.
ISBN 978-0-9942290-9-0

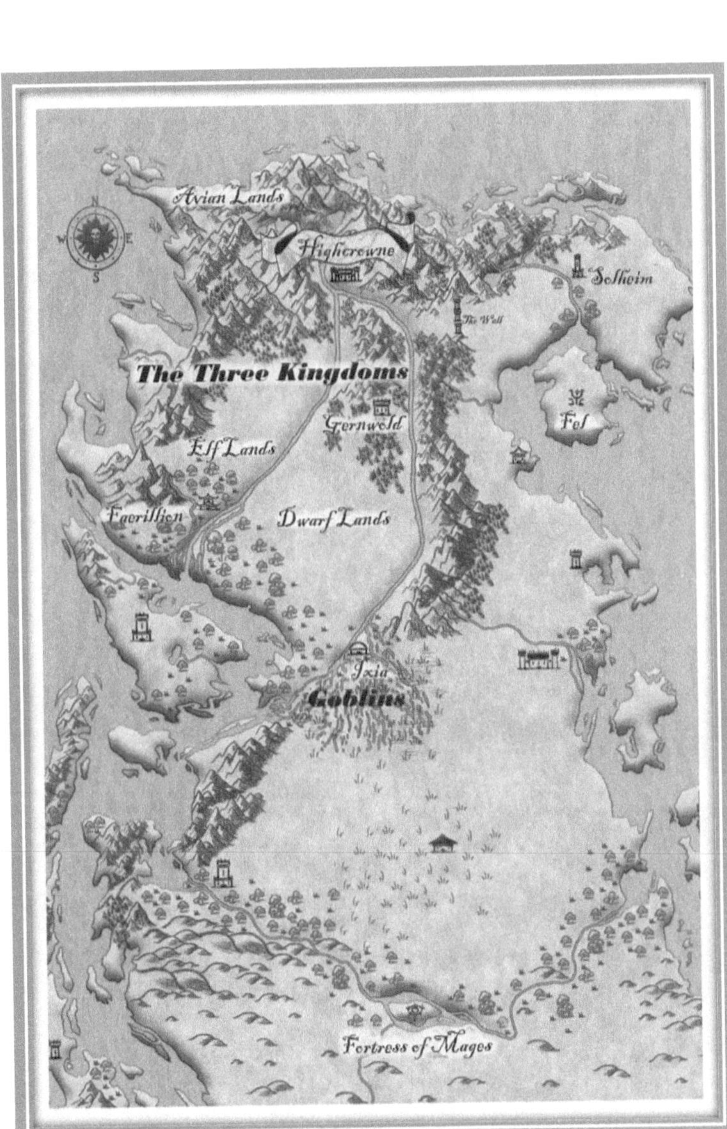

Avian Lands
Highcrowne
Solheim
The Well
The Three Kingdoms
Gernwold
Fel
Elf Lands
Faerillion
Dwarf Lands
Ixia
Goblins
Fortress of Mages
N
S
E
W

*ACKNOWLEDGEMENTS*

*Thank you, Glen Cook, for Garret PI. We spent many rainy days (and sunny ones too) curled up together and reading aloud as we enjoyed his surly adventures, wondering what the Dead Man was, and dying to visit the Cantard. Eva Thorne and Highcrowne are our homage—with a twist. Who cares if hardly anyone else loves hard-boiled detective novels set in a pseudo-fantasy world? We do! So, let's have some fun...*

# 1   Highcrowne Noir

I've read a few of those hard-boiled detective novels. You know, *The Maltese Griffin, Murder on the Troll Road* ... the classics. None of them ever mentioned the smell. Mister Hylar, my last hope, smelled like old sweat mixed with fermented stomach contents, some of which stained his shirt collar. City elves were like their country cousins, filthy.

The detective lounged at his desk, cigar in his mouth, glass of whisky at his elbow. When he took a swig from the bottle, the caramel alcohol scent swirled with the cloud of cheap cologne he wore, and I thought I might pass out.

I pinched my nose shut and tried to bat my eyelashes like every femme fatale should. The effect was ruined by the hand clamped over my nose and how green I was turning. I wasn't a good femme fatale. That's another thing those detective stories never told you—how tough it was to be the dame with a problem.

"I'm in trouble," I said nasally.

Mr. Hylar turned his full attention to the near empty glass, seeming to wonder if he should bother with the sip remaining. He shrugged and chugged it back, decision made.

"Look." I tried again. "My brother died and left me a fortune." All my life I'd been told to keep Thorne troubles in the family, not to show weakness. Yet, here I was asking for help and hating it.

"A fortune? How is that bad? Other than your brother being deceased of course. Though, with you people, it might not be." The detective curled his lip. I was accustomed to the expression and the way he said, 'you people'. He meant Solhans, like me. We were a whole different category of human, one other races tended to hate. Not without good reason.

I needed the elf, so I closed my nose tighter and went on. "Viktor was attacked in an alley ... his heart cut out."

He perked up with professional interest. "Odd for a robbery."

"Nothing stolen, not even his jeweled dagger. Where did Viktor get one anyway? My brother always had the same vow of poverty as me."

"You're broke?" The detective sat up, ready to see me out.

"Not anymore. Remember?"

He slouched back in his chair and eyed me head to toe, not like he was appraising a client but more like he was looking to buy property. "Right. I'm listening. What's your name, gorgeous?"

"Eva Thorne."

"Thorne." He stood all the way up this time, crossed the room and held open the door. "Sorry."

Was he kicking me out? "My brother was murdered. People are saying it was me, but I loved him. I need to find his killer. You are a private investigator?"

"Private means I choose my clients. I don't choose you or your troubles."

I wanted to smash that cigar into his face, but I kept my anger in check. "What should I do then?"

"Talk to the City Guard." He took my arm.

I pulled away, not about to let him push me around. "Why won't you help me?"

"I'm not the first person you came to."

I should have known. These jerks were all in the same business and talked to one another. "The other guy took off with my money. He never got back to me."

"Your last detective, Oberon, is dead, murdered, and he was better than me. Whoever killed your brother is making sure no one finds out. I advise you to go home, have a good cry, and be done with it.

Your brother isn't coming back, assuming he was cremated. He was, I hope?"

"Of course." I was off balance from hearing the dwarf I'd hired was dead, Gypsum's brother-in-law. She would be upset when she found out.

"Best if we all get on with our lives." The detective took advantage of my daze to usher me to the exit.

I was stunned. Other people were dying? What had Viktor been into? The elf nudged me the last few inches out the door. I wobbled on unfamiliar heels and then there was nothing but unvarnished wood in my face. The lock clicked.

The shock wore off along with any desire to keep up the pretense I was a lady. I was mad. I kicked off the heels, tore the large, decorative pin out of my hair, and stabbed it right into the 'P' of 'Stanley Hylar Private Detective' painted on the door. It *thunked* like a throwing knife hitting its target.

"If you're going to sit around all day and do nothing, Stanley, you might as well take a bath," I screamed, making sure he heard me. I turned on my bare toes and fumed down the hall and all the way out to the street.

Talk to a guard? Some advice. Guards were mostly elves and dwarves, paid by the Three Crowns to police the Central City, which meant no profit, no incentive to help those of us who lived in the Outskirts. What I needed was a human guard, which was impossible.... I paused, remembering something: Karolyne's cousin.

That would be my next stop after I grabbed a pair of decent shoes.

There was dirty snow and ice in the cracks of the cobbles. Solhans loved the cold, but we didn't like going around barefoot in it. I put the atrocious high heels I'd pinched from Ilsa back on and headed for home, trying not to break an ankle. My sister bragged about the shoes' no slip enchantment, but it didn't guarantee I wouldn't fall off them.

It was early morning, the district busy with elves going to market, human servants trailing, arms laden with baskets of produce or bolts of cloth. Their smiles were as fake as Stanley the detective. All he could detect was the bottom of a bottle. Why had I come here?

Everyone stared as I cursed my way across the treacherously uneven cobbles. I wasn't a servant, dressed as I was, but I certainly didn't look like any of them. Ilsa could have glided through the crowd, charming her way into any company. I imagined her mocking laugh as she chided me, saying something like, 'Sugar, don't even try. You're not in their class.'

"Eva?"

The wall I'd run into was talking. I looked up at a guileless expression and recognized the slab of muscle, Gormless, a thug from the neighborhood. Why had he followed me here?

"Please move. I'm in no mood." I was always courteous to Gormless. I like to think it's because I have a heart—who could be angry with someone so simple—but, really, it was my survival instinct.

Someone stepped up behind me. I hadn't heard him coming. That would be Grim, Gormless' smaller, more slithery companion. He was the unlucky one. I didn't like having him at my back. I didn't like having Gormless at my front either. If only I could get these shoes to work, I might escape sideways.

"We worried you was Ilsa, what with the dress and all. You look just like her," Grim said.

"Don't ever say that!"

"You's twins," he reminded me.

"Well, I'm Eva. Now, what do you want?"

"Boss wants to see you."

I rolled my eyes. "Duane? He's not my boss."

"Don't call him that. He don't like it." Grim shook his head.

"I'll call him whatever I damn well want. Get out of my way." There was no pushing past Gormless, so I mowed over the little one.

I shouldn't have touched him, because his notorious bad luck rubbed off on me, and I fell on the hard stones. My palms were scraped, arms twanging, but I'd saved my chin. Grim was less fortunate. He landed on a pitchfork. Where did that come from? One tine was poking into a buttock, and he spit blood.

"I 'it my 'ongue!"

"He bit his tongue," I translated.

"Oh no." Gormless helped his friend to stand, pulled out the short pitchfork—it was the size of a trowel, really—and flung it behind him.

Miraculously, it landed back on the table in the blacksmith's stall from which it had fallen. That's where Grim's luck went: Gormless sucked it all up. I didn't know which of them I was more nervous being around.

My shoes were standing where I'd been. Definitely non-slip. Gormless lifted me up and set me back in them, easy as dressing a doll for him.

"You's gotta be more careful." He was genuinely concerned for me. "I'll helps you walk."

Meaty hands clamped over my shoulders, guiding me and lifting me into the air every few feet. Grim cursed eloquently, though it was the kind of eloquence the elven ladies weren't accustomed to, judging by their aghast expressions, and limped along behind us.

Looked like I was going to see Duane.

I dreaded this meeting for three reasons. First, while he and my brother had been best friends their entire lives, he and I ... 'clashed' would be the polite way of putting it. I was seldom polite, so I called it 'hating his guts'. Second, Viktor's will gave Duane guardianship of my five-year-old nephew. My uncle was contesting it, as the boy was his only remaining male heir. I didn't care to choose sides, not when Duane and Ulric were equally evil.

Although, Ilsa could teach them both a thing or two. I shuddered. Best not to think the Dark One's name. My twin was extra grouchy these days after being excluded from Viktor's estate. She didn't like all this 'male heir' talk either. With Viktor gone, my sister assumed she would inherit Uncle Ulric's nefarious enterprises. I wanted no part of them.

Of course, with no alternative prospects, I was living in a dingy room above the tavern where I worked. Cleaning tables at Karolyne's wasn't enough to pay for both her over-priced food and supposed friend's rates. After six months, I'd squandered all my savings on rent.

Viktor's will could save me, which is why some people believed Ilsa's stories about me having him killed. I'd started moving into Viktor's old house, just to watch out for Nanny, but none of it sat well with me. I was stupid that way. I knew from being a member of one of the oldest and richest Solhan clans, there was a long trail of blood behind any fortune. I tried to avoid money, and in return it had avoided me—until now.

Viktor had never accepted family money either. He'd had a legitimate job as a bookseller. Yet, somehow, he managed to leave me a house in the expensive section the neighborhood and enough silver coins to keep me footloose and fancy-free for a year. Not to mention the pile of gems he bequeathed to Little Viktor's new guardian, and the fund held in the

Highcrowne bank for when his son came of age. My brother's gains were ill-gotten; they had to be.

By the time I and my unwanted escorts passed through the Market Gate and into the Outskirts, I allowed myself to consider the third reason I didn't want to see Duane. He may have been the one who killed Viktor.

I didn't know whether to be sick or fall back on my old favorite, furious.

Even when Duane was nothing but a grimy street urchin, he had been shrewd. He knew who Uncle was and befriended his heir, a real coup. The urchin grew up to be a thug and killer. Now he ran a gang and extorted protection money from the local businesses, including my friend's tavern.

The money, the violent end.... Viktor had been pulled into Duane's world, and he died because of it. All I needed was proof.

More than convincing everyone else, I needed to know what happened. I missed Viktor. No one else could make me smile.

Gormless set me down in an ironworks, one of many fronts for Duane's real business.

Such places never existed in the Three Kingdoms before the tide of human refugees came to escape the Dead God's war. Why melt metal with fire when it was so much easier to craft swords from magic?

Now there were whole nations where those with knowledge of magic had been obliterated on the battlefield, leaving behind the untalented. Human ingenuity found other ways. Less efficient and stupid ways with no place in a civilized society, like Highcrowne, but I could see how they might be useful when you had no other choice.

The heat was suffocating. Sweaty workers manned contraptions with long, mechanized arms and poured molten iron from smelting pots into molds for ingots, which would be used to make more implements like the one that had skewered Grim. Ah, the circle of life.

I recognized a diminutive form in the distance wearing soot-smeared overalls. Plaits of blonde hair bounced up and down as Bell shouted over the boom of automated bellows and the clanking of mechanoids. When one started jittering about, she donned her goggles, scrambled up its side, and ripped out some hoses to make it stop.

Bell was Duane's most intelligent flunky. She operated the ironworks, and they wouldn't have a legitimate business to hide behind if it weren't for her. I never understood why she worked for him when she.... Okay, there weren't a lot of options for human women in Highcrowne.

Elves and dwarfs could join the Guard, own land, even rule. One of the Crowns, the Avian, was a female, though it was difficult to tell with birds. But human society was ruled by men—you could tell by looking at the state of it. Duane was one of those who added to the mess.

He perched agilely on a high platform, watching me with jade eyes. Black hair hung halfway to his shoulders, framing a strong jaw. He had presence, I could say that about him.

I didn't know how he withstood this place with the heat and noise, but it was his preferred office. His ancestors came from the shores of the Western Sea. It must have been sweltering there, because his bronze skin was dry. Gormless, Grim, and I were all sweating as profusely as the iron workers.

"Since I'm here, I can tell you to your face I don't want to see you, Duane." I emphasized his real name, hoping to irritate him as much as he irritated me.

Message delivered, I twisted around, trying to spot the door. Gormless took up most of the space. A ladder leaned above the only direct route to the exit. Damn, those things were hazardous. Walking beneath one was tempting fate. People told me I was superstitious, angry too, but I usually told them to go to hell.

"You're searching for his murderer. Stop it." Duane's voice was as smooth and dangerous as the liquid iron sizzling through the air.

Here it was—the intimidation. Would he kill me too? Had he killed Viktor? After fifteen years of friendship, was Duane cold enough to have butchered him over money or some childish street gang nonsense?

My voice was steady. "No."

"Eva, stay out of it. I know who's responsible, and I'll take care of it."

"Is the murderer in this room? Someone he trusted? Is that why he never drew his weapon?" I was too angry to shout, but my voice dripped venom.

"You think it was me?" Wide eyes faked innocence.

"Are you saying it wasn't? It wasn't you who got him gems and a big house? I bet you ripped it all away for some stupid reason, some disrespect he might have shown, something I would never understand."

"Viktor was my friend. I'm going to get the bastards who did it." Duane jumped down from the platform and landed as graceful as a cat, or in his case, a cat burglar. He brushed past me and brazenly walked beneath the ladder.

I grabbed his shoulder, and he spun around, anger making his eyes gleam. He said, "How can you think...?"

"Maybe you're a great actor, maybe you're not. Even if you didn't kill Viktor, or have him killed, you're the reason he's dead."

Duane let black hair hide his features. "You're right." He started walking again, Grim and Gormless falling into step behind him.

I stood there. It was the first time he'd ever told me I was right about anything. My chest tightened, and it was hard to breathe in the searing air.

I realized I was under the ladder. "Oh, crap."

I ran after Duane and his goons. "If you know who did it, I want to be there."

"I told you to keep out of it," he repeated.

"Tell me all you want, but I do what I like."

"You can never leave anything alone. This is something you don't want to see."

"What are you going to do?"

He didn't answer.

"Who was it?" Perhaps it was my black, Solhan heart talking, like the one that beat in Ilsa's chest, but I wanted to see Viktor's killer suffer. I fought the feeling, and my nature, as I'd done all my life.

Solhans weren't called the Dark Race because of color—we were pale as death—it was because we had a reputation for cruelty. Our people were the ones who summoned the Dead God, the reason Solheim fell and half the world had been conquered. It all happened while I was a child, so I was innocent. Still, malice was in the blood.

Duane didn't answer me. Instead, he set a brutal pace, hoping I'd fall behind. Highcrowne was built on a crag of rock. The inner city was tiered and connected by steep, switch-backed roads. The Outskirts weren't as bad, having grown across the lower foothills like a cancer, but the streets were still hard on the calves. I gritted my teeth, fighting to stay balanced, and kept moving so my toes wouldn't freeze.

We left the neighborhood, Duane's neighborhood. I knew enough about street politics to know it meant trouble.

"Who did Viktor know all the way over here?" I asked.

"Killian's crew."

"What? Why would he mess with them?" I clued in. "You sent him."

"No. I didn't own him, and I didn't run his life. Vikky did what he wanted. He was working with someone, but when I learned he had business here, I asked him to feel the place out."

"You're expanding." I knew it. I knew he had gotten my brother killed.

I wished I had my usual boots on, and my hairpin back, then I'd kick Duane to the ground and shove the needle in his eye. He had put Viktor in the middle of a brewing gang war.

I looked around nervously. There were only four of us. Gormless was as big as two people, but Grim's diminutive form evened things out. Duane had never been stupid, but here he was challenging another gang on their turf, and he had no backup. I had no backup.

## 2  THE WRONG CROWD

"Wait a minute." I squeezed my way between Gormless and his boss. "Are you sure you should be here? Won't Fink, Bell and the rest of your people feel left out?"

His stony gaze hit me, and I realized this was my fault. My accusation had set him off.

"You don't have to get yourself killed to convince me you're telling the truth," I said.

"I've decided to stop second guessing and act. It has nothing to do with you."

"Second guessing? You mean it might not have been Killian?"

"It had to be. By the time I'm done with him, I'll know for sure, and I'll find out what he did with the heart."

Some people believed souls were trapped in flesh, which was why corpses strived to reach the Dead God's side. Cremation was the only way to release them. Had Viktor's soul been stolen along with his heart?

We were deep in the Slave Quarter now. I didn't know why it was called that, because slaves lived everywhere. Most worked fields in the valleys of the Three Kingdoms, or manned barges trading up and down the river.

They were so dim-witted it made Gormless look like an Avian sage. It wasn't their fault. They were branded with magic to smother their will. Slaves weren't useful for any work requiring thought. Still, if you wanted one, this was where you came to buy.

I turned my gaze away from the cages crammed with people and the stage where 'merchandise' was beautifully presented in silks and fine linens. Duane headed right for it.

There was a small group of shoppers, and we merged with them. He whispered something to Grim, who grabbed Gormless, and our only protection vanished into an alley beside the slave pens.

"What are you doing?" I hissed.

A lady glared at me. I glared back. Like most elves, she appeared beautiful, but it was all glamour. I caught sight of her shadow and saw it was twice as wide as mine. Her unwashed odor was poorly masked by cloying floral perfume. City elves were fake. The loveliest creature didn't look so great with an extra forty pounds, and they compensated for their hedonism with expensive charms and natural glamours.

"If you're going to be here," Duane said, "blend in."

"That's impossible." Three-quarters of the crowd was elves.

I'd never known an Avian or Dwarf to buy and sell people like property. They didn't think that way. But elves? This was their favorite type of human—servile. They say a poor elf owns only one slave.

Sadly, it wasn't difficult to go unnoticed, once I stopped glaring at everyone, because humans made up the remainder of the buyers. We were worse, I thought. We did this to our own kind. Hell, we probably gave elves the idea in the first place.

The four-inch heels I wore made me two inches taller than Duane and a foot taller than most of the people around me. Well, maybe not that easy to blend in. For once, I wished Gormless was here. I could hide behind him and use him as a shield in case Killian's gang attacked.

"You look nice," Duane said.

I started. He was checking out my stocking-clad legs, black dress, and white fur jacket. Some rich girls had formed a club and went around badgering people about wearing furs, saying it was wrong. What were you supposed to wear? It was winter.

"I'm not nice," I told him.

"I know. Appearances are deceiving. Why you all dolled up? You think you need to look like that to talk to an elf detective?"

"I hate it when you spy on me. You call me nosy, but you know everybody's business. You send your cockroach friends scurrying around, fetching me whenever you want to argue. You act like this whole city is your domain, like the Elf King, but I'm not a slave with a brand on my arm."

Being here was stupid and dangerous, and the company was worse. I wanted to leave, but it would mean obeying Duane, who had wanted to exclude me from the start. If he was going to stay here and be stupid, I'd prove I could be equally dumb.

"If you're not going to tell me what you're doing, then don't tell me anything."

He went quiet, staring at the alley where his henchmen had vanished.

"Stay here." He couldn't speak without it sounding like an order.

My stubborn reflex took over and I followed. We weaved through the crowd, which murmured as a new slave was directed to the block. He was the same race as Duane and muscled, but the similarities ended there. The slave had a faraway gaze and meekly stood where the slaver told him to. My glare came back when I recognized the slaver, Randall Kingsman, a Solhan and an old business partner of my uncle's.

Surrounded by stinking elves, in a slave market in Killian's territory, with Duane and Randall? A deep-down grime settled in my every pore.

I wasn't the only person to have recognized someone. Duane brushed by Killian, who stood to the side of the stage. The slave market was Killian's cash cow. He watched the proceedings with avarice, but he did a double take when he saw his rival.

"Hey!"

Duane took off, headed for the alley. Oh no, we were running. I didn't have time to remove the shoes, so I tottered along and tried to keep up. Killian was almost beside me, but like a hungry predator, he was focused on his real quarry.

Two of Killian's people caught sight of the chase and joined in. Not good, since one was headed for me. I reached the alley. It took a moment for my eyes to adjust to the gloom. Heavy breathing a few steps behind me, then one of the pursuers pinned my arms to my side. I was caught.

Killian barreled after Duane, but Grim stepped out of a recessed doorway and whacked the gang leader in the stomach with a small club. He doubled over, and Grim thumped him again on the back of the neck. Duane turned around, pulled a dagger and strode toward me.

"I'll kill her!" the one holding me said. He clamped one hand around my throat and squeezed.

Enough of this. I elbowed my captor, stomped on his instep and then whipped my head back to crush his nose. There was a satisfying crunch, and he screamed. Duane was fast. He pulled the guy away from me and buried the knife beneath his rib cage. I put a hand to my mouth, stifling a yelp. This was serious. What was I doing here?

The straggler tore into the alley, a metal bar raised in one hand and ready to strike. A brick crashed squarely on his head, and he crumpled like a broken toy. Gormless smiled from a second story window. He stepped back and, a moment later, came through one of the lower doors, excited to see what he'd done. He gave Killian's thug an inquisitive kick, and the man groaned.

I noted the pool of blood spreading around Ilsa's shoes. Duane wiped his blade on the dead man's shirt and glanced up at me, no trace of guilt in his eyes.

Highcrowne was the most civilized place in the world, but we were in the Outskirts. Here, generations of refugees had established their own city in the shadow of the Three Crowns. We had a crude police force, paid by the merchants to keep order, but they were corrupt and useless. It was people like Uncle Ulric, Killian, and Duane who actually ruled. He could get away with murder, and he knew it.

Still, if enough people died, like in a gang war, the Guard would get involved. Humans were the city's workforce, its servants and slaves; too much chaos would not be tolerated. How far was Duane going to take this?

Grim found a frayed hunk of rope and trussed up Killian.

Duane turned his back on me and went over to examine his prize. "Just the person I want to talk to."

I thought I gave good glare, but Killian could carve stone with his dark eyes. "Go to the Dead God! What do you want in my territory, Adder?"

Was that what Duane called himself these days? It would have been funny, if I weren't standing in blood.

"Territory is one of the things I'm here to talk about. Your ranks are thinning." Duane pointed out the dead man. "I don't think you can handle this place. Fortunately, I'm willing to help out."

Killian spit. "You're overreaching, and your hand is going to get chopped off."

"Not by you. Good idea, though." He grabbed Killian's bound hands, wrenched a thumb up, and rested his dagger against the exposed webbing.

"Get off me. You mess with me and you'll have both my crew and Jessup's to deal with!" Killian bucked and tried to pull away. Gormless locked one hand on the captive and all struggle ceased.

"You think I can be reasoned with? Haven't you heard? I recently lost a friend of mine." Duane cut into the thumb, and Grim held Killian's jaw closed to smother his cry.

I was transfixed. This was one of those situations where my brain was telling me to get out of there or do something to stop this insanity, but I couldn't move. My heart ached, ached for Viktor and ached to hear whether this was the man I could blame for his death.

No one came to investigate. Grim gagged Killian during the interrogation, removing the rag only long enough to hear answers to Duane's questions. Even so, there were enough stray shouts and pleading sobs to have attracted someone's attention. People in the Slave Quarter must have learned not to be curious.

By the end, Killian wasn't holding anything back. He tripped over his own tongue trying to answer fast enough. He told Duane everything about his operation and his allies', but he swore he had nothing to do with Viktor. The state he was in—he wasn't lying. Duane put him out of his misery.

Gormless had the remaining thug, who was still unconscious from being brained, slung over one shoulder. "What I do with this one, boss?"

"Leave him. All Killian's men get the option of working for me."

"What about the other one you murdered?"

Duane flinched at the scorn in my voice. "He threatened to kill you, and you're upset he's dead?"

"Not upset, more like disgusted." I wanted to lay all the blame on Duane, but I was disgusted with myself as well. Had wearing Ilsa's clothes turned me as pragmatic as her? "They were innocent."

"Only of this. If Killian didn't take Viktor's heart, then who did?"

"You don't care. This was all an excuse for your takeover."

"No. I want vengeance, Eva. For both of us."

"Leave me out of this from now on." I would not allow myself to slide this far into the gray again. Gray? I was kidding myself. Murder and torture made this black, very black. This is what being around Duane did to you. This was how Viktor got mixed up in things he shouldn't have.

I was going to the Guard.

I started walking, planning never to look back, but a question niggled at me. I stopped where the alley opened on the square, midday light before me, shadows at my back. "You said Viktor had his own business in the Slave Quarter. Did your cockroaches tell you what he was doing?"

Duane frowned. "Freeing slaves."

Plenty of people wouldn't like that. I eyed Randall and other slavers in the distance. Instead of making progress, my list of suspects was growing. I'd keep my suspicions to myself for now. Nobody else deserved Duane's baleful attention.

I stumbled into the open, my legs rubbery. I had already witnessed so much; my gaze did not shy from the cages when I passed them.

The merchandise smiled vacantly, and I envied their contentment, even knowing it was due to magic. Did some deeply buried part of them understand what was happening?

Randall pawed an attractive slave girl a few years younger than me. I knew how he liked them young. She was shiny as black shoe polish, made for a sunnier land than this. It was cruel to bring her here, where winter never ended. Randall combed her hair, preparing her for the evening sale. I shivered, remembering his fingers reaching for my hair when I was nine. I couldn't stand to watch any more.

My head swam. I clutched metal bars to steady myself. Something soft and leathery moved beneath my fingers, and I snatched them back. The place where my hand had been shimmered, revealing a small creature with hairless, ashen skin and eyes like ripe cherries. A bogle.

*Ick!* I wiped my palm on my dress, afraid of disease. The pests were everywhere, camouflaged, and impossible to eradicate. It snickered and scampered away.

I stood unevenly, a heel broken off. Great. I snapped off the other one, so the shoes matched. I must have exuded a miasma of anger, because no one disturbed me as I made my way back to the neighborhood.

The City Guard should have been my first stop. My untrusting nature made me suspect corruption everywhere, but they were the good guys. I really needed that right now. Still, I could improve my chances of being heard if I spoke to Karolyne's cousin.

I trudged into the restaurant where I worked most of the week. I was a customer today, so I took a seat and leaned back with a sigh.

Karolyne was tending the tables herself. With her deep red hair and stylish clothes, not to mention perfect deportment, she looked like she should have been surrounded by servants rather than doing the serving. She came over as soon as she saw me. "Were you sat on by a grall or something? You okay?"

"I will be, once I get a kick in the gut. Whisky, please." It worked for Stanley the detective.

"Not before dusk."

"What? Since when?" I had only taken a few days off for Viktor's funeral. Left to her own devices, Karolyne tended to get strange notions. I should have been here to reason with her.

"It brought in the wrong sort. I'm trying for a better clientele."

I shook my head. "*Clientele?* Sounds like an elf word."

"And I'm catering to the elf crowd." She pointed to a new placard mounted on the wall: *Authentic human food available.*

"There's inauthentic human food?"

Karolyne fidgeted with energy, and I practically saw her thoughts buzzing with calculations.

"Gypsum told me about this new fad in the Central City—Southern food cooked by human servants. Plus, lots of young elves come to the Outskirts these days looking for some excitement. I thought I'd seize the opportunity. Elves have all the money."

"Except what my uncle, or Duane, has stolen. Well, what do you serve in the day then?"

"Food."

"No, I need a drink."

"Try some kaffe."

"What is it?"

"Southern. I'll get you a stein. On the house."

On the house? My old school chum never gave anybody anything. Since her parents went broke, thanks to bad caravan investments and gambling, she was stingy, keeping every last silver hidden. While the cut of her clothes was stylish, it was three seasons ago style, and her favorite shawl was moth eaten. She wouldn't replace anything that didn't disintegrate first. If the kaffe was free, it must be crap. But I was willing to drink sword polish right about then.

She came back with a steaming stein.

"It's hot?" I was dubious.

"Yep, perfect for winter, which is about all we have here. Try it."

I took a drink and a bitter taste sucked the moisture from my tongue. "Blaahhh." I was right; it was awful. Yet ... there was something, a kick. "It needs sweetener."

"How much?"

"Eight sugar ants."

"Eight!" She would subtract the cost from my next pay I was sure.

After I sweetened the drink with a few popped ants—disgusting but better than the green cane they used in the South—I downed the whole cup. Wow. Now I understood why she was giving out free samples. It was addictive. I paid for the second one, and Karolyne grinned. She had a winner.

Feeling better, I said, "I wanted to ask you about your cousin."

"Which one?"

"The one trying to join the Guard. Did they let him in?"

"Oh yes. Conrad. I already told Gypsum. It's wonderful! They say he's an example for his entire species. His dwarven captain said if he maintains his current level of performance, he'll not only be the first human guard but the first lieutenant. An officer. Things are looking up, opportunities everywhere. We just have to keep our eyes open."

I didn't want to dampen her enthusiasm, but a token guard posting and an interest in human food did not mean equal rights was on the horizon. Solhans had further to go.

I forced a smile. "Great."

A pewter mug clanged off the stone wall. "Kek!" A goblin retched at a corner table, a mercenary or caravan guard judging from his leathers and the sheath on his hip. Not everyone liked the kaffe.

"You trying to kill me?" The goblin accused Karolyne.

His friend made a phlegmy hacking sound that was supposed to be a laugh. It was best when goblins didn't smile. They were all teeth: just two beady eyes, a pug nose, and a freakishly huge mouth brimming with ivory needles. Why bother with a restaurant? They ate their enemies.

Karolyne went over and spoke to them. After a few heated words, she handed them a bottle of fermented milk and blood from the back and asked them to leave. They knocked over the table before obliging her.

When she had righted things and calmed her other customers, she came back to me. "See what I mean? Wrong crowd."

"Can I talk to Conrad? Where do I find him?"

Karolyne gave me his home address. I thanked her, freshened up in the bathroom upstairs, still technically mine until I moved out the few boxes of things I owned, and started for the city.

I had been ready to sleep the rest of the day away earlier, but the kaffe invigorated me. Some of Karolyne's optimism had transferred as well. Perhaps her cousin could help?

# 3  Knuts

I found Conrad's boarding house in the Goldsmith's Quarter, north of Market Square, one tier up, and as deep into Highcrowne as our kind was allowed. He really must be the new poster boy for humanity. It was primarily a dwarven neighborhood, children running around, the corner pub crowded at noon.

The town clock chimed. It was louder the closer you were to the inner city. Purportedly, it was made of pure gold, crafted and fueled by magic of course, and mounted on the highest tower of the palace, but few had ever seen it.

I had to wait minutes before an elderly man answered the door. He barely reached my navel yet managed to look down at me.

"Quit that racket!"

I had been knocking continuously, waiting for someone to respond.

"I'm trying to find Conrad Faulconbridge."

"He's not here!"

"Do you know where he is?"

"I'm not his mamma!"

I could only take so much abrasiveness before my thin veneer of civility got stripped away. "What would your mamma say if she caught you being so rude to a lady?"

I didn't actually consider myself a lady, despite having been to finishing school. I only wore a dress when I needed to show off my legs or attend a funeral. I couldn't pour tea worth a damn either. Still, I knew how much dwarves respected their mothers.

"I'm," his face turned sour, "sorry."

"Apology accepted. Now...?"

"He's at work! Sorry. He mentioned the Red Precinct."

"Thank y—" He slammed the door before I finished. I bristled, but, if I couldn't take it, I shouldn't dish it out.

Red Precinct was the other side of the city. I wished I had a horse. I could come back tomorrow, but I had a fire burning in my belly and not just from Karolyne's drink. I needed to see this through, needed answers, and I couldn't get them sitting on my behind.

Highcrowne was like a layer cake with a mountain at its center, not the most scrumptious filling, but that's as far as I wanted to take that analogy anyway. The fat, bottom piece held everything important to most people: pubs, markets, craftsmen, mills, foundries, steamworks, wetworks, dryworks ... the works. The road penetrated the outer wall in one well-guarded place and then spiraled around to the upper levels, where less useful things could be found. Like elf detectives and dwarven Guardhouses. Staircases connected the different levels at random points.

The inner city, the center, where the Three Crowns and nobility dwelt, was a fortress made of marble and stone. The walls were twenty feet high, most of it cut into the mountain, with no entrance, except through heavily guarded gates. I smiled at the soldiers, but they didn't smile back.

It would be a terrific short cut, going through the middle, but I decided against sending a message to Gypsum. She would happily give me an escort, but I had hired her brother-in-law and gotten him killed. I felt guilty and wanted to put off sharing the bad news. I'd have to take the long way around. The newer, flatter version of Ilsa's shoes would survive the trip, so I got walking.

It was a shorter distance than if I'd started from the bottom layer of the cake. I still wanted to drop the analogy, but it was stuck in my head, and I don't let go of things easily.

The Outskirts didn't qualify as a part of the dessert, not even a pretty doily around the edge, and was more like a ramshackle pile of garbage. So, picture Highcrowne like a layer cake with a mountain in the center resting on a pile of garbage. And everyone would rather be on the prettily frosted top where the Avians and The Crowns lived than down in the muck, but you had to start somewhere.

I was warm and breathing hard when I set foot in the Red Precinct. The dyers' vats stunk up the place, red being the most popular color.

I figured Conrad would be guarding the main square, where dripping cloths hung to catch the feeble warmth of the sun. I saw dozens of human workers, but they were slaves.

This was an elven-owned area. It took ten slaves to operate every mechanoid that hefted cloth from vat to vat or churned the liquid to keep the rare dyes in suspension. More inefficient human technology spreading like the plague.

A glint of golden hair and white, lacquered armor caught my attention. Was that Conrad? I wove between the clotheslines, dodging splatters. As I drew near, I really started to heat up. I completely forgot my recent decision to swear off men. He gleamed.

"Hello," I said.

He was watching a group of traders gathered around a wagon but turned and smiled when I addressed him. "Hello, yourself."

Wow. He was the reason I was off balance this time. "Conrad?"

"How come you know my name and I don't know yours?"

"It's Eva. I'm a friend of Karolyne's."

"You're the Solhan?" There was no distaste in his tone when he called me a 'Solhan'. He was scoring very high on my test for perfection.

"Isn't it obvious?"

"I don't know why you've come looking for me, but I'm glad you did."

I stared at him for a moment before I remembered why I was there. "I need a guard."

"Trouble?" He instinctively put a hand on the hilt of his sword. I noticed the shield strapped to his back. He was ready to take on an army.

"Nothing immediate. It's my brother—he was murdered."

"I'm sorry. What can I do?"

"Find his killer."

"Tell me everything." He wiped off a seat for me, making use of a deep lintel in the window of the nearest building.

After hours of hiking around the city, it was a relief to sit. Conrad listened attentively to my sob story, his eyes regularly checking our surroundings. He was on duty and didn't let my legs distract him.

I explained about the inheritance, although I chose not to mention it was my sister spreading rumors of my guilt. I told him about Viktor, his kindness, how he was a good father … but I left out the part about freeing slaves. It was illegal and, as much as I wanted to trust Conrad, he was a guardsman.

When I finished, Conrad thought for a moment, absorbing it all. "Anything else?"

I remembered Duane murdering Killian and one of his henchmen right in front of me, but I bit down on my tongue. Perhaps I was afraid to reveal the neighborhood's business to the authorities, or maybe I did believe Duane had done it for Viktor. Either way, I couldn't betray him.

I shook my head. "That's it. Can you help?" I'd told him almost nothing useful.

"I'll report this to my sergeant, but I can't promise anything. I'm new, still learning the system, and no one owes me any favors."

My hopes sunk. Who was I kidding? This would be classified as 'a human problem' and forgotten.

Conrad must have seen the dejected look on my face and rested a hand on my shoulder. "I swear I will do everything I can. I put on this uniform because I believe the Outskirts needs the rule of law. Someday, we will all live as safe as the Central City."

He meant it. I sighed. Where had that come from? I hadn't sighed since seeing Tommy the stable boy working with his shirt off when I was thirteen. I was not a sigh-er. Then I blushed. Blushed!

"Thank you." I stood and took a few steps towards home.

"Eva, is it all right if I call on you? In case I have any more questions, I mean."

"I'd like that. I mean, yes of course, if you need to."

I floated away. Could it be all men weren't the same? Was there hope?

I ran into a robed merchant loading bolts of dyed cloth into a wagon. I recognized the keen brown eyes, crooked nose, and beardless chin. Ahsaed. Not my first disaster, but the latest. My burgeoning re-interest in men was quashed all over again. What were the chances of running into my ex right after meeting someone who might well be the ideal man? Was the universe trying to tell me something?

"Eva!" He put his arms around me, and I stiffened. "You've changed your mind!"

He didn't believe I was here to see him, did he? The arrogance. "Get your hands off me."

He obeyed immediately. He knew me well.

There was a time when I thought Ahsaed was as perfect as a man could get—only a few dozen things wrong with him—then I discovered he was married. A traveling merchant could have a woman in every town with none of us the wiser. He claimed it was an arranged marriage, and he didn't love her, but I'm not the type to be anyone's mistress. So, I broke up with him there and then. Oh, and I broke his nose.

"Are you well?" he asked carefully, like he was tip-toeing across a floor covered in snakes.

I folded my arms. "I think your nose is better this way."

He stepped back, putting more space between us. After a moment of heavy silence, he took a bolt of sky blue linen from his wagon and held it out to me. "A peace offering. It's your favorite color."

"I know what my favorite color is."

He cringed and held it out further. I yanked the bolt out of his hands and tossed it back on the pile. It was awkward, and I made a mess of the roll as I levered it over the wooden side panel, but it felt good to throw something. I straightened my hair and stomped off without another word.

"Wonderful seeing you again," Ahsaed called.

This day was getting on my nerves. The sun was a few hours past its zenith, and I willed it to move faster. I had investigated a dead end with Duane—not funny, I told myself—and spoken to Conrad. What else could I do?

I should go home, clean Ilsa's clothes and finish packing. I was moving into the house Viktor left me. Part of me thought it was wrong, gaining from his death, but I'd be broke if I had to pay to live above Karolyne's place much longer.

I caught sight of the Merchant's Bank. My feet carried me inside before I was aware of what I was doing. This was where the silver Viktor left me was deposited:

five hundred coins. I'd never seen so many in one place, so I spoke to the manager and asked to see my strongbox. The thin container was brought out and opened. Candlelight glinted on polished pieces.

"You don't clean them, do you?"

The elf snickered. "No."

"I'm taking it with me. Can I have the key?"

Nonplussed, the manager resealed the box and handed the key over. He eyed the other customers, most of them focused on the money counters, double checking their numbers. "Are you certain you should be carrying this alone?"

The strongbox was little larger than a loaf of bread, but I knew what he meant. I lived in the Outskirts, and I'd grown up with Duane, so I wasn't an idiot.

"Can I borrow that vase?" I indicated a large urn, filled with dried flowers, which rested on a plinth behind his desk. "I'll return it tomorrow."

When he continued to stare at me like I was mad, I opened the box and dug out a coin. It was foreign, an unfamiliar image of a winged woman stamped on its side.

"I'll buy it then."

He shook his head, flabbergasted, but handed the vase over. I pulled out the crackling stalks of lavender and dropped the strongbox inside. After shoving some flowers on top, leaving the rest on the manager's desk, I walked out cradling the vase with the strongbox safely hidden inside.

I slowed going downhill, as I had to peer around long stalks of lavender to see where I was going. The city clock tolled dusk, which came early in winter. I hurried, making it to the slave block just as the bonfires were lit.

The bidding hadn't started yet. I was in time.

Maybe it was because of what I let Duane do in Viktor's name. Or maybe it was the way Randall brushed her hair. Whatever the reason, the world felt wrong, and I had to do something to make it right again. I planned to rescue the slave girl. One good thing could come of this bloody money.

I set the vase at my feet and waited as other buyers gathered.

The usual complement of slave guards was bolstered by the presence of a grall. My hair stood on end looking at him. He was eight feet tall, bulging with muscle and had tusks the size of my forearm. Gralls had a mean reputation, and few were allowed in the city. I'd only ever seen one before.

There was something sinister about the flames, the cloaked figures around me, shifting with anticipation, and the caged people staring out at us with innocent eyes.

The night market was where concubines were sold, the buyers masked or hooded to keep their perversions secret. The place stank of hormones, and any faith I might have had in men vanished when the first girl was brought out. People leaned forward hungrily. To be fair, it wasn't only men: women were there too, elf and human buyers, male and female slaves.... It felt like I was in the middle of a fully clothed orgy.

There were four concubines for sale, all young and beautiful, and the bidding was frenzied. I began to worry my strongbox would be light. Too bad I couldn't help every one of the men and women paraded on the stage before me. How had Viktor done it? Freed them? And why had he never told me?

The young girl I'd been waiting for was brought out last. She was the prettiest of the lot. I was sickened by the way the crowd looked at her. I bid, willing to give up every silver I owned to save her, and then I bid again. The hatred of the other buyers warmed me.

I'd won, but it felt more like facing the chopping block as I strode over to the flesh merchants and the grall to collect my purchase. Had I just bought another human being? Gray, Eva, very gray.

"Listen, Randall. I don't quite have five hundred, more like four ninety-nine..." I'd forgotten about the vase when I was bidding "...but I'm good for the last silver."

"You don't have it?" The slaver had been leading the girl over to me. Now he pushed her back towards the cages, where two of his associates were packing things up. "I have an immediate payment policy, Ilsa."

"It's Eva. I'll throw in this vase." I held it up like a potter hawking her wares.

"I might take something in trade, but not that." He reached for a lock of my black hair and brushed my cheek.

I froze for a second before pulling away. "Don't ever touch me again."

He frowned. "You're wasting my time. Get out of here."

"Not without the girl." I emptied my small purse and found a few silver quarter knuts and coppers inside, just enough. "Here." I held out the change and the vase with the strongbox. I was now officially broke. I guess what I'd considered a fortune wasn't one among those who bought and sold humans. That was a whole new level of rich.

"There's a surcharge, document transfer fee.... How you want to pay it?" He wouldn't take the money I offered, and his leer made me tremble with fury.

"You can suck on your fee." I beckoned to the girl, and she obediently took a step forward.

Randall's flabby arms rippled as he shoved her back again. "Keep causing trouble, Eva, and you'll end up like your brother."

"What do you know about Viktor?"

"Just that he was as big of a pain in the ass as you."

"You don't know me very well then. I'm worse." I dodged Randall, ignored the grall like I'd ignore a pallet of bricks hanging over me—unable to do anything if it happened to crush me, so why worry? —

and grabbed the girl. We made it a few steps before the slaver whipped me around by my shoulders.

He shook me until my teeth rattled. "Stealing from me!"

Did he think I was still the scared little girl he'd caught spying outside Uncle's study years ago? My new policy was when in doubt, get mad. "Like I said, you can have the vase." I smashed it over his head.

# 4   Mysterious Stranger

The strongbox popped open. Silver coins and shards of clay showered Randall as he toppled to the ground. I tossed the knuts and coppers on the pile.

The grall laughed.

The slaver held his bleeding scalp, but he was still conscious. He grabbed the hem of the grall's tunic. "What do I pay you for? Get her!"

I held up a hand. "I'm not a thief. You've got your silver."

The other two slavers came to investigate. "Let the customer go, Randall. You know there's no surcharge."

"There's not? It's not right to lie," the grall said.

Randall fumed. "I don't care what you think...."

"Jorg. My name is Jorg," the grall reminded him.

"I don't care about that either. You're not supposed to open your mouth. You're muscle."

"This job is too violent. I thought I would be learning the mercantile trade."

It was my turn to laugh. A grall merchant? I hadn't laughed in a long time, and it felt good.

"You're useless." On the verge of apoplexy, Randall swayed and held his head. "Pick this up."

"I'm not a janitor."

"I don't care!"

"I'm leaving," I said. The female slaver nodded, indicating I could go. Randall was red, but he didn't contradict her.

The big grall was pitiful on hands and knees, obeying his boss. I told my new purchase to come along, and we turned our back on the scene. Coins jangled behind me.

"I couldn't hurt her. She was only a girl." The grall's deep voice faded as I walked away.

I felt sorry for him, but I didn't like anyone calling me 'only' anything. If he weren't an eight-foot-tall mountain of muscle capable of snapping my bones and using them for toothpicks, I would have complained. I didn't know why he allowed Randall to push him around.

Once out of the bonfire-lighted square, I felt twitchy. Everyone had vanished after the night market ended. The other buyers had bodyguards and carriages to escort their unspent silver or new slave home. I was only a girl.

"Let's hurry," I whispered.

"Yes, Mistress." The slave kept pace with me.

Now I had her, what was I going to do with her? "What's your name?"

"Whatever you desire, Mistress."

This was going to get old quick. I envisioned the next few months trying to teach her concepts like 'free will' and 'independence' while she nodded vacuously. I'd really done it this time. I didn't only mean the slave. I was unarmed in the Outskirts at night ... and figures were emerging from the gloom to encircle us.

"Run!"

"Yes, Miss—"

I made it between two of them, but the girl was easily caught. I turned around. "Let go of her."

Someone grabbed me. I kicked him in the gut and sent him sprawling.

The girl didn't move as lascivious thugs petted and grabbed her.

"This is how I like 'em, docile," one said. I yanked him away from her by the hair and felt lice crawling across his scalp.

Half a dozen blades, oiled and glistening in the wan light, were drawn and pointed at me. I stayed perfectly still.

The lousy one blew fetid breath in my face. "I think she's the one what was with The Adder this morning.

You killed my pal, Fox. Now, I'll cut you." Gormless shouldn't have let this one go.

"Adder, Fox ... can't you guys come up with better names? I suppose they call you Jackass." I laughed.

He didn't find it as funny as I did, and a second later I was dodging a knife. This had been my least favorite part of Morgan's lessons as a child.

Fortunately, I'd been paying attention. I avoided skewering, and I could have taken him down, but his friends closed in. I had no room to maneuver. The place between my shoulder blades itched, and I imagined six inches of steel sticking out of it at any moment.

I hadn't realized how accustomed I'd grown to the dark until a phosphorous glow bloomed around us. We all covered our eyes. I peeked as the light faded and caught sight of a glowing cord unknotting itself at my feet. It grew larger and larger until it was the size of a python. Silver fangs emerged from one end and struck the nearest street thug. He collapsed, wracked with agony. Magic. The rest of them took off.

Cord magic. I'd heard of it but never seen it before. Everything sold in Highcrowne was either potions, conjurations, or enchantments, usually Avian made. Cord and knot magic wasn't in their repertoire. Should I be running as well?

A man taller than me stepped into the artificial light. He un-stoppered a flask and forced it down the injured mugger's throat. "This will stop the poison. You can thank me for my mercy."

"Th-Th-Th-" was all the thug could manage through chattering teeth. At least he stopped writhing.

The newcomer turned to me, and for a moment I thought I knew him. He was Solhan, tall and fair, about fifteen years older than me. I had never met him before, but I couldn't shake a sense of familiarity, of inevitability.

"You were a fool to wander here with your slave, my lady."

I don't like being called a fool, and the 'lady' bit wasn't much better. Did I look that useless?

"I appreciate the help but not the lecture," I said.

The magic-bitten thug passed out, while the slave girl watched everything incuriously. It felt like the Solhan and I were the only two people there.

Self-conscious, I absently combed fingers through my tousled hair. "I'd best get home. Thank you again."

"I'm afraid you misunderstand me. I can't let you leave with your purchase. I intend to set her free." He pulled another knotted cord out of a small pouch on his hip. "You would be just as foolish to resist as you were coming here in the first place."

Wasn't this a shocker? Mistaken for a filthy slave buyer, rather than the idiot do-gooder I saw myself as?

"No, no, no. I only bought her to set her free."

"You expect me to believe that?"

"Why not? You think you're the only emancipationist in existence?"

"I think you're trying to be clever, but you are only looking more foolish, my lady."

"Enough 'fool' and 'my lady'! My name is Eva. Watch, I'll cross my arms and stand here while you set her free. I doubt she understands the concept, so I'm looking forward to seeing how you do it."

"Eva?"

"That's what I said."

"Thorne?"

"Yes." My last name summoned fearful visions of Uncle Ulric's wrath in most people's imaginations. While I hated being overshadowed by my uncle, I didn't mind the resultant terror the name instilled. Such intimidation could be useful when you were unarmed and facing a wizard.

He put the cord away. See what I mean? Sometimes it paid to be a Thorne.

"I knew your brother, Viktor."

I uncrossed my arms. "What? He was freeing slaves with you?"

"For quite some time." He bowed. "My name is Erick Karsten, and I am honored to meet you, my la— Eva."

"Um, likewise."

Did I mention I almost flunked out of finishing school? All these manners made me feel like I was facing one of Lady Halcyon's deportment lessons. I stood straighter and nodded my head. Why hadn't I done it so well when I was being graded on it?

Erick held out an arm to me. "I suggest we retire before courage returns to any of your attackers. I will escort you home."

I hesitated before putting a hand on his arm. He felt incredibly warm, and I had the strange urge to let his warmth enfold me. I was tired was all.

I turned my head and said, "Come on." The girl followed.

Once we were safely out of the Slave Quarter and back in the neighborhood, I told Erick, "How are we supposed to free her? She seems so helpless."

"It is only the slave mark. The symbol is seared deeper than the flesh, passed from parent to child, so there is no escaping it. It smothers the soul."

"Sounds worse than I thought."

"I can remove it." He let go of me, and I was momentarily at a loss. Touching him had felt so natural.

Erick went to the girl and placed a palm over the crosshatching of lines etched in bright red on the ebony skin of her upper arm. Her liquid eyes watched him with complete trust. A few moments later, she began to fidget. Soon she gasped and tears poured down her face.

"You're hurting her." I wanted to stop him, but I knew better than to interfere with a spell in progress.

"She's waking up."

The red mark flared. The light of it shone through Erick's hand, and an ear-splitting scream escaped the girl. She collapsed, but he caught her. Suddenly, the night was quiet. A shriek like that would have caused everyone who heard it to lock their doors.

"What happened? It didn't work, did it?"

"She'll be fine." He showed me her arm. The brand was erased. "When she wakes, she will be confused and frightened. Let me carry her to your home."

I thought about Karolyne. She would object to my bringing an illegally freed slave into her place of business. I didn't even know her stance on the slavery issue. She might insist I return her to Randall.

"Better we take her to Viktor's. Do you know where that is?"

"Yes." He strode ahead, the unconscious girl held gently in his arms, her head against his shoulder.

Why did I feel jealous? It was innocent. Besides, I wasn't interested in Erick. At least that's what I repeated to myself on the way.

I'd forgotten my key, so I rapped on the door loud enough for Old Nanny to hear. She wasn't deaf, but she did tend to ignore things she didn't like. The cover over the peephole slid aside and a rheumy eye, pale yellow and surrounded by wrinkled skin, stared out at me.

"Is that the young master come so late?"

"No, Nanny. It's Eva. Let me in."

The eye moved up and down and side to side, inspecting me. "No, you're not! You're Ilsa. Don't try and confuse me. You're not allowed."

"By the Light Bringer." I groaned. This could take hours. "What do I need to do to prove to you...?"

"Madam Olinov, it is I, Erick."

"Oh! Erick, why didn't you say?" The old woman opened the door, the grin on her face as welcoming as her gesture. How come she never looked at me that way?

I'd inherited Nanny along with the house. She had been Viktor's nursemaid and Uncle's before that. She was devoted to my brother but cracked: unable or unwilling to admit he was dead. I could forgive her eccentricities but not the way she treated me like an unwelcome guest. She kept confusing me with Ilsa or my mother. She never liked either one of them.

Erick laid the ex-slave on the largest couch in the sitting room and propped her head up with a cushion.

"Another one?" Nanny said.

"Yes. You don't mind caring for her, do you, my dear lady?"

Nanny waved a hand dismissively. "Of course not. I only wish Viktor would give some warning of these things. Seems there are always strange people coming and going without a care for my privacy." She eyed me when she said the last bit. Nanny believed this was her home, and there was no telling her otherwise. I had no intention of kicking her out—she was an institution—but sometimes....

"Thank you." Erick turned to me. "It is late, and I will take my leave."

I felt a jolt. "Wait. I have to ask you about Viktor, how he died, and what you're doing with these slaves."

"I am perfectly willing to be interrogated, but it has been a long day." I could tell him a thing or two about having a long day, but I kept quiet. "May I call tomorrow at noon?"

"Fine. I mean, yes. I can wait. I'll be here."

"You are most gracious." He kissed my hand.

Gracious? He must not have been paying attention.

Erick went to the door, navigating the dangerous, shin-high furniture with ease, familiar with the layout of Viktor's house. He gave me a last, parting look that got my heart beating faster.

Who was this mysterious man who'd helped my brother right wrongs? Part of me didn't want him to leave, and not because I had questions. I knew the warning signs of an impending crush—I'm well aware of my addictions—and firmly reminded myself I wasn't looking for a man. I was looking for a killer.

With Erick gone and the slave girl passed out, I was all alone with Old Nanny. She stood in the middle of the room with her hands clasped, staring at me. She seemed to expect me to go as well. I'd had enough of knife fights in dark alleys for one day and had no desire to walk back out into the night.

"I'm going to my room," I headed for the stairs. None of my things were here yet, so I'd sleep in one of Viktor's shirts.

"What do you mean, 'your room'?" she asked nastily.

"By all the gods, I've told you a dozen times, Nanny. Viktor left me this place and asked me to look after you. His room is now my room."

"No, you don't. You are not to disturb a thing in there! I want something to remember him by." The old woman had her lucid moments, and sometimes I thought they were worse. She was happier when she thought Viktor was still alive.

"Then where am I supposed to sleep?"

She indicated the smaller lounge across from the one on which the slave girl rested. Its once lavish upholstery was ancient and moth-eaten. So much dust had stained the cloth, the birds embroidered across it appeared to be caught in a tornado.

"No. My feet are killing me, and I need a bed." I headed for the stairs before I caught another accusing look from her.

"Use the guest room then. For if I catch you in Viktor's, you will die a slow death by poison, Ilsa."

"It's Eva!" I stamped my way up the staircase.

I did not want to use the guest room, but I ended up there anyway. There was something scary about Nanny. She must be the one who had taught Uncle Ulric his charms, or lack thereof.

I sprawled on the bed, wishing I had the energy to draw a bath. There was no time for dreams. I only knew I'd fallen asleep because I was bewildered and slow to rise when the screams started.

# 5   FAMILY

"Ahhh...Ahhh...Ahhh!" Each shriek from the girl was punctuated by huge gulps of air. I stared at her, not knowing what to do. Old Nanny tottered down the stairs in a nightgown, hands over her ears. She didn't hesitate before slapping the girl across the mouth with all her strength.

The ex-slave put a hand to her cheek and sobbed. I patted her shoulder awkwardly. "You didn't have to hit her," I told Nanny.

"Only way to quiet them down. Viktor's brought a few like her through here."

"Are you alright?" I asked the girl.

She nodded, but her wide, tear-filled eyes said otherwise.

"What's your name?"

"... I don't know. Where am I?"

"Her name is Kali," Nanny said.

"How do you know that?"

"I have a list." She pulled out a sheet from the writing desk in one corner of the room. "Yes, the next girly name on the list is 'Kali'."

"You're randomly naming ex-slaves?"

"It's alphabetical." Nanny said, as though it explained everything.

"Didn't their parents give them names?"

"I remember my mother." Kali's elvish disintegrated into an excited string of foreign words. Seeing my confused expression, she switched back to the standard dialect. "She's dead I think."

Old Nanny shook her head. "Born to slaves with the mark, just as addle pated as they are, who's going to name them if we don't?"

"I know what 'addle pated' is." Kali scowled at the old woman. "I remember lots of things now, but they're ... hazy. You broke a jar on his head."

"You're safe." I tried to smile reassuringly, but it frightened her more. I didn't smile well, plus I had circles under my eyes and hair sticking up everywhere. She must have thought I was an overgrown bogle. "What do we do now?"

"Give her some money and send her on her way," Nanny said, dismissively.

"No. She has nowhere to go."

Kali was born a slave, her mother was dead, and she was a long way from the land of her birth. I couldn't simply toss her on the street with no means of surviving on her own. Besides, I didn't have any money to give her, not anymore. I've always been terrible with it. Whenever I found a coin, I'd lose three. She would have to stay here, at least for the time being.

Kali's stomach growled. "I think I'm hungry."

"We'll take care of you." I looked at Nanny.

She threw up her hands, saying, "I'll warm up the stew," and headed for the kitchen.

I rummaged through Viktor's closet and came out with some oversized clothes for Kali and myself. With two of us, I could justify the work involved in heating water for a bath. When it was ready, I let her climb into the huge copper tub first.

"I love to bathe," Kali said. "They gave me a bath at least once a month."

Sounded almost as bad as elves. "Our custom is once a day. Maybe a bit longer in between if I'm lazy and not giving a damn. Of course, it's often a cold bath for similar reasons."

I scrubbed Ilsa's clothes and hung them to dry. When Kali was done, I shooed her out and took my turn in the tub, letting the hot water relax my sore calves. I seldom hiked around the city, and my muscles were shouting at me not to do that again.

A yummy smell enticed me downstairs, but it was false advertisement. A traditional Solhan stew, made from every part of the animal normal people chose not to eat, awaited us. I didn't enjoy seeing bits of brain and intestine nestled together in the same spoonful. Especially for breakfast.

"What's wrong?" Nanny frowned. "It puts fire in your blood."

"I have enough fire already." I set my spoon down. "I'm going to Karolyne's to finish packing." Not that I had many things to pack. I'd left most of my stuff behind when I'd stormed away from Uncle Ulric's over a year ago.

Nanny's eyes narrowed. "You're not moving into Viktor's—"

"—I know! I'll take the guest room." I stood.

"Where are you going?" Kali grabbed my hand. She glanced nervously at Nanny. "You haven't told me what to do."

"You don't have to wait to be told anything ever again. Do what you want. But I recommend staying indoors until Randall and the slavers leave town. They'll recognize you, and if they see your slave mark has been removed, we'll be in real trouble with the law. Branding for you and something worse for me for freeing you. I'll be back tonight, and we'll figure something out for the long term."

Slowly, after another nervous look at Nanny, Kali released my hand.

I felt terrible leaving her, but the home-cooked meal frightened me off. I needed real food, which meant I needed to go back to work this afternoon. I also needed my own stuff. Viktor's shirt still carried his smell, but as comforting as it was, it also reminded me I would never see him wear it again.

A detour first.

Even more important was returning Ilsa's things before she noticed them missing. I donned the shoes and gathered the dress, coat and accessories I'd washed, but I couldn't find the hairpin. Then, I remembered leaving it in Stanley's door. Not smart. Still, it had been our mother's, so I had as much claim to it as Ilsa did. I could leave it anywhere I wanted. Hadn't mother left me behind as indiscriminately?

Viktor's shirt was long enough to be a dress, a very short one. The weather was cold, as usual, but I could endure a brief exposure. I scurried up the cobblestone street, hoping to avoid anyone I knew, which was impossible, since I knew everyone, and it was full morning.

I frowned at the miniature locomotive pulling an ice scraper across the cobbles. I hated those things. These new technologies were ruining the place. This one was particularly bad, because it was covered by goblins hitching a ride. I recognized them from Karolyne's place. They were still drunk and showing no signs of sobering. One tried to whistle at me, but with a mouth full of teeth and no lips, he just slobbered. The human operator inside the glass bubble at the front of the locomotive huddled in his seat and had a better view of the drool than I did. I hoped they broke the noisy eye sore. I smiled and waved as they drove away, the goblins excitedly waving back.

When the quiet of falling snow returned, I took a moment to breathe in the icy air and coughed on the stinking smoke left by the locomotive.

This was supposed to be the best neighborhood in the Outskirts. No shanty houses here. Foundations were brick or stone. The sturdy wattle and daub walls were painted white to contrast with the black wooden beams that crisscrossed the surface and framed real glass windows. The neighborhood didn't have a special name, like the Slave Quarter, but it was where every self-important human tried to live. Merchants, hostellers, master tradesmen, less savory businessmen, priests ... I smiled enticingly at the High Priest of the Light Bringer temple when I caught him looking at my legs. He went livid and stared stiffly ahead.

I heard other people whisper as I passed, "...her own brother". They must have recognized me from my disheveled appearance. Ilsa would never be caught without her face painted and hair perfectly 'so'.

"Murdering Solhan pig." That comment felt like a punch to the gut. I couldn't see who said it, but I walked faster.

Murder. The scene leapt into full recall. Morgan had found me at Karolyne's with the wagon. I was one of the first to see.... We drove to Uncle Ulric's, and he gently carried Viktor's blood-covered body inside and laid it on the marble floor. I couldn't bear to look at the mess made of Viktor's chest, but Ilsa ... Ilsa crept forward, eager. Ulric took hold of his lifeless hand. "Who did this?" Morgan had no answers, but I burned for them from that moment.

Later, when we heard the will read aloud by the magistrate and what was bequeathed to me, Ilsa shot me a knowing glare. I could ignore Ilsa's suspicions. I spent most of my life ignoring her. But she turned the neighborhood against me. Most people respected Viktor, even those who mistrusted Solhans. After he died, they had nothing but rancor for his supposed killer.

Solhans, and the Thorne family in particular, had a reputation. While we didn't have a monopoly on dark magic, we were good at it. When I was a child, my uncle showed me a twisted effigy of wood and blood and sinew, ready to start my lessons. I ran and hid under the house.

I wasn't like Ilsa and the rest: I liked ponies. Viktor and I were the only sane ones, and we fought hard to avoid being entangled in Ulric's web.

I didn't cut Viktor's heart out, but someone had. I saw other fair-skinned Solhans strolling the street, all a head taller than the humans around them. Thornes weren't the only ones who knew what to do with a captured soul.

I knocked and Morgan answered the door. When I thought of home, I thought of Morgan. He was Uncle's manservant, although 'bodyguard' was a more accurate description. He looked the part, with his wide shoulders and huge hands capable of smashing nutshells one at a time. When our family fled the fall of Solheim, he carried me in one arm and Ilsa in the other and never set us down until we were safe. He was still looking out for me.

"Those are Ilsa's shoes you're wearing. At least they used to be shoes. She's still asleep. You had better move fast, Eva." He held the door open for me.

"Morning." I did a little jump to reach and gave him a kiss on the cheek as I swept past.

He wiped it away with a scowl. Morgan wasn't good at smiling either.

Tiny feet pattered across the polished marble floor. "Papa!" It was my nephew, Little Viktor. He saw me and stopped, his face falling. "Where's Papa?"

I felt my heart clench and my throat constrict. This was the worst part. As hard as it was for Nanny to accept he was gone, it was harder for a five-year-old to understand. "Sorry. Only me."

Morgan hadn't closed the door yet, and someone crossed the threshold behind me. Lil' Viktor's eyes widened, and his mouth fell open.

"It's 'Ane!" The boy ran past me and hugged Duane.

Duane wasn't alone. Bell smiled, tucking her thumbs in the straps of her soot-stained work overalls. Massive goggles dangled from her neck, like they were the latest fashion. Duane tossed Viktor in the air and swung him on his back.

I instantly cocked a hip and felt my lip curl, ready to snarl. Him again. "What are you doing here, Duane? Following me?"

He laughed and set the boy down. "Not only dressing like Ilsa, you're sounding like her. Think you're the center of the universe now?"

Morgan and I shared a frown. He understood how much Duane irritated me.

"If you must know..." Duane paused to give Viktor a tickle. "...I'm here to see this little guy. And your Uncle."

"What about?" I was curious—and suspicious.

A deep voice rumbled behind me like thunder. "Mister Adder." Ulric stepped into the foyer, which was getting crowded. My uncle raised an eyebrow at seeing me there

, but he chose not to comment. He stepped past me and kissed Duane on each cheek before extending an arm for a businessman's handshake. "Please, come to my study."

My uncle claimed to be a shoemaker, which was why he was on the council of merchants that ruled the Outskirts. I'd never seen him pick up a cobbler's hammer in my life. The only business he conducted was closed meetings with the powerful. Priest, merchant or criminal, he pulled all their strings.

Ulric appeared to be the same age as Morgan, although I knew he was older, and he was almost as tall, but the similarities ended there.

Where Morgan's pale, Solhan skin was tinted gold from too much time spent practicing in the yard, Ulric was white as a cadaver. His eyes were white too, and if his hair was any fairer, he'd be monochrome. At least it must have been so in his youth, for now there were enough distinctive threads of silver and gray among the shoulder length locks to spoil the albino effect. Nevertheless, all the white in contrast to his immaculate black suit gave him an otherworldly appearance, like the Harvester of Souls Himself.

Ulric let his guests precede him. Duane's smile vanished. My uncle had that effect on people.

"What's going on?" I had to ask.

"You should be more concerned with making yourself presentable." Uncle eyed my borrowed shirt and sack of damp clothes slung over one shoulder. "You are an embarrassment."

*Yeah, well, you're an evil old coot,* but I kept my thoughts to myself.

When they disappeared into Uncle's study, I told Morgan, "I'm worried about Little Viktor. Can you keep an eye on him for me?"

"I will take care of the child. I always do. You should be more worried about Ilsa."

"Trust you to stay focused."

"Never take your eye off your opponent, and never let a dog's bark distract you from its teeth." He was quoting an old lesson.

"Right." I headed upstairs. I understood the first part but wondered about the second. Did he mean Uncle was worse than I thought? My thoughts were pretty bad, so I didn't see how it was possible.

On the way to Ilsa's room, I passed the family shrine and felt a chill. I made myself go back and bow my head in obeisance before continuing.

Uncle would have whipped me if he'd caught me walking by so brazenly. He was a very religious man, but he didn't only worship the usual gods, such as the Light Bringer, Hearth Mother, and Riverwalker. He told us to respect the other ones too—the Devourer, in particular. Worship of the Dead God was banned; otherwise, I think my uncle would have had a statue of his winged form in the shrine too.

I blew out the hall lamp and went into silent running as I neared Ilsa's door. Tiptoeing, I cushioned each footfall and slowly turned the knob. It wasn't locked. It never was. What did Ilsa have to fear?

I slipped inside, shut the door behind me and waited a moment for my eyes to adjust. Thick curtains were drawn across the windows to allow Ilsa to sleep off another night spent surrounded by her admirers. The outlines of the four-poster bed became visible and then the lump of soft, downy blankets.

I started when I saw Ilsa staring right at me with cat-like eyes, the irises as pale as Uncle's. It was my own face, but a cold and unforgiving version. I was ready to run, when a soft snore eased my fear. Sometimes she slept with her eyes open, just one of the creepy things she did.

I felt like a knight raiding a sleeping dragon's lair as I skulked past her to the closet. The clothes were still damp, so I hung them to the side, where she was likely to overlook them for a while. I put the shoes back in their box and hoped she forgot they were supposed to be heels and not flats.

On the way back, I tossed a few words of gratitude at the shrine. This was turning out to be a far better day than yesterday. I had avoided Ilsa completely.

A neatly folded stack of my old clothes awaited me at the top of the stair. Morgan no doubt. How thoughtful. I'd abandoned my things when I left Uncle and his twisted world behind months ago.

I ducked into another dark alcove—Ulric's place was full of them—and changed clothes. It felt good to be back in my own skin: brown riding pants, for the pony I never had; sky blue knit top; furry white jacket; and best of all, knee high leather boots with no heel. I was me again.

I took in the austere surroundings. I'd been imprisoned here throughout my childhood, and there was nothing I missed. Just these few cherished garments, forgotten in my haste to escape.

I went downstairs, looking to thank Morgan and see if he'd kept any more of my old clothes. Was it my fault I passed Uncle's study on the way? Or that, with my ear to the door, I could hear everything they were saying?

"It's settled," Ulric said. I disliked the satisfaction in his voice.

"Except for this." I couldn't see what Duane was doing, but I heard Bell exhale.

Ulric chuckled, dismissive. "He left those to you. I have no need of them."

"They were meant to be spent on Little Viktor, to care for him. I'm not doing that. You are. You've won. The responsibility is yours, and so are these." Stones clattered against Uncle's desk, chairs shifted, and I backed down the hall.

My uncle stayed behind in the study. I went up and grabbed Duane before he reached the front door. "You're giving up? I thought you would have fought harder than this for Lil' Viktor."

"You sound disappointed. I thought you didn't want me to have him?" Duane was the one who sounded disappointed.

"Better you than Ulric." Part of me was wondering what the hell the other part of me was saying.

"You turned out alright."

"Only because of Morgan."

"Well, Little Vikky will have Morgan—and me. I'm his godfather. I'll see him as often as I can."

My temper heated up. "You couldn't handle taking care of him every day. Raising a child was too hard, so you quit. You couldn't do the one thing your best friend wanted?"

"You don't know what you're talking about." He told Bell, "Come on, let's get out of here."

"Duane is doing what he has to do, Eva." Bell glared at me, but she was an amateur. My glare sent her for the door. When she opened it, Conrad was standing there, hand poised to knock.

"Hello." He looked from Bell to Duane and then to me. "Am I interrupting something?"

  VISITORS

uane froze at sight of the Guard uniform. Or, was it Conrad's effortless smile and golden hair? "Yes, you're interrupting. Why don't you leave?"

"This isn't your house." I strutted over to Conrad, nudged Bell aside, and said, "Come in. They were going."

"Actually," Duane said, "it's not your house either. And I want to check in on Little Viktor."

"I thought we were headin' back?" Bell was halfway out the door.

Duane shook his head. "I'll catch up."

I stared at Conrad; it was hard not to. "What are you doing here?"

"I need to speak to Mister Ulric Thorne and your sister. Just being thorough." He raised a questioning eyebrow at Duane.

"He can find his own way around the house." I took Conrad's arm and dragged him inside. "I'll show you to the sitting room."

Duane's disapproval was palpable as I brushed by. It wasn't my fault he was a criminal and uncomfortable around good people.

When Conrad was ensconced in the satin loveseat with a glass of weak mead in his hand, I said, "I didn't expect to see you working so hard. I mean ... the Guard isn't well known for expending resources in the Outskirts."

"Your story affected me. I spoke to my sergeant ... and he's allowed me to investigate whenever I'm not on duty. I got a few details from Karolyne, spoke to the witnesses who found your brother on Cliff Street...."

"Whoa. Since yesterday?"

"Since this morning. I don't have to be at my post until the afternoon."

"Thank you. I didn't believe anyone would help. No one seems to care about Viktor, or the reputation of a Thorne like me."

"I do."

Was I blushing again? Come on.

Uncle's clock ticked. The plague of inefficient human inventiveness had spread even here. It was some mechanical thing from the south and horribly inaccurate. But it distracted me long enough for my cheeks to cool.

"You should know the detective I hired was killed over this. Whatever my brother was into, the people behind it are willing to stop anyone who comes looking for them. Be careful."

I almost warned him about Duane too, as individuals tended to die in his company as well. But as much as I loathed Duane, I didn't believe he had anything to do with Viktor's death, other than introducing my brother to another dark layer of the world. It wasn't as dark as Ulric's, though, which is why I wished he'd fought harder for Little Viktor. Better a murdering thief for a guardian than a Solhan … whatever Ulric was.

"Of course." Conrad paused. "What makes you say 'people' instead of 'person'?"

"As soon as I heard he was freeing slaves, my first thought was all the unhappy slave owners and slavers who would want Viktor punished."

"They have a right to be upset when their property is taken."

I stiffened. I shouldn't have let that slip. Best not to forget Conrad was a representative of the law, and I had been party to the illegal removal of a slave mark only last night. "Is theft justification for murder?"

"No, of course not. I'll question the merchants in the Slave Quarter next. What do you know about your brother's activities? How did you find out about them?"

"A rumor on the street." I didn't think Erick would want me to mention his name. I would be questioning that source myself soon enough, anyway. Speaking of which.... I hoped Uncle's clock was wrong. It couldn't be that close to noon?

Conrad sipped his mead once, for my benefit, before I offered to take it. My fingers met his as the glass changed hands.

"Eva."

"Yes?"

"I hoped to run into you today. I wanted to see you again."

"Oh?" I meant to say, 'thank you' one more time to the household shrine, but it was important a girl not look too interested, or desperate. Besides, I told myself yet again, I was not looking for a man ... or two.

"Eva!" A high-pitched child's voice pierced my eardrums as footfalls hammered on the hardwood. I jumped and sent mead spilling over Conrad and the silk cushions beside him. He stood, swinging his sword back into place on his side. I looked for something to wipe off his formerly gleaming armor.

"Help, Eva!" Little Viktor cried again as he made another circuit of the couch.

Duane pounded into the room. "I'm going to get you!"

Giggling uncontrollably, Viktor ran around and around with Duane at his heels. I felt trapped inside a whirlwind. He lifted the five-year-old into the air, the boy's legs kicking uselessly.

"Sorry." Duane was breathless. He pulled a grimy handkerchief from his pocket and handed it to Conrad.

"Thanks. Is he your son?" Conrad mopped up the spill.

"No," I said, decisively.

Duane frowned. "I apologize for the interruption. Let's go Vikky."

What was his problem? We exchanged dark looks. "I have to go too," I said.

"Can I escort you somewhere?" Conrad smiled. I hesitated, thinking about my date—I meant appointment—with Erick.

"Sure." Was it wrong to be interested in two men? Or wise to shop around? You didn't buy a new pair of boots without trying on a few pairs.

I grabbed my mother's old walking stick from beside the door. My feet were aching, and I would need it if I trekked through the Slave Quarter again. Wait. I wasn't planning on it, was I? I had Conrad looking into things. I could go on with my life and leave the detective work to the experts.

Still, Duane had been right when he said I couldn't leave anything alone. It wasn't nosiness so much as a fear that no one else cared as much as I did. Conrad looked impressive in his armor, competent, but the law could get it wrong.

I wasn't going to turn in Viktor's emancipationist friends. And I wasn't going to let any slaver off the hook, no matter how 'justified' they might be in looking out for their 'property'. Two irons in the fire never hurt a thing.

Morgan opened the door for Conrad and I. Duane followed, carrying Vikky. I leaned over and gave my nephew a farewell kiss on the cheek. I felt the heat that emanated from Duane, like he carried the ironworks with him, and his breath disturbed my hair, so I pulled away.

Little Viktor cried when Duane set him down.

"I'll see you tomorrow," he told my nephew. Was Duane going to come by Uncle's every day now? It wasn't my problem, I told myself. I didn't live there anymore.

Conrad bowed. "A pleasure meeting you all."

Morgan returned the bow. Little Viktor was still crying, while we—the criminal, the guard, and the Solhan devil—smiled uncomfortably at one another for a few moments.

I took Conrad's arm and said, "Let's go."

When I glanced back, the door to my old home was shut and Duane was walking in the opposite direction. I forced myself to look ahead. Even my favorite boots could trip on the irregular cobbles.

"When I've found your brother's murderer..." Conrad began.

"You're confident."

"I am. When I've done this for you, proven myself, I hope we can be friends."

"Friends?"

"I mean, I hope you will be interested in getting to know the man inside this uniform."

Worse than blushing, I giggled. "You want me to see what's inside your uniform?"

"By the gods, that was awful!" He laughed too. "I didn't intend ... I—"

"—I know what you meant, and, yeah, I'd like that." I slid my hand from where it rested on his armored elbow, found his fingers, and squeezed.

When we reached my new home, I noticed one of the windowpanes was missing. The lower story was Viktor's bookshop. One door led in there, the other to a staircase and the main house, which took up the second and third floors of the building. I tried the door to the shop; it was unlocked and the doorjamb splintered.

"It's been broken into," I said.

Conrad gently pushed me aside and went in first. Over protectiveness gave me the urge to strangle someone, so I darted around him. I wanted to see whatever there was to see before he did.

The place was a mess, books torn off shelves and loose papers scattered everywhere. Did Viktor leave an inventory? I had no way of telling if anything was missing.

"Vandals?" he theorized.

I sniffed. No nasty smells and no paint on the walls. "I don't think so."

I clambered past overturned chairs and drawers pulled from Viktor's desk. "They were obviously looking for something. Damn it!"

"What is it?"

"I'm going to have to search every wall and floorboard, hoping to find whatever they missed, not knowing what I'm looking for. Then, when I don't find anything, I'll wonder if it was a waste of time. At which point, I'll assume they already got whatever it was." I took a deep breath.

Conrad shook his head. "If you know how it's going to turn out, why do it?"

"I like pain. It's a Solhan thing."

I lifted a board angled across my path—it had a map of the world engraved on it in colorful inks—when something hairy brushed against my shins.

"Eek!" I dropped the map board.

A black cat streaked out of the shadows and fled through the empty windowpane to the street. My heart was racing. Why did it have to be black? Just when the day had been going so well.

A bogle suddenly dropped from the chandelier and landed on top of a precariously positioned stack of books. They toppled over, and the furless creature gave a cackle.

"Eek!" I squealed again. "Shoo!" I threw a pamphlet at it, and it scampered off after the cat. The place would be infested soon if I didn't board up the window.

Had I really said *eek*? The guardsman brought out my most insipid, girlie behaviors. I didn't like it.

I poked the piles of paper around me with the walking stick, hoping to scare off any more nesting creatures before I stepped on them. I'm not superstitious. Oh, who am I kidding. If one more black cat crossed my path.... Let's just say, I would be taking a pilgrimage to the temple of the Luck God before things got worse.

"Can you help me push one of these shelves in front of the window?" I didn't have any tools or wood with which to board it up, so I hoped the bookcase would do for now.

Conrad did most of the moving, but I shifted books around and told him when it was placed properly.

I had inherited the shop along with the house. Maybe I should quit working at the tavern and take up bookselling? Of course, I knew nothing about the business, or any business for that matter.

I'd never been able to get excited about money, unlike Karolyne, whose eyes shone whenever a silver was dropped into her palm.

Whether I wanted to run the place or not, it had been Viktor's, and it was my job to clean up the mess and set things right. But I would do it later. I heard the distant noon call of the city clock and knew I had to get rid of Conrad. Now.

"I need to…" I didn't want to say, 'talk to a source' or 'meet with another man', so I said, "…get ready for work."

"You want me to go?"

"No, but yes. For now. Can I see you tomorrow?"

"Any time you want to see me is fine." He smiled rakishly, gave me one of those chivalrous bows that look terrific in polished armor, and set off up the street.

Moments like this made me believe he was utterly perfect, and I should throw myself after him. Instead, I sighed, which was almost as bad.

I locked up with my spare key and turned to the busy street. The shop was fine when I left in the morning, so in the last few hours someone had managed to break in without alerting the neighborhood. How?

"Watch out below!"

I froze, which worked out for the best. If I had moved a few inches to the right, I would have been drenched in liquid from the chamber pot Nanny tossed out the window. I could have sworn she was grinning.

Stinking water drizzled into the gutter, and I stepped out of its way. Conrad was fortunate to live in the city. They had real sewers there, and plumbing. I shrugged. At least Nanny had given warning and it missed me—no permanent damage from the cat then.

My gaze searched the avenue. Erick was late. I went inside and climbed the creaky stairs to the sitting room. I intended to find Old Nanny and tell her what I thought of her cleaning techniques, but it sounded like someone else was already doing the shouting for me.

"You are slow and archaic! Melli flowers in the water makes it putrid! If I could go outside, I would go to the well and show you how easy it is to have fresh water!" Kali? I'd never heard her speak above a whisper, other than when she woke screaming, so it was hard to tell who it was.

"I won't listen to a child in swaddling! This is my home, and I do things my way!" That was Nanny for sure.

Maybe it wasn't too late to head back to Uncle's. Ilsa might kill me, but at least I would die surrounded by quiet.

"You!" Uh oh, Nanny had spotted me. "I know what you're trying to do. First, you move in a new servant, next you'll take Viktor's room and give her mine. I won't be pushed out!"

"I'm only trying to help!" Kali shouted over her.

I put hands to my ears. "I'm not doing anything, Nanny."

"You and your machinations, Ilsa."

"It's Eva!" Great, now I was doing it. "*Shhh. Everyone, act civilized.*" I'd flunked Lady Halcyon's class, and even I knew this wasn't close.

In a quiet, reasonable, tone, I added, "Erick is supposed to be here any minute."

"Why didn't you say? Help me with the biscuits, now girl!" Nanny dragged Kali to the kitchen.

She needed some reminding the girl was no longer a slave.

A knock on the heavy front door made me jump. He was here. I ran to the mirror and straightened my hair. My fur jacket made me look too big, so I threw it on one of the armchairs. I hurried down the steps but stopped to catch my breath before opening the door wide.

The smile on my face vanished as soon as I saw the frown on its mirror image. Ilsa. The beast was awake, and she'd hunted me down.

# MEET MY EVIL TWIN

I recognized the shoes she held up. I'd hid them in her room just that morning. They were smeared with dye from the Red Precinct and encrusted with blood. I'd forgotten to clean them when I'd washed the clothes.

"Ilsa..." I began.

She walked past me as though I didn't exist and tossed the shoes into the embers of the fireplace. The flames came to life.

"That blood wasn't yours or Viktor's. Murdered someone else recently, have you, Sugar?"

Ilsa had to know I was innocent, but it didn't stop her from trying hard to cause me pain in whatever small way she could. She took such enjoyment from it. Of course, ruining my life and having me hanged for murder would be the icing on the cake for her. Which is why I couldn't understand her burning the shoes. They were evidence of something, so why not keep them?

"Why are you here?"

Once again, she ignored me as she casually reached for a picture on the mantel. She stroked the elegant frame of a vignette featuring Viktor and Emily, Emily's hands resting on her stomach, with Little Viktor yet to be born. Without warning she tossed it into the fire along with her shoes.

I gasped. "What are you doing? It was Viktor's."

"No, Sugar. It was something you cared about, like I cared about my inheritance. Now it is about to go up in flames too." Her usual relaxed and sultry demeanor vanished for a moment as she looked at the charred image of the once happy family. Her expression feral, pitiless and inhuman. "Why did Viktor have to have a son?"

"Stay away from him. He's only a child."

The sweet expression she cultivated like a mask fell over her features again.

She tossed back her hair in the fluid, languid way she always did, as though she was Queen and had not a care in the world. "I'm only saying. Some poor children are not strong enough for this world and should never have been brought into it. Just like

Mama knew you were never meant to be a Thorne. Why else would she choose to save me from the cradle and leave you behind? If Morgan hadn't gone back for you.... You were meant to die in Solheim."

I slapped her so hard half her face turned red, but she didn't flinch or try to touch the spot that must be throbbing with pain. She made me feel inferior for resorting to blows.

It's not like I hadn't heard all her theories before, or Morgan's version of the events that day which, sadly, didn't contradict hers. It was the rawness I felt at Viktor's death and the burned photo that had me so exposed. I crossed my arms and resumed the particular glare I reserved for my twin.

Nanny hurried in from the kitchen, a ladle held menacingly in one hand, a confused Kali at her heels. "Be gone you!"

I didn't think Ilsa was a bogle to be scared off with kitchen implements.

Ilsa curled her lip. "Nanny. Still not dead? Or are you only shambling around because people forgot to cremate you?"

I smiled. Not that I thought Ilsa was funny, but I did enjoy the way Nanny stripped her civilized veneer faster than anyone.

"I'd like to do more than cremate you." The old woman gave her the Evil Eye.

Ilsa held up a wrist, the bracelet around it dangling with charms and bits of charred bone. "Don't, Dearie.

Else you'll get a taste of whatever you send my way." Her sharp gaze cut across to Kali. "Who's this?"

"Get out," I said. Ilsa was only here to play with her prey, but I knew she was capable of real harm if she learned about Erick's activities in the Slave Quarter.

Ilsa ignored me. "I recognize this one from when Julietta was browsing for a new maid, but it was in a cage then. Why is it here? You've turned perverse, sister. Then again, you always did like playing in kek."

"You're the piece of kek!" Kali threw in a few incomprehensible foreign curses as well.

Ilsa's eyes narrowed suspiciously. "A lot of nerve for a slave."

"Leave before I do something that will make me an only child." Once more, I was attracted to the simplicity of violence.

"Tsk, tsk. No need to strike me again. I'm going. I made my point."

Nanny spotted the charred photograph. "Viktor." She flung the ladle at Ilsa, who dodged without stirring a hair on her carefully groomed head.

My evil twin straightened her immaculate silk dress and long fur coat, not that they needed straightening, and flashed diamond earrings as her nose went up in the air. "See you around, Sugar."

Ilsa strode out the front door with an air of accomplishment.

"What an awful person," Kali said. This coming from a girl raised by slavers to be a concubine.

I stared at the spot where Ilsa had been. "She's up to something. She was too nice."

Kali's eyes widened.

My cheek suddenly stung in the same place I had hit Ilsa, and I thought about her dark charm bracelet. She dressed fashionably, but every stitch of clothing and bead of jewelry she wore was etched with runes. Unlike me, Ilsa embraced the Solhan arts wholeheartedly, the darker the better.

I wondered about the rumors she'd been spreading. Was there a hint of truth in them? Had one of the Thorne twins murdered her own brother?

I had no idea what was required to construct her spells, what components. Forgetting about magic ingredients, Ilsa could use a replacement heart. I should add my sister to the list of suspects, but I didn't want to. Ilsa and I were identical, as much as I hated to admit it, and I didn't want to believe either one of us were capable of something so awful.

Nanny was still upset by the destruction of the portrait and turned on me. "Why did you let her in?"

"It wasn't by choice. We'll mend it, buy a spell, whatever it takes." My brother's face was intact, the image looking right at me. The dead wanted justice, and so did I.

Nanny and I fought about everything, but she was like family. She and Morgan had raised all three of us while Uncle Ulric was busy with plots and power plays. Plus, we had common ground in our love for Viktor. Fearful suspicions wouldn't leave me, and Nanny was the only one I felt I could share them with.

"I never realized how much she resented Viktor. You don't think Ilsa...?"

"You think she killed him?" There was more anger than shock in Nanny's words. This time she didn't hesitate to admit Viktor was dead, and I wondered how much of her forgetfulness was an act and how much was her method of coping.

"I'm doing everything I can to find out who's responsible." I felt a chill anger of my own rise, and I stiffened. "Whoever it is, they will pay. I swear it."

Nanny's tone was colder. "They'd best pray you're the one who finds them—or her—because if it's me.... I swear to the Devourer I'll tear the eyes from their sockets and feed their souls to the crows."

She picked up a candlestick, pulled off the wax and jabbed her index finger on the sharp needle of metal protruding from the holder. Red blood began to drip as she went to the fireplace. She let a few drops fall on the charred image of Viktor's family.

Kali gasped at the dark pact Nanny had made and moved her hands in a protective gesture, making a circle around her head and around her heart.

The magic hadn't been directed her way, but it was always prudent to shield yourself whenever the Devourer was invoked. I should have done the same, but I sensed Nanny didn't respect me. Probably why she was so nasty to me. I didn't want to look any more childish in her eyes.

The scent of something burning sent Kali scurrying off to the kitchen. She seemed relieved at the excuse to get away from the old woman.

"Even if Ilsa didn't kill him," I said. "Do you think Ilsa was the one who busted into Viktor's shop? What could she have been looking for? A safe?"

"What's this?" Nanny's hackles rose. "Viktor's shop has been violated?" It must be a worse offense than disturbing his bedroom. Viktor was Nanny's little boy and always would be.

"I don't think anything was stolen, but it's a mess. Bogles got in too."

"Kali!" she cried. "I've got a job for you, girl!"

"She's not a slave anymore. You know that, right?"

"It doesn't mean she shouldn't work to earn her keep."

I thought Kali needed at least one day to enjoy her new freedom. I was about to say something along those lines, when the girl returned from the kitchen, Erick behind her.

"Mister Karsten is here," she said. "He was at the backdoor."

I stood straighter and hoped arguing with Ilsa hadn't messed up my hair more than it usually was.

"Erick. Why didn't you come in the front?"

He glanced at the scene, Nanny's finger still dripping on the wood floor.

"I have enemies. I thought it unwise to allow anyone to see me enter your residence. I already feel responsible for what happened to Viktor."

"Freeing slaves will piss people off. I bet my brother loved it." It was exactly like Viktor to take up some romantic quest in opposition to authority. He'd spent his entire life testing lofty ideals against Uncle's pragmatism. Now, he was dead.

"Didn't he realize there would be consequences?" I added. "Why didn't he consider his son? Why didn't you?" Some of Ilsa's cruelty had infected me, and I couldn't help rubbing some salt in Erick's wound.

"Viktor was a brave man, but a foolish one. I—"

Nanny sobbed, interrupting. "I miss him so much!"

Her tears made me uncomfortable. I preferred her when she was casting curses, and so I said to Erick, "Let's go to the other room to talk."

"Yes." He bowed to Nanny. "I cannot bear to upset you more, Madam. If you will excuse us?"

Nanny waved him off with a handkerchief drenched in snot.

In the dining room, Erick pulled out my chair then sat across from me. I felt his warm leg a few inches away from mine under the table. He leaned toward me, forming his fingers into a triangle. "I endangered Viktor. For that, and for all your tears, I will be forever penitent."

I wasn't crying. I hadn't been able to cry for years, but I knew what he meant.

After a few moments, he said, "I don't believe Viktor cared about the danger, because I think he was hoping to die."

My brother would not abandon his son. Still, it was true he hadn't recovered from Emily's death. A cough that wouldn't go away, a slow wasting disease.... Little Viktor had never known his mother when she was well, and now he would have few memories of his father.

I thought about the detailed instructions my brother left, telling me to care for Nanny and help Duane watch over the boy. He had known it might end this way, but that didn't mean he wanted it to.

"No." I shook my head. "It wasn't suicide. People don't cut out their own hearts. He might have enjoyed the thrill and danger, but I'm sure he never truly believed he would die. Besides, the punishment for his thefts was bizarre. The slavers could have simply cut his throat, or had the Guard arrest him. I think there's more to it than that. Tell me everything the two of you were doing."

"Should I trust you, my lady...? Eva?"

"I'm not going to give your name to the Guard, if that's what you're worried about. I had that chance and passed. So, tell me."

In the light from the chandelier, I detected strands of gray in his hair. He sat erect, chin raised, and appeared distinguished and utterly reliable. Hard to believe he was some sort of rebel, skulking the night and rescuing the down trodden. I saw why Viktor had been drawn to him. While both Solhan gentlemen, Erick was the opposite of Uncle Ulric in every way that mattered.

Erick sighed and visibly relented, his shoulders drooping. He said, "We met in his bookshop. Your brother's collection of philosophy tomes and political rhetoric would have been banned in Solheim. He noticed how engrossed I was, and we began to talk.

"I am slow to trust, and it took months before I broached the subject of freeing slaves. Even then, I waited until we imbibed too many strong drinks one evening, allowing my words to be blamed on drunkenness. It turned out we were agreed. If there was a way to remove the slave mark, then it was our duty to free them. I knew it was possible, because I had been secretly freeing slaves for years."

"The way you removed Kali's brand. You don't just buy knots; you have your own magic."

"Some. Though, I did purchase the cords. Only the Kells of Eastern Darrub and a few great wizards still possess the knowledge of their manufacture."

"Do Kell traders travel this far?"

"No. I acquired them myself."

"A wanderer, are you?" I imagined him on a dark horse, cloaked, stopping in one exotic land after another, learning the local dialects.

"Yes. I've been travelling since the fall of Solheim."

"That's a long time. You remember it, the fall?" I had often asked my uncle about it, about what happened to my mother and father. Ulric would only tell me they died. They all died a torturous death, and the land of our birth was best salted and left to the Dead God. That pretty much ended the conversation right there.

"Would you prefer to hear of Viktor or of that cursed place?" Erick didn't seem too keen to talk about it either. Besides, I shouldn't allow myself to get side-tracked.

"Viktor," I said.

"We began by buying people, as you did. I work as a trader from time to time, and, if you will excuse my braggadocio, I am quite prosperous."

"The silver coins Viktor left me—they were yours. I'm sorry, I spent them on Kali."

"Then you used the money as it was intended. No, I did not squander all my wealth bolstering the slave trade. I absconded with those poor creatures most times, and Viktor was an accomplished thief. He would sneak into the merchant's coffers at night and steal back my silver."

"Cat burglar, huh?" Now, I wonder where Viktor learned that? I could throttle Duane.

Kali came in smiling, carrying a porcelain platter covered in blackened biscuits. "The tops are okay to eat," she said. "Want some?"

My instant reaction was to wave them away. "No."

Erick was more diplomatic. "They look far too rich, but I will try one for your sake, child."

She beamed when he took a nibble without spitting it out.

"Thank you, Kali," I said by way of a dismissal. She didn't leave. "Can you check on Nanny for me? Make sure she's alright?"

"The old crow stopped blubbering the moment you left the room. If I go in there, she's going to make me scrub the kitchen tiles again."

"You don't have to do anything you don't want," I told her.

"You hear that!" Kali called to the other room. "You can eat gravel, you old witch!"

"What did you say!?" Despite Nanny's tiny feet, she stepped as heavily as a grall. She was coming in here.

"We should find another room," I whispered to Erick.

"Is there any place safe?" he asked drolly.

I smiled, unable to stop myself. "We can always go to my friend's restaurant. You can try her kaffe. Only thing to worry about there is fractious goblins."

"I would like that, but another time. I think our current topic is too sensitive to continue in public."

"Of course."

"They didn't like your awful biscuits!" Kali told Nanny as soon as she appeared.

Indignant, the old woman said, "It's your fault they were ruined! Five turns of the small hourglass I told you!"

"You pointed to the large hourglass!"

"I did not! I was preparing biscuits before you were born!" I winced as Nanny shouted right next to my ear.

Erick noticed my discomfort and said, "I have a solution."

He removed a vial from another small pouch at his waist and un-stoppered it. A drop of black liquid was beaded on the lid. He touched it to his lips then held it out to me. I leaned forward and felt cold spread from the place of contact over my entire body. It felt like I was enclosed in an ice cave, and the argument between Kali and Nanny faded away.

Erick's voice was rich and clear as he said, "No one can hear us now."

"Better yet, we can't hear them. I like it, but a privacy potion has got to be expensive. You shouldn't have wasted it for this."

"I like having you to myself."

I felt uneasy. Erick had a lot of magic, which he threw around without hesitation. "What do you know about trapping souls?"

He frowned. "Why?"

"A theory about why Viktor's heart was taken. You don't have any idea what someone would want it for, do you?"

I didn't believe Erick killed my brother, and he wasn't going to admit it if he had, but I felt like pushing a few buttons to see what I could see.

"There are countless uses for a trapped soul, and I know many of them."

I swallowed. "Okay...."

# 8   Authentic Human

rick wasn't admitting to stealing souls, was he? I tensed up, wondering about the liquid he'd placed on my lip.

"I mean I have knowledge of many types of magic, not that I know how to perform them, like with the cords," he said, soothingly. "Souls are an ingredient in many of the most potent enchantments, curses, bindings.... The slave's mark, as I said, is a binding on the soul. There are few things worse."

He seemed disturbed by the thought of using souls, so I relaxed, as much as a naturally uptight person like me was able. "So, do you know why someone wanted Viktor's soul?"

"No. As I said, it can be used for anything."

I bit my lip, thinking. "I'm working on the assumption slavers were involved. What might they use it for?"

"Build potent protections into their cages, kill an enemy from a distance, heal a fatal wound or illness, extend their youth...."

"Wow. Now I'm wondering why people's souls aren't stolen all the time."

"You must be able to invoke the spell involved. Such knowledge is rare. Find a slaver capable of it, and you will discover your villain."

"My villain? Don't you want to know who did this? Was Viktor your friend, or were you only using him?"

He winced. "Your words wound so effortlessly, my lady. Yes, I considered him a true friend, and I will aid your search for vengeance in any way I can. However, I have not been endeared to those particular merchants, so I am unlikely to be entrusted with knowledge of their magical prowess. If anything, I should worry they intend me to be their next victim."

"You're right. They killed one detective I put on the case, and they may not be done. If more lives are at stake, then it's even more important I stop them."

"If you wish, I can make some enquiries about these slavers. Although, useful information is unlikely to be public knowledge."

"I appreciate anything you can do, Erick." I smiled, trying to blunt the effects of my earlier suspiciousness.

I could see, but not hear, Kali and Nanny screaming at one another still, so I asked, "Any suggestions for what I should do with Kali now she's free?"

"I can give her a small purse and secure a place for her in the next caravan travelling to Lallaloka. I assume from her accent that is where she's from."

"You'd do that?"

"Of course."

"I'll tell her. Thanks."

It was pleasant, enclosed in our snug little ice cave together, but I felt the day wearing on. Erick could afford to be generous and finance adventures to Lallaloka, while I could barely afford to keep Nanny and me in biscuits. This time I really did have to get ready for work. After enjoying a few more blissful moments of quiet, I said, "I have to go. Sorry to kick you out so soon."

"I understand." He wiped his lip on a napkin, which soaked up the drop of potion, and did the same for me.

The outside world came crashing in. Nanny's heavy footfalls were in the sitting room now, and I heard Kali singing in the kitchen.

"For the last time, be quiet!" Nanny screeched.

"When will I see you again?" I asked.

"I will seek you out as soon as I learn anything. If you have need of me for any reason, you can contact me at the Bowl and Crown in the Coppersmith's District."

"Nice inn," I said. "I hear they make those pastries that look like little bow-wrapped presents with meat and vegetables inside."

"Yes, the mistress there is a fine cook." He poked the half-eaten biscuit he'd left on the table. "You will not take offense if I choose to dine there before coming to see you next time?"

I smiled. "No. As long as you bring me a pastry too."

"Agreed."

I walked Erick through the kitchen to the back door. He was unwilling to use the front during daylight hours. He kissed my hand again before walking away. I thought he was the sort of gentleman any girl would want—handsome, wealthy, devoted to a cause—except I wasn't any girl. Plus, he was Solhan, and I didn't trust my kind.

Dammit. I forgot to ask if he was married.

Kali was humming and stirred the stew desultorily. I bet it was the same stew from the morning, only bulked up with a few extra entrails.

"Can I talk to you for a moment?"

"Me?" Kali set down her spoon, giving me her full attention. "What do you need, my lady?"

"It's not about what I need. You've got to stop acting like a servant. I want to share good news—you don't have to put up with Nanny much longer."

"She's dying!" I didn't know if her expression was shocked or exultant or both.

"No. At least, I don't think so. Listen, Erick is willing to pay your passage back home and give you some money to get started. It's perfect. You can return to your family, to sunshine and better weather."

Kali's reaction wasn't what I hoped. She nodded. "Whatever you want, my lady."

"It's what you want that's important, Kali."

"I know, my lady. I need to stir this."

"Call me Eva."

"Alright." She focused on the pot.

Thus dismissed, I stood there for a moment, not knowing what to do. I kept telling her she wasn't a servant, so I couldn't demand she talk to me. I wanted to know what she was thinking, though. I bet this was all too much for her.

I wasn't good at being comforting; I never knew what to say, so I quietly left the kitchen. It wasn't my natural habitat. As much as I hated Nanny's cooking, mine was more frightening.

"Did Erick leave?" Nanny asked, disappointed.

"I have to go to work."

"Who cares what you're doing. Erick could have stayed for dinner. It's that serving girl and her blasted cooking that scared him off. I want to choke that warbling neck of hers."

"I think Kali's singing is beautiful."

Nanny stopped fluffing the cushions on the divan and stared at me. "I suppose you're staying for supper? Again."

"I live here now. But, no. Like I said, I should go to work. I'll get something at Karolyne's."

"You won't have a paycheck left after forking out for her overpriced swill." If I didn't know better, I'd have thought Nanny was concerned for me.

"I'll tell her you said hello."

Even though it was my choice to go to work, I felt driven out. I wasn't welcome at Ulric's or Viktor's. Would I ever have a place to call home? Poor me. I kicked a frozen chunk of dirty snow out of my way as I walked. I had nothing to complain about, but I usually found a way to do it anyway.

The short walk from Viktor's to the tavern wasn't long enough for me to digest the shock of Ilsa's visit, nor the information Erick had given me.

I'd always disliked the slave trade, always avoided the Quarter. Now, I was being forced to face my feelings head on. I had rescued Kali for undefined reasons, but I felt good doing it. Could I go back to ignoring the things I didn't like?

I toyed with the idea of continuing Viktor's work with Erick.

The roaring hearth in the tavern made me overly hot, so I stripped off my jacket as I made my way to the kitchen. Karolyne was there, haranguing the new dwarf cook she'd hired, Reginald.

"It's fine for you to char the vegetables when it's a dwarf customer, but humans like their vegetables raw-er," she said.

"It's unhygienic," he insisted.

"Authentic human food cooked by a dwarf, huh?" I chuckled.

"He'll get the hang of it," Karolyne told me.

Reginald's hairy arms were crossed. "I won't be liable for getting anyone sick."

"Don't worry. People will be fine. I'll take the responsibility."

Mollified by Karolyne's assurances, he pulled a fresh bunch of carrots from a crate. The burnt remains of his last batch smoked.

"Let me give him a hand." I could do a better job, even with my poor knowledge of cookery,

Karolyne hesitated, but the growing murmur of hungry voices in the common room must have convinced her. "Give it a shot. I need to get back out there."

I grabbed a pot, filled it with water from the barrel and hung it above the fire. "Boil the carrots—don't put them directly in the fire."

"Thinks she's a chef now, does she?"

"I'm trying to help you keep your job. Gypsum is a friend of mine."

Reginald was a relative of hers—or was he a husband? I couldn't keep all Gypsum's family connections straight. She had asked Karolyne to give Reginald this job to keep him out of her hair. But Karolyne would only tolerate so much ineptitude before the siren call of silver forced her to put profit above kindness.

"What? I should peel them too!?" He'd seen me doing just that, and it was too much for him. "Enough of this madness!" He pulled off his apron and threw it on the floor.

"You can't leave." I moved to block the door.

"Watch me." He ducked under my arm and went past me faster than a bogle with its ears on fire.

This was not good. I looked at the arcane implements around me: pans, spatulas, barrels of oil, and crates of produce. A caged chicken squawked. A pile of raw fat meant for an elf customer who preferred traditional fare oozed. Boiling water was the extent of my knowledge.

I bolted after the dwarf, but he was long gone.

Karolyne faced me. "What did you say?"

"Nothing. You better get back there. I can handle the tables."

She shook her head and cursed under her breath, before heading for the kitchen.

The patrons were looking at me, clearly wanting something, and I doubted my choice for a second. Maybe it would have been better trying to boil everyone's meal. I wasn't a very good barmaid, either, not that this was much of a tavern anymore.

It was close enough to sunset.

I grabbed a bottle of whisky from the cupboard and held it up for all to see. "Who prefers a glass?"

There were a lot more smiles after that. Orders for drinks I could handle. A glass, a slosh of alcohol and 'viola', as the elves said. By the time Karolyne had the food ready, cheerful songs were belted out around the room, and the general mood had improved. It had the opposite effect on my friend.

"Eva." Her steely boss tone was a bad sign.

"I panicked, sorry."

"You are not cut out to work here." She sighed. "Is this even what you want to do with your life?"

"Are you firing me?"

"No, of course not, you're the only one working tonight. I mean, this isn't exactly your calling. You have money."

"Uncle's money, not mine."

"Still, you must have other options? Since coming home from school, you've been kind of..."

"What? Angry?" I folded my arms. She could do steely boss, but I could do scary.

"...Drifting. You know, Conrad was asking about you. My cousin has real prospects."

"I am not getting married so a man can support me."

"He likes you. Consider it an option."

"Why are you trying to fix me up? You don't have anyone either."

"I'm focusing on my career."

I didn't have the same excuse. But even if I had no clue what I was doing tomorrow, I would not define myself by the man on my arm. Marriage was not a career option.

I knew Karolyne was only parroting back what had been drilled into our heads: 'be a lady and snag a man'. So, I couldn't yell at her. Especially when she was my boss. I should get another job then come back and yell at her.

Karolyne headed for the kitchen, saying, "Think about Conrad. No one would call him settling."

I did think about Conrad, in between thinking about Erick and having cautionary flashbacks of Ahsaed.

The guardsman seemed too good to be true—golden looks, a paragon of virtue, shining armor—which was the reason I hesitated at the thought of pursuing him. Thornes were anything but paragons. I could never introduce him to the family.

A few hours after the dusk bell, Gypsum came in surrounded by a gnat-like cloud of children. It was frightening how quickly their numbers were expanding, but that was dwarves for you. Pregnancy lasted only six months, and if a dwarf girl got a kiss, she was certain to have twins.

"Reginald told me what he did." Gypsum shook her head, ashamed. "He is so contrite. I told him I'll do what I can to placate Karolyne."

"This was his idea? Really?"

"Of course not, but he is contrite. Now. Of all my cousins, he's the most infuriating..." So, he was her

cousin. I had to remember that. "...and I can understand if Karolyne won't forgive him, but I must get
him out of the Central City. I'd send him on a one-way
march to the Eastern Line, let him vent his rambunc-
tiousness, but my aunt would kill me if I got him
killed."

"I'll back you up with Karolyne," I said. "I think
my peeling carrots is what scared him off."

"Thank you."

"Don't thank me. I'm feeling guilty about a lot of
things. You remember your brother-in-law, Oberon?"

"The one who was knifed by the docks the day after
you hired him? Yeah, I remember, and I can see why
you might feel guilty." She knew. At least I didn't
have to break the bad news.

He had been at the docks?

"What was he doing by the river?" I asked.
Gypsum raised an eyebrow, so I put my curiosity aside
for the moment. "I mean, I'm sorry about what
happened. The people who killed Viktor are extremely
dangerous, and I won't be hiring anyone else. I spoke
to the Guard instead."

"They're incompetent, but if you want, I can put
some pressure on them. My third cousin is second in
command of the North Precinct."

"You've already done enough. Besides, Conrad is on
it."

"Ah. Karolyne talked me deaf about him. Sounds like he'll be able to bring your brother's killers to justice and slay a dragon before teatime tomorrow."

"I hope so, except for the dragon part. Poor creatures."

Gypsum shook her head. "I'd better order. Karo prefers paying customers at her tables."

Remembering my job, I told her the menu, as much as I could recall of it. This definitely wasn't my calling. The most esoteric facts stuck in my brain, but dinner menus weren't among them for some reason.

"I'll try the 'authentic human food platter' and give me a round of honeyed milk for the little ones. Their energy is flagging. How many did I bring today?" She counted the streaks that ran around the table, hid under chairs and wrestled before the common room fireplace. "Six, I think."

"Sure. Anything to take home to the rest?"

"No, the husbands are cooking for them. I would have blissfully come alone, but these ones were dying to visit their 'Auntie' Karolyne's place."

It was too busy for conversation for a while, but when I grabbed the orders, I let Karolyne know Gypsum was here to apologize for Reginald.

She said, "Good. Tell her to tell him to get back here and quit hiding under her skirts."

I relayed the message, as Gypsum dug into her plate.

"Human food is disgusting," she said. "But I'll have another helping of this."

"The roast pork?"

"Yes, more, but send these green things back. I won't get diseases. I need my vegetables cooked!"

I smiled. "I've seen you eat human food before."

Gypsum smiled back. "Yes, but if Karolyne is going to complain about my skirts, I can complain about her cooking."

"Got it."

I played messenger for the next hour, in addition to my usual work. In the end, Karolyne agreed to accept Reginald back, after he'd had time to cool off.

Dwarven men were known for their temperamental natures, the result of having too few women. Males outnumbered females ten to one, which is why the women were revered, and why they had so many husbands. Many missed out anyway, which made for some unhappy men-folk.

Gypsum, satisfied, gathered her offspring into a whirlwind around herself. Before she stepped outside, I asked about Oberon's family. "I feel like sending flowers or something."

"The Burial Boat was sent downriver this morning, plenty of beautiful flowers arrayed around him."

I shivered at the thought of leaving the dead unburned, but I reminded myself it was a human plague. Other races had other customs.

Gypsum gave me a cautionary frown. "Don't mention to his family that Oberon was working on a case for you. I'm the only one who knew. Others might resent it."

I could translate that. Gypsum's family was dwarf royalty. While they were far more accepting than elves, they were still inundated with anti-human rhetoric. Many of them would not like hearing Oberon had died helping one.

I spent the remainder of the evening dealing with a particularly boisterous crowd, my own fault for breaking out the booze early. It had turned into a special occasion, everyone soaking up enough juice to keep themselves preserved well enough to last the next day. Maybe it was yet another devious aspect of Karolyne's plan, but scarcity had certainly made the hard stuff more popular. At closing time, it was a nightmare trying to get everyone outside while leaving the tableware inside.

The door bolted, I took a deep breath and said, "I'm going home."

Karolyne eyed the dirty dishes, but I was no busboy. Let her hire another one of Gypsum's cousins for that. I shook my head, and she relented. "Fine. See you tomorrow."

I groaned in farewell and left through the backdoor. Tomorrow was today. I hated the late shift. I hated the morning shift too. If only I could make a living doing something I enjoyed, like glaring and intimidating people.

I had brought my walking stick at least. I was glad of it, not only because I was a little tired and wobbly on my feet heading back to Viktor's house, but because it was dark, and I could thump bad guys over the head with it.

This was my neighborhood, and I knew every sound and deep alcove where a person could hide. The silence had a quality that made me watch the shadows closely. I felt the hairs along my scalp rise, so I gripped my weapon in both hands.

# 9   NOT HIS GIRL

The Ashur was a traditional Solhan lady's weapon, made of carved bone and tempered steel, which could also serve as a walking stick. It was three feet long, with a polished orb of metal at one end that fit comfortably in the palm of my hand. That bit worked well for head knocking.

The piece with the orb attached could be twisted and pulled out just so, revealing twenty-four inches of steel with a razor-sharp blade on one side and serrations on the other, each saw tooth shaped like a rose's thorn—a play on the family name. It was excellent for disarming an opponent or gashing them terribly. Solhans usually did first one and then the other. This Ashur had been my mother's and part of my training with Morgan. I had missed it. I should have stolen it from Uncle's earlier.

I stopped in the street, illuminated by lamps and the larger of the two moons. If someone was stalking me, I preferred to wait for them here, where I could see them. I could wait until the sun rose if I had to.

Tense minutes passed. I'd halfway convinced myself that I was paranoid, when I saw an elbow incompletely hidden in a shadow.

"You afraid of me?" Mocking villains probably wasn't the smartest thing to do, but I wanted to get home to bed soon, or the guest room, whatever.

"Go!" someone said.

There were three: two coming at me from the sides, one from behind. They must have felt inadequate, needing so many buddies to back them up. I said as much, maybe something a little ruder, and then one of their knives was in range. I struck out with the Ashur and cracked a wrist. The knife clattered against the cobbles as the thug hissed with pain. One down.

All I registered about their faces was yellow teeth, hungry eyes, and bristled chins. They seemed more like wolves than men. When I got the next one across the jaw, I expected a snarl, but it was a human sound of pain he made as he spit blood.

The third one stood out of range, waiting for his companion to gather himself together. Never give your opponents what they wanted. I lunged forward and rammed him in the gut. The air went out of him with a whoosh. I got some distance and swung the Ashur in a pattern meant to force the other two back.

The one with the broken wrist had a throwing knife in the other hand. I blocked it, and then went after him special. He dodged, but I got Broken Jaw upside the head again when he tried to sneak in from the side. He went down on one knee.

"Hey!" a too familiar voice called from a nearby alley. Duane came in fast, way ahead of the rest of his gang. His footfalls echoed off buildings shuttered and closed for the night.

"Let's go!" the one suffering nothing more than a blow to the gut said. He took off, his two friends at his heels.

I had questions for those goons, such as, why had they jumped me? Now, they were getting away. I'd go after them, except running wasn't my specialty. I got winded after a hundred feet.

I turned on Duane. "Look what you did. I wanted to talk to them."

Without a word, he uncoiled a bola from around his waist and sent it flying after the one with the broken wrist. It wrapped around the thug's legs, felling him and causing him to slide a few feet across icy stone.

Grim, Gormless, Fink and a few others I didn't recognize thundered past us and kept after the other two. They wouldn't get far.

Duane smirked.

Show off. I wanted to learn how to use a bola, but Morgan wasn't trained in it, and there was no way I would ask Duane to teach me. I pretended to be unimpressed and went over to question my assailant.

I cracked him one across the knee. Morgan always said it was best to start with an incentive to talk. I figured avoidance of pain was a good one. "Why in the nine hells did you come after me?"

The injured thug clutched the bruise and looked from me to Duane. He said, "You took down Killian. Jessup sent us with a message."

"What message?" Duane and I asked at the same time.

I glared at my undesired rescuer. "Shut up and let me ask the questions."

"Why should I?" He crossed his arms.

"Because I'm the one who had to dodge knives after a grueling day of honest work."

Duane threw up his hands. "Do what you want."

I repeated the question, "What message?"

"We were supposed to cut the Adder's girl."

I stared blankly for a moment before the absurdity registered. "Me? I am not his girl!"

Duane laughed at my reaction. A second later, his eyes turned hard, and he kicked the thug in the ribs. Something cracked.

"Stop it," I said. "Let him go back to his boss and explain I am not your girl."

Duane crouched down, eyes locked with the other man's in a staring contest that lasted only a few seconds before fierce-eyed Adder won. "Go home, Eva."

"I won't let you hurt him."

Duane wouldn't look at me.

Finally, I said, "Promise me you won't kill him, at least. Any of them."

"Alright. I won't kill them, but they are going to get an education. Now, go home."

The urge to disobey was there, but I was too tired to listen to it. I took a few steps, turned back and said, "You promised."

"I know. Go."

He was far too bossy, but no point sleeping on the street just to spite him.

My angry boot stomps echoed off stone walls as I headed for Viktor's. I soon worked myself into a righteous fury. 'His' girl indeed. But the worst part was, by stupidly following Duane to the Slave Quarter, I had ended up as one of the targets in his little war. Didn't I have enough problems?

I was on edge, so when Bell jumped me, I had the Ashur half drawn before I knew it was her.

"Eva, can you help me with something?"

"What?" I was tired, grumpy and not feeling helpful.

"I'd rather not say here. Come to my place and I'll show you." She took off and didn't look back to see if I was following. I groaned and went after her. More of Jessup's people could be about, and she'd left Duane and the rest of her crew behind. Stupid girl.

We detoured to the border of our neighborhood, where there was a new shanty town recently erected for the latest influx of refugees. They were still under quarantine—who knew what nasties they carried with them from the war zone, or if they were nasties themselves—so the area was cordoned off. All I saw were a few flickers of firelight through the gaps in the high wooden fence.

Our destination was a metal shack nestled between two abandoned factories. I couldn't see the shack well, because of the head high piles of metal junk barring the way. There were broken wagon parts, rolls of resin tubing, and other paraphernalia beyond my comprehension. I'd never been to Bell's home before, if you could call it a home.

"Where do you sleep?"

"Not here in the yard. Inside, of course." She wiggled through the maze of scrap, and I followed awkwardly, catching my sleeve on sharp wires and rusted metal sheets every few steps. I wasn't as petite as Bell, but I did have the advantage of height and, on tiptoes, could peek over the obstacles to get a better perspective on the maze.

We finally reached the door, and I stepped through, gratefully stretching my shoulders.

Bell's place wasn't just the shack but the whole factory itself. She had a cot in the shack section, along with a small kitchen, consisting of a water barrel sprouting pipes and a dripping faucet that overhung a ceramic bowl. Next to it was a black metal stove that emanated heat, the copper kettle on top nearly fused to it.

"Frazzle," Bell semi-swore. "I left the tea on." She grabbed a thick pair of gloves from atop a nearby gas tank that had hoses attached to it. Some sort of homemade acetylene torch. I backed away from the flammable container nestled a mere arm's length from the cooking stove. She cut the kettle free and set it aside.

Bell was a mystery to me. "How does a girl like you end up outside Karolyne's in the middle of the night waiting to jump Jessup's gang? Does Duane bang on your door when you're sleeping and say, 'it's time to knock a few heads'?"

"Pretty much. But I'm not assigned head-knocking detail. I'm the bomb-wielding back up." She pulled several orbs from the huge pockets of her work overalls. They were tarnished brass and covered in an ornate pattern of interlocking gears.

"I hate to ask, but what sort of bomb is that?" I knew of magical fire bombs and poison flasks, but a mechanical bomb was unheard of.

"It opens up like a flower and shoots out a cloud of tiny needles coated in sleep powder. I'll show you...."

"No, no, no." I said quickly when it appeared she might activate the damn thing. "Your description was clear enough. Now, why am I here?"

"I'll show you."

Bell pulled her gloves on tighter and reached for a copper lever mounted on the wall. She flipped the switch and sparks flew. A glass jar next to the lever glowed with more of the green goo I'd seen at the ironworks. A line of it ran up a wire that stretched into the other room, up brick walls and to giant lamps dangling from the rafters. They weren't oil lamps, because they shone with the same yellow-green light put off by the goo, only brighter.

I could see the full contents of the old factory now and my mouth fell open. There were grall-sized mechanoids in neat rows, dozens of them, as well as other contraptions I didn't recognize. A few appeared to be based on the same locomotive design as the ice scrapers. Some sprouted metal arms, others wielded shovels or hammers.

Bell was creating mechanical replacements for almost every line of work. There was even a mechanoid with a serving tray attached. I would have worried about my job and everyone else's, if I didn't know how useless those things were. It took twice as many people to operate one mechanoid as it did people to do the job the regular way.

"Impressive," I said. "It must have taken a while to build all these. I hate them, but I can see why you'd be proud. Can I go home now?"

"I didn't bring you here to brag. There's something you'll find very interesting. Magic."

"I don't like magic any more than I like mechanical abominations. Combining the two, as everyone in Highcrowne seems to be doing these days, is worse."

"Is there anything you do like?"

"Sleep."

"Well, let me rephrase then. You'll be interested in what I have to show you because it involves Viktor."

That did catch my attention. "Go on."

"This way."

The inside of Bell's place was more organized than the outside, and I had plenty of shoulder room as I walked between the rows of her creations. "You plan on selling any of these, or is Duane building an army?"

"This was all my idea," Bell said, as she removed her gloves and dropped them on a worktable we passed. I noticed she didn't answer my question as to the purpose of creating so many mechanoids.

I thought there were plenty in the main room, but she took me to a bricked off section and another door. Inside, there were two more machines. These were smaller than the grall-sized versions, nearly human or elf in proportion and shape, but with rods for legs and gears for hips and joints. The body cavity and head were disturbingly life-like: The metal casings for each sculpted with the detail sometimes seen with fine marble statues. Their bronze skin exuded living warmth.

The humanness of the machines made it even more disturbing when Bell grabbed the chest of one and cracked it open. Inside were shiny wires and clear tubing, as well as glass jars for more green goo, but they were currently empty. The whole thing looked new.

"If you want me to help fix that thing, it's not my area," I said. "But here's a tip. Maybe you need to fill the jars with green goo. I don't think any of these clunkers work well without the enchanted fluid the Avians are selling for a fortune."

"Ha, ha, not so funny. This is one of my pet projects, and I'm trying to keep it goo-free. I'm planning to implant a miniature steam engine, one fueled by microfyrite crystals from the new mines north of the Kingdoms. If I can get the combustion and pressure chambers small enough, air intake and water circulation worked out—maybe they can drink it? — not to mention attaching gears to link the other appendage servos, a guidance switch system...."

"Whoza whaddit?" I said. Bell had lost me. Although I think I might have drifted off into a bizarre dream. I really needed to get to bed. "Can you skip to the part about Viktor?"

"Just giving you a glimpse of what one of these should look like. This one's mine. It's a special project

Viktor ... helped finance." The way her voice caught when she said Viktor's name this time made me cock my head.

"I saw you at the funeral," I said. "There were a lot of dry eyes there, typical for Solhans and Thornes, especially, although Duane managed to respect our ways too. But you and Little Viktor must have soaked through a dozen handkerchiefs. I didn't know you and my brother were so close."

"We aren't. I mean weren't. Well, not as close as I would have liked. He loved Emily so much. I understand completely. But from the moment Duane took me in, Viktor was there too. I looked up to him. He deserved to be happy. At least ... he would have made me happy, if only he could have moved on. I waited for three years after Emily. I tried to be his friend, but...."

"So, you were jealous of Emily's ghost? Men can be so infuriating. I bet you hated Viktor after he turned you away." I was trying out a new theory. Love, hate, passion. They were strong motives for murder. I liked Bell, but it didn't mean I trusted her. I didn't trust anyone.

"What? No. I could never hate him. Never mind. None of it is important now. What I need to show you is the other automaton. Viktor's."

She indicated a machine identical to the one she had rummaged inside, except its chest cavity was intact. The casing was dented in a few places and smeared with dirt, but it looked functional.

"What use would Viktor have for an 'automaton'? What is it?"

"It's a more elegant mechanoid. One that doesn't need an operator. It obeys your commands."

"What? Like a living person?"

"Like the golems built by dwarfs and powered by magic. I wanted to experiment with one, as I said, but it had to be imported from the Fortress of Mages. You know how impossible it is to get someone to send a message that close to the front, let alone drag back a wagon of rare, automaton cargo? Very pricey. Viktor offered to buy two. One for him and one for me. If I taught him how it worked. I did. He took it home with him."

"You didn't think that odd?"

"It was easier not to question too much. I told myself he wanted it to stack books in his shop or take over some housecleaning from Nanny."

"And now it's here?"

"Arrived last night. By itself. I don't know how long it's been wandering around, the way it's scuffed up. Maybe since Viktor died? It banged its way in here, woke me, but then marched past everything until it reached the other automaton's side. I started making tea to wake up and get my head around what had happened, when Duane showed. It was perfect timing rescuing you, because I could use your help."

"Duane didn't rescue me. You're telling me machines can go walking around on their own and know how to find their way home? That creeps me out more than Nanny's cooking or Uncle's shrine. Way more."

"It's not the creepiest part." Bell reached for Viktor's automaton, her fingers trembling ever so slightly as she cracked open the casing. She took a big step back, giving it some distance and allowing me to peek inside.

I thought I might be sick. There were organs in there. At least lumps of flesh that looked like organs. Veins pulsing with blood.... Symbols were etched into the metal and smeared with black charcoal over the living tissue. I knew enough to recognize necromancy when I saw it.

"This one's powered by magic too, just a different sort," I said. I thought the green goo was disgusting enough but, evidently, there were worse things to animate a machine with.

"Is it human?" Bell shivered. "Is that Viktor's heart in there?"

I saw the pumping chunk of flesh she was referring to, but it was too big to be human. Nothing inside was. "Most necromancy uses animal components. Since the Dead God's invasion, no human flesh is controllable. It's His domain."

"I knew when I saw dark evil necromancy stuff, you'd be the one to talk to." She smiled.

"Hey! I don't do magic of any kind. I would never do anything like this. Neither would Viktor."

"Well someone did. Come on. We all know you're destined to go dark. You're Ilsa's twin. You're a Thorne."

I wasn't very happy with Bell right now. "I'm going."

"Wait. I don't want this weird thing around. It might wake up again and try to kill me."

"Why would it do that? Besides, you know more than I do about machines. Shut it down."

Yes, Bell was the one who knew about automatons. It would be much easier to send a machine to rip out the heart of the lover who spurned her rather than get her own hands bloody.

I didn't think she knew necromancy, a flaw in that theory, but there were plenty from Solheim who did. Even Nanny used it to keep the stew fresh. Bell could have paid for the work to be done, to throw blame onto a Thorne and off her. She hadn't expected the abominable creation to come back here and find her though.

"This is magic," Bell said, as though she considered it more dangerous than brass bombs in her pocket. I wasn't so sure. "If I start tearing stuff out, I might curse myself. Right?"

Was this petite girl Viktor's murderer? I couldn't just leave her to be killed by a rampaging mechanoid—unless I had proof.

"Let me look at this thing." I ignored the chest cavity and reached for one of its arms. The metal was heavy, but after a moment the weight vanished. The thing was holding out its arm for me. I shivered.

Grime was smeared along its once-polished surface. It wasn't sewer muck: not smelly enough. The dirt had a grayish cast, like damp ash, and was mixed with rust-colored streaks of fine crystal. Pot ash. It was used to make soap and to bleach clothing white. More knowledge inadvertently picked up from Nanny.

One thing for sure, the automaton hadn't been cleaned by anyone or been out in the falling snow for long. That meant traces of whatever else it had touched would remain. Such as blood stains.

I pried open its fist and examined the fingernails. It had them, made of brass, a bit shinier than the rest of the human-like bronze hand. It was amazing how the metal bent and flexed like flesh, when it should be stiff as a statue.

There was nothing under the fingernails or inside the palm. Pot ash smeared the knuckles, but wherever the automaton had been, it hadn't touched anything with an open hand. So, it hadn't reached into Viktor's chest and ripped his heart out.

At least not since its last bath. If machines had regular baths.

"Sorry. I told you, I don't know much about magic. And what I do know I don't want to know." I couldn't help Bell the way she wanted, but I could give her some advice. "You should lock up this room and bar the door from the outside. Maybe Duane can help you dump this thing in the river or send it back to the Fortress of Mages? Whatever you do, do it soon. This thing is definitely alive ... because it's holding my hand."

I yanked free of its grip and shoved Bell out of the room. I followed my own advice and barred the door behind us. The automaton banged on the iron door, the sound echoing through the open warehouse. The rhythm was that of polite knocking, which I found more disturbing than if it had tried to break the door down.

"Do you have any bigger bombs?" I asked Bell.

"Yes, but we're not blowing up my workshop. Or the good automaton. It cost a fortune."

"Are you sure there's such a thing as a 'good' automaton?"

Bell threw up her hands and stamped off to retrieve her stash of explosives. She returned with a stick of dynamite.

"No fancy brass contraptions or mechanized what-zits?"

"Sometimes simpler is better," she said.

I thought there might be hope for Bell yet.

I lent her my sparker. Once the fuse was burning, a much shorter fuse than I would have liked, I yanked open the door long enough for her to toss the stick of dynamite inside. I closed the door as quick as I could and ran all the way back to the shed section, dragging Bell behind me.

We took cover, but there was no need as the explosion was contained to the workshop. A loud bang, smoke creeping through the edges of the door, and an automaton-shaped dent in the metal were the only signs the bomb had worked.

We stared at the misshapen door.

"Do we open it?" Bell didn't seem too eager.

"I hate not knowing. We have to check." I crept forward, arm outstretched, when the door came flying off its hinges. It whacked me good, and I went down, bruised all along my right side.

The automaton stepped out of the smoke. I hadn't noticed in the dim workshop, but it had a woman's face, delicate and kind. The eyes were the same bronze as the rest of it, so I didn't know how they could see, but they did somehow. It noted me on the ground and Bell standing frozen and open-mouthed.

It had survived a bomb and destroyed an inch-thick metal door. I was sure it would smash us next, but it took off running. It slammed through the nearest brick wall, a cascade of debris falling. An upper story window shattered, and glass rained down. I closed my eyes to protect them from the dust and glass fragments, but nothing large hit me. When I opened my eyes, the automaton was long gone.

"Duane will find it," Bell assured me.

I wasn't so confident, but I really didn't care anymore. It hadn't hurt us. Maybe all it wanted was to find its way back to the Fortress where it was created. It wanted to go home; I wanted the same thing.

I didn't bother telling Bell goodbye. I just left, taking the shortcut through the brick wall the automaton had created.

# 10  KALI

When I reached Viktor's house, I made sure the front door was locked securely behind me before I trudged up the stairs to the sitting room. Not only were Jessup's goons on the loose, but a creepy, living automaton thing was roaming the streets as well. Could this city get any worse?

It was black, except for a faint glow from the stoked fire. I wasn't familiar with the layout of the house yet, and I tripped over something. It was soft and too low to the ground to be one of the hardwood salon chairs or the sofa. I felt the outlines of the object, and realized it was a suitcase.

Morgan had brought my old things over. Yay! There were two suitcases. I hefted the largest with both hands, dragged it up to the guest room and then went back for the other one. On the way up the second time, I saw Nanny standing at the top of the stairs with a candle and a frown.

"What are you doing? Shifting dead bodies around in the middle of the night?" She was in a huff.

"Having raised Ulric, you're no doubt familiar with that sound. Why didn't you ask Morgan to carry these upstairs for me?"

"I told him to take them back to your uncle's, and he wouldn't oblige me. This is my home, and no one asked me whether you could move in, you and your disrespectful slave girl."

"You think anyone who disagrees with you is disrespectful."

"They are, and stupid too."

"Well, I am stupid, and I am staying in the guest room because it's what Viktor wanted. Probably not the guest room part, though. Where's Kali? I didn't see her on the couch."

"On a rug, next to the kitchen hearth." She gave me a smug smile.

"In the cinders? Your nastiness is dangerously close to cliché. Tell her she can sleep in the guest room with me."

"I'm not telling her anything, besides, I lied. She disobeyed me and went to bed in Little Viktor's old room."

"Good." I grunted, having levered the suitcase over the final step. Nanny stood there, blocking my path. "Goodnight, Nanny."

She looked at me, looked at the stairs behind me, looked at me again....

"You better not be thinking about pushing me."

"I wouldn't trouble myself." She spun around, sending wax from the candle splattering across my boots, and did a stately walk back to her room.

The next morning, I woke to the sound of crows screeching, but it wasn't Nanny and Kali arguing this time. The scarcity of human sounds was unnerving. Once dressed, I crept downstairs, expecting to see a horrifying scene of murder: the girl and the old woman locked together, hands around each other's throats, dead.

Nanny was on the settee, darning socks and humming to herself. Maybe there would be only one body.

My gaze searched the room, but there was no sign of Kali. "What's going on?"

"Mending. What's it look like?" Nanny's tongue hadn't lost its sharp edge.

"Where's Kali?"

"Working her behind off." The old woman sounded pleased.

"You didn't sell her back to the slavers, did you?" Nanny was a Solhan woman through and through, and I expected her to be cunning.

"Oh, I wish I'd thought of that. No, she's straightening up Viktor's shop. And before you tear into me about ordering her around, she volunteered. That one may be trainable."

I grabbed two apples from the kitchen and went down the back stairs to the alley. I understood now why Erick liked this route: the steps were covered and kept free of ice; the alley was clean and narrow, with several exits, and it would be easy to spot anyone lurking. I used my key, one of a handful on a small ring I kept tied to my pants, and went into the shop.

Kali sang as she worked, but she croaked discordantly when she saw me.

"Sorry," I said. "Didn't mean to startle you. Want something to eat?"

"I have to work."

Kali had straightened papers. All the books were in neat piles, and the broken furniture was stacked in the corner. The only real work left to be done was to right the overturned shelves Kali had been unable to move alone.

"No, you don't. I should be the one cleaning this place up. You've done so much. A break is the least you deserve."

She put her broom aside and took the apple I held out. She gave it a perfunctory nibble.

"No appetite?" I asked.

"No."

"You feel all right?"

She nodded.

After praying for quiet around here, I didn't know why I was so disturbed when I got it. Once again, I wished I was better at comforting people. With a loud cracking sound, I took a big bite of my apple before setting in on a clean looking bookshelf.

"Let me help," I said with my mouth full.

I spent the next four hours moving furniture around and sorting through Viktor's papers. Part of me was keeping an eye out for anything that might have prompted this ransacking. All I found were orders and accounts that made me cross-eyed whenever I tried to make sense of the numbers. I could do math, but debits and credits and net totals and Crown tax rates all made me weary with boredom.

"Maybe this is important?" Kali handed me a stack of documents.

She couldn't read, so it was up to me to make sense of everything she came across. I could see why these had caught her attention. There were pictographic symbols next to every line. It represented printers, the trademark found on the spines of their books next to their names. The price Viktor paid to purchase each of the titles in his inventory was also listed.

"This is useful," I said. "Now we know what to charge for the books. I don't know how to keep this place running, but I can figure out how to sell what's already here."

"Can ... can you show me?"

"Show you what?"

"How do the symbols tell you things?"

Teaching her to read would take a while, and there was no point if she was leaving. What need would she have for elvish in Lallaloka? Her home was deep in human territory. Still, she looked so enraptured by the sheet of paper in my hands I wanted to encourage her.

"Those pictures are the bookmakers." I grabbed a history from the shelf and showed her the mark on the spine.

She spotted the corresponding symbol on the list before I did. "There!"

"Right. Now, if you follow the line horizontally, the name is spelled out and says, 'Ferdinand Brothers'. Here is the book title, 'Raiders of the Northern Wastes', and the price Viktor paid, 'five silvers'."

"So, you will ask people to give you five silvers for it?"

"Not if we want to make a profit. Karolyne is always prattling on about profit margins. We should charge eight or ten silvers so that we make more than we paid."

"I see. Randall paid my last owner one hundred silvers, so he made a profit of ... three hundred and ninety-nine silvers."

"You can count?"

"I watched people counting my whole life—teeth, toes, coins and slaves. But no one ever talked about trapping words on paper."

"How sad. Words are far more interesting than numbers. Wait a minute. Randall made that much profit?" I hated being fleeced, but it wasn't my fault. Everyone was bidding too much. All I did was keep up. "No wonder Ilsa was so surprised."

"I didn't like your sister."

"No one does. Actually, that's not true. She has plenty of admirers but few of them know the real her."

Kali looked at the paper in my hands again. "Will you teach me to make sense of those? Please?"

"I'm not the best teacher, because I wasn't the best student, but you won't need elvish when you get home. You should learn your own language."

Her face went blank before huge tears formed in the corners of her eyes and cascaded down her face. She was crying more than I had ever seen anyone cry, but without making a sound.

"Kali? What's wrong?"

"Don't make me go home."

"Why?"

"I will work so hard and be so good. Let me stay with you. Please," she begged.

"You are aware Nanny is still here and not showing any signs of keeling over soon? You really want to stay?"

"I can be good. I'm working like she said, no arguing."

"I don't want you to work: I want you to be free."

"I won't be if you send me back. My mother died and they dragged me away from her and gave me to the man who burned me with the mark." She rubbed the place on her arm where the slave mark had been. "I screamed and screamed until I could do nothing but what they told me."

"You were sold into slavery?" I was aghast. "In Highcrowne, only hereditary slaves can be traded, thus the official papers showing bloodlines ... which I forgot to get from Randall."

"I don't care what my papers say. I know what happened."

"I believe you, but I want to see them. They've got to be forgeries. Maybe that's what Viktor found out!" I stood, ready to go back to the slavers, but Kali grabbed my hand.

"Please, don't send me away. It is much better here, even if I must work. I don't remember much, but the place I came from was horrible. I never want to see it again."

What was I doing? It was hard to counter my insensitive nature, but I sat back down and put my arms around Kali. "Don't worry, you don't have to go. You can stay and learn to read elvish if you want."

"Thank you. Thank you, my lady."

"I'm not your lady. I'm your friend." I let the hug go on until Kali's tears ebbed and she pulled away. I was proud of myself—my usual reaction to tears was to run.

Finally, Kali asked, "Do I have to be kind to Nanny?"

"Not if you don't want to."

She smiled broadly. "Be right back." She tore out the backdoor. I heard her feet pound up the staircase, and the screaming started. "Guess what, you old witch...!"

She left the backdoor open, so I went over to close it. I spotted Erick in the alley, looking dashing in a gray cloak and high, black boots.

"In here," I waved.

He ducked inside and stood close to me as I shut the door. Comforting waves of warmth poured off him.

Erick's smile lit up his whisper blue Solhan eyes. "I discovered something startling."

## 11 ANTICIPATION

"What?" I couldn't stand the suspense after a dramatic sentence like that. I also couldn't bear leaving gifts unwrapped for long, waiting for the punch line of a joke, or the agonizing expectation before a first kiss.

"I went to the Slave Quarter," Erick said, "hooded so no one would recognize me, and eavesdropped on conversations, hoping to learn more about the slave merchants."

"What did you hear?"

"It's what I saw that surprised me. Several weeks ago, your brother and I daringly freed a slave named Olaf. He was ancient, with little time left to enjoy the freedom we would give him, but he seemed important to the slavers. He worked all day in their covered wagon, doing accounts, dealing with official documents.... We thought taking him would be a blow."

"So, you stole him," I said to hurry him along. Nothing Erick had told me so far was all that startling, other than a slave with some brains left intact after being marked.

"Yes, we took him from the wagon while he and his masters slept. Olaf was less docile than the others, so it was an effort to keep him from calling out. We got him to Viktor's, where I removed the mark, and once he had regained his senses, he was very grateful for the rescue.

"He had been a scholar, captured by pirates on his way to the Abbey at Carlton, and sold into slavery. He had an abundance of tales to relate, all trapped inside his skull for too many years. I left him in Viktor's care.

"The Quarter was in an uproar after that: angry merchants bawling out the Guard, ordering them to do something about these 'thieves'." Erick chuckled.

"Viktor and I had to take a brief respite from our activities, wait until things had quieted down before resuming." His smile faded.

"What's wrong?"

"Viktor and I never went on another adventure. He was dead after that."

Erick's sadness cooled my impatience.

I touched his shoulder. He put his hand on mine.

After a while, he said, "I assumed Olaf was sent out of the city, like the others. Yet, today, I saw him again in the merchant's wagon. The slave mark was on him. They have recaptured him. You know what this means?"

"They have an awful lot of non-hereditary slaves, and they have the audacity to mark a free man in the shadow of the Three Crowns. They are so gonna get it."

Erick nodded. "Yes, but more than that, one of them has the ability to place a slave mark. It is soul magic. Slavers will hire a necromancer for such work, but I know of none in this city willing to do it. One of the slavers has hidden power."

"The one who took my brother's soul." My eyes narrowed. I wanted to run to the Slave Quarter and tear apart whoever was responsible. Only, the person I wanted to hurt had magic, and I didn't. I had to be careful.

"Will you help me find out who?"

"Anything you ask, darling Eva. But there is no simple test for magic. A skilled practitioner can hide anywhere."

"Well, there are only ten slave merchants operating in the city. Which ones had Olaf?"

"The Solhan Circle."

I frowned. "Of course."

Solhans were masters of dark magic, and that just happened to be the company Randall worked for. If he was the one.... Let's just say I'd prefer for him *not* to be locked away in Northcliff Prison. A deadly 'accident' would be better.

"I have news of my own. I found out Kali, like this Olaf, was sold into slavery. Yet, Randall boldly auctioned her off."

While slavery was tolerated in Highcrowne, more than tolerated by the elves, depended upon, there were rules. Calka, the Avian Queen, and Rutgard, the Dwarf King—his representatives actually, but the Rutgard situation was another story—had decreed no new slave lines could be created within the bounds of the nation. Only the descendants of slaves could be sold and employed here. That had not been popular with the Elf King, Fharen, but he'd been outvoted. I loved that, because Fharen was the biggest jerk of them all, not that I'd ever met him. His policies told me all I needed to know about him.

"You think her slave papers were forged?" Erick said.

"They had to be, and I wonder if your Olaf might know something about it."

"He has been marked again, thus he is their devoted servant, and he will tell me nothing, even if I were able to get a private moment with him."

"I'll speak to him myself. I'm going back there to get Kali's documents."

He frowned. "That would be unwise. They are watching Olaf now. They may decide you pose a threat."

"You're worried about me?"

"I could not call myself a gentleman if I were not."

"So, it's nothing personal, just a policy of yours, keeping girls out of trouble? I can handle myself, don't worry."

"It is personal, Eva." He moved closer and touched the side of my face. My heart sped up, thinking he might put his mouth on mine, and I hated the anticipation. I stepped a little closer, but he didn't lean down. All he said was, "Viktor would want you safe."

"He's gone, so he doesn't get a say. I'll do what I want." I grabbed the back of Erick's neck and kissed him.

He made a surprised sound but didn't push me away. After I released him, he stared, stunned and at a loss for words for once. I smiled, feeling the power.

"I have to go to work, but I'll find you after I've had a chance to talk to Olaf." I sashayed out the door.

Kali was coming down the back stairs. "I have to take off. Can you close up?" I asked her.

"Yes."

"Thanks. There's a stunned wizard standing in the bookshop. Feel free to kick him out before you lock the door." I couldn't stop smiling, despite the strange look Kali gave me.

I felt light on my feet, making my way to Karolyne's in record time. I was early, so I took a seat next to the well in the center of the courtyard. I leaned back, appreciating a patch of blue sky in the omnipresent blanket of gray clouds.

A bakery, cheese-maker's shop, and tallow sellers all shared the courtyard with the tavern-turned-café. I savored the scents of bread mingled with beeswax and chimney smoke. Sometimes, I loved this city.

I'd wandered the streets of the neighborhood as a child, but I'd never explored further. The Markets and a small section of the Outskirts were all I'd known. I changed all that when I came home from school over a year ago.

One good thing about Ahsaed, he was an excellent tour guide. He was the visitor to this city, but he loved it and called it the only civilized place in the world. He showed me everything, and I had been attracted to his knowledge and confidence. I was naïve. Amazing how a few months older made you wiser. Guess it depended on what you learned in those months.

I had kissed Erick, and I had no idea if he was married or soon to be hung by the Crowns for freeing slaves, but it had been wonderful.

Was I making the same mistakes? Erick was even older than Ahsaed, so who knew what secrets he kept? I wasn't sure if I was going to kiss him again. If I decided to, I could give him a thorough interrogation.

Right now, it didn't matter. The city was vibrant and new again, and I felt the same way.

As the meagre light dimmed and twilight approached, I heaved a resigned sigh. Time to get back to work. I was starving and wondered if Karolyne would give me an employee discount if I bought some dinner to eat during my break? Probably not.

The evening shift meant I didn't have to worry about food and kaffe and all that nonsense. Everyone started drinking mead for a little sustenance, and then ordered a glass of something harder to get them through another chilly night. There was another tavern a block away, but Karolyne's was closer to my part of the neighborhood, the pompous part. All those pious tradesmen and priests would prefer to say they dined at the cafe than caroused at the pub.

After working the bar for three hours, I nabbed a vacant table and took a break for supper. I was near the bottom of the bowl, enjoying some southern dish Karolyne forced me to try, made with cheese, tomatoes and hot spice, when Conrad came in.

I'd been pouring food into my mouth in a most unladylike manner, so I set the bowl down and wiped my face on a napkin. Some sort of legume was stuck between my front teeth, so I didn't open my mouth when I smiled at him. His white teeth gleamed like his armor, and he waved before coming to join me at my table.

"I'm glad to find you here," he said.

"Oh?" I couldn't show teeth, so it was easier to say that than anything else.

"I wanted to update you on my investigations."

"Oh?" I played with the food in my teeth with the tip of my tongue. Still stuck.

He seemed unconcerned with my monosyllabic replies. "Yes. I've only now returned from the river. I think all the fog has seeped into my bones."

He waved to his cousin. "Karo, can I have a mug of kaffe?"

Karolyne glowered at me, but I was still on my break and sitting with my back to the wall, hemmed in by Conrad's sword hilt. I folded my arms and raised my chin defiantly.

"Sure," she finally said. She grumbled something indecipherable on her way to the bar.

I coughed delicately, put a napkin to my lips to hide my mouth as I spoke and said, "Gypsum's brother-in-law was killed on the docks."

"The riverfront isn't inherently dangerous. But I like you being worried about me."

Not what I'd meant. I didn't worry about Conrad getting ambushed, not with that gleaming breastplate and giant sword he wore everywhere. I wasn't going to correct him, though, so I simply said, "You do?"

"Yes." Was he blushing now?

Still hiding behind the napkin, I picked the bit out with my pinkie nail. Success.

"Did you find out why my detective went there?"

"I asked around, and no one remembered seeing him. The white of the uniform always seems to petrify witnesses' tongues." He leaned forward conspiratorially. "But, being a guard has some advantages—I was able to examine the dock master's log. There were only five ships berthed there that night."

Karolyne came with the kaffe, forcing Conrad to sit back so she could set it before him. She shot me a look. I ignored it. The place was busy, but I had at least another five minutes, or maybe it was two. I didn't have a timepiece. Other than the chimes of the city clock, I relied on guesstimates.

"Which ships? What were they carrying?"

"Most were traders heading deeper into the Three Kingdoms, an ore hauler headed south ... and one passenger ship. The passengers in this case being slaves."

"Told you the slavers are involved," I said, smug. "I figured out a few things myself, such as the fact the Solhan Circle, which includes Randall Kingsman..." I almost spat his name "...is selling captured slaves. They're forging the breeder's paperwork."

"Really? I can arrest them for that alone and then question them about your brother when they're in prison. What's your evidence?"

"Well...." I thought about my sources: an illegally freed slave, the rogue wizard who had freed her, and documents I suspected were forged, but which I didn't have in my possession yet. "Let's just call it a hunch at this point."

Conrad was halfway out of his chair. He sat back down and shook his head. "You shouldn't get me excited."

"Is that what gets you excited?"

"Catching bad guys, yes—and quite a few things about you." His eyes sparkled, and his insouciant smile was perfect. Everything about Conrad was perfect. I was such a damned flirt.

I stood. My break was over, and I didn't need Karolyne's glare from across the room to remind me. "I have to go, but I'll let you know if I get anything solid."

He raised an eyebrow. Ah oh, he was making me blush again. Not where I worked, please. He moved aside for me, but there was little room; I had to press against him as I slid past.

A question occurred to me. "The Solhan Circle came overland, by wagon, not by ship. Why was there a slave ship in port?"

"Oh, it wasn't bringing slaves here, it was taking them away."

"A ship full?"

"That's what the manifest said."

"Where were they headed?"

He thought for a moment before recalling. "Toulon? Some little town to the east."

East? Odd. Other than a few mining towns, worked by teeming hordes of male dwarves, not slaves, there was nothing there. The wall was east, of course. The front had been stable for a decade, but pickets still guarded the approach to Solheim. What use would soldiers have for so many slaves? A few concubines, maybe, but not a ship load. They needed food not farmers.

"Thanks," I said, knowing I didn't sound thankful, as I was stumped. "You don't have to report to me every day, you know. I trust you're doing all you can to help me."

"I like seeing you every day. Until tomorrow." Conrad bowed, his sword goosing a patron behind him. The man's angry response was cut short at sight of the armor.

I went back to filling steins and wiping spills.

Karolyne was much happier when she saw me working. "You do like him."

"Conrad? Yeah, I do." I watched the machinations whirring behind her eyes and knew she was planning the wedding. It wasn't going to happen, but I wasn't going to mention I had already kissed someone else today. She might cut me some slack for my poorly timed breaks if she thought I would be joining the family someday.

The trip home that night was, thankfully, uneventful, but I kept my eyes and ears open in case more of Duane's rivals showed up to harass me. I also kept thinking about what Conrad had said.

For some time now, I'd had the feeling Viktor's death wasn't simple vengeance enacted against a thief. Something bigger was going on. I felt it like a tingling in my fingertips. The detective I'd hired had stumbled on it right away and died right away. My own investigation was progressing a bit slower, but I hoped it would turn out better. I might not be a pro, but if I managed not to get myself killed, I'd be happy.

Conrad and Erick were helping me, but there were things I needed to do myself. First thing tomorrow, I was going to see Randall, get Kali's documents, and then give the proof to Conrad. He could put the merchants under lock and key before they moved on to the next city and out of Highcrowne's jurisdiction.

My 'to do' list sounded straightforward enough, but nothing ever is. The chaos began well before breakfast.

# 12   LOOKING FOR TROUBLE

I planned to get a solid eight hours sleep, but Nanny was oblivious to the fact I had worked the night shift. It wasn't dawn yet when she opened my door, shouted "Get up!", and pulled my blankets off, putting them into a basket to take to the well for washing.

I lay there shivering, needing rest so bad my eyeballs ached, but after a few minutes of fleeting dreams, in which I was buried up to my neck in snow, I tumbled out of bed and put on my clothes, trying to get warm. The stove in my room was useless. There was no fuel for it, and Nanny had the only key to the coal cellar. Getting a copy of that key was my first priority.

When I went downstairs to complain, Nanny shoved her key ring down her brassiere and said, "You can warm yourself by the hearth in the morning like the rest of us, miss High and Mighty Wants Her Own Fire."

I looked over at the massive fireplace sheltering a miniscule flame. Kali was practically sitting inside the hearth, stirring a small cauldron of porridge, her teeth chattering. Obviously, Nanny's plan was to see us all catch cold and die of pneumonia so she could have the house to herself.

"Unlike you, we're not Ice Queens. You will give me the key, or so help me, I'll send you all the way to the mines to fetch the coal for Kali and me."

Her mouth gaped. "You're going to turn me out! How can you live with yourself, treating an old woman like this? I'll die of the black lung, you heartless...." She stopped in mid tirade, bursting into tears. I thought she was laying on the melodrama a little thick, but then I heard her whisper Viktor's name. She was old and insecure, I got it, but I didn't want to suffer for it.

"I'm not literally going to send you to the mines. You wouldn't be able to heft a pick worth a damn." She sobbed more violently, and I really felt like crap, so I said, "Sorry. Forget about it."

She heaved in a big breath of air and choked back the tears. Kali was right; Nanny could turn the water-works on and off at will. Despite what I'd told her, I had no intention of giving up. I would add buying my own coal to the list of things to do today, as well as buying a lump of wax, so I could get an impression of the key while Nanny was sleeping.

I suffered through a bowl of porridge. Kali couldn't cook either. It was salty and lumpy, but it was better than Nanny's stew.

I had an overwhelming sense of homesickness for Morgan and the roast tomatoes on toast he made me for breakfast every morning. After tasting it in my memory, I couldn't finish the clotted chunks at the bottom of my bowl. I was going to starve living here.

It wasn't only the cooking I worried about. We were all going to starve. Supporting three people with the amount of money I earned was impossible. Gruel would soon be a luxury. I needed to hold a book sale soon, but that wasn't a permanent solution. I hoped there was a solution.

I boiled water for a sponge bath, got cleaned up, put on my other blue shirt and riding pants rescued by Morgan, and set off for the Slave Quarter.

If facing potentially murderous slavers wasn't bad enough, the area was now a war zone between Duane and Jessup's gang, so I brought my mother's Ashur along. Not that I thought I could take on the whole district by myself, but it was better than stumbling in there wearing Ilsa's heels like last time.

As I was about to cross the invisible line between my neighborhood and the Quarter, Gormless stepped in front of me. The itch between my shoulder blades told me Grim had snuck up behind. I considered myself observant, but somehow those two always managed to get the jump on me.

"Tell Duane you couldn't find me. I'm busy," I said.

"Boss wants us to keep you safe," Grim said. "You can't go over there. It's dangerous."

"How long have you been following me?"

"Two days."

Gormless smiled. "It's been easy. You's only go to work and home."

"But if you go into the Slave Quarter, things will get real hard," Grim added.

"I don't plan my day around making things easier on you two. And I don't want you following me anymore. Go back to Duane and tell him he is really pissing me off."

I was wearing proper footwear this time and managed to dodge the two of them. I walked quickly past the invisible border and kept walking. Gormless jogged beside me.

The slightest exertion made him break into a sweat, and he was panting when he said, "Please. We can't disobey Boss. We supposed to keep you out of trouble."

"Too late." I stared resolutely ahead as I walked, and it was a few moments before I realized I was alone again. They had vanished. I saw wagons and pedestrians but no mismatched pair of thugs. I hoped they had listened and left, but more likely they had returned to shadowing me in that eerily effective way of theirs.

I was entering a contested area in a gang war, but I was not Duane's girl, and I was not going to let his little intrigues interfere with what I had to do. The gall of him, having his flunkies guard me like I was part of his territory. Still, it might not be bad having Lucky and Unlucky watching my back.

I reached the slavers' encampment and immediately spotted the old man Erick told me about. He was climbing into a wagon, a tin of water and a breakfast roll in his hand. This was my chance to talk to him, so I followed him inside. That's when the day really soured.

"What are you doing here?" Olaf cried, "Help! Thief!"

"Shhh!" I said. "I'm not here to steal anything. I only want to talk to you."

"Help!"

"Viktor was my brother. You know Viktor? The one who set you free."

I caught the briefest flicker of recognition in his eyes, but it was too late. The curtain across the back of the wagon was flung aside, and both Randall and his grall glowered at me. Of course, with the grall I couldn't be sure of his expression: those tusks made it impossible to tell the difference between a smile and a snarl.

"You," Randall said. "Stealing means I can see you stripped naked and whipped."

"Whoa there with the whipping. I'm only here to get..." I almost said, 'Kali's papers', but she was property to these people, and they wouldn't recognize the name. "...I'm here for my slave's documentation."

"You didn't pay the fee."

"They said there was no fee," the grall pointed out.

"Thank you, Jorg." I reappraised his expression and decided it was a smile after all.

"You remembered my name. What a nice lady. How do you do?" Jorg held out a giant hand, each rounded knuckle and taut sinew as smooth as though they had been molded from clay. The yellowed claws were striated and flaking and appeared tacked on the surface.

I reached out to complete the handshake, but Randall yanked the grall's arm back down. "You work for me, remember? Stop making friends and get her out of my wagon."

I wasn't about to let anyone drag me anywhere, so I flung back my hair and climbed down the small ladder to the cobbles. I straightened my shirt and stuck my nose in the air. When I realized I was doing a fair impersonation of a lady, I stopped acting insulted and gave Randall a straightforward glare instead. "Now, give me the documents."

"You know?" Randall folded his arms and looked me up and down. "You aren't as pretty as Ilsa. Too skinny."

There was no room to draw the Ashur, which was my first reaction, so I cursed him in Solhan. A good, long string of epithets Nanny used often. It's not as though I cared what Randall thought, but anger was my automatic response to hearing Ilsa's name. I hated how she always brought out the worst in me.

"Get her out of here," Randall told to the grall.

"You need to leave. Sorry." Jorg reached for me.

"I'm only here for what's mine. Why are you so reluctant to give me those papers, Randall? Hiding something?"

The slaver narrowed his eyes. Ah oh, I had aroused his suspicions. "You need to stay out of things, girl. If you weren't your uncle's ward, I'd have even less tolerance for your stupidity."

I wouldn't let anyone call me stupid but me. "I know you're a lying, conniving, criminal. I know my slave was born free."

"Shut your mouth."

"That's why you won't give me those papers. You know I ask too many questions and would expose you if I found out. Well, it's too late. I already know and so does the Guard." I wouldn't mention that by 'the Guard' I meant Conrad, or that he wouldn't act without proof.

"Know what?" The female slaver from the other day said, stepping around the wagon. I could see her better in daylight and realized she was half-elf. Such mixes were rare, or rarely allowed to live.

Common belief was a half-elf child was a changeling, a corrupter. The elves did not want the purity of their race despoiled, and so the illegitimate spawn of their romantic pairings were put to death. At least that was the story. I had known a strange half-elf girl at boarding school, with an elvish mother, so I suspected it was more a matter of difficult breeding, like generating a fertile mule, rather than a carefully planned elf conspiracy.

The half-elf slaver put a restraining hand on Randall, who was ready to attack me. I wanted him to come charging, so I could skewer him in self-defense. There were plenty of reasons the world would be a better place without him. I shook my head. The bloodlust I felt for Randall was a dangerous thing. I tried to calm myself and started by taking my hand off the hilt of the cane.

"She's spreading vicious rumors," Randall said, spitting at my feet.

"I only want the documents owed me," I told her.

"I heard your accusation, and I'm happy to allay your fears." Focusing on Olaf, she said, "Give Miss Thorne the paperwork for the Lallalokan."

Olaf nodded, ducked inside, and began to rummage through a lockbox he took from a drawer of his desk.

"You'll find everything is in order," she said.

"The old man is your bookkeeper?"

"Yes." She was smiling, but I saw how her large eyes watched me, trying to read me.

"A lot of responsibility for a slave. How did you teach him? Mine seems impossibly slow. I doubt she understands the reasons for her beatings." Just us slaveholders here, I was trying to say, old chums exchanging information on how to make those pesky servants do our bidding.

"They're very individual," she said carefully. "Some are easier to train than others."

"Of course." I nodded.

I turned and caught Olaf staring at me. Had Viktor died because he helped this old man, or because he'd found out about the forged documents? How far would I be allowed to go with them before a stiletto was slipped beneath my sternum?

"Thank you," I said, taking the parchment. On a whim, I asked Olaf, "Do you like your work?"

"He doesn't like or dislike it," she said, answering for him.

"This one is like her brother," Randall said into the woman's ear. "An emancipationist."

"Don't get nasty now," I told Randall.

"I'd show you nasty..." He licked his lower lip.

"...if it weren't for my uncle," I finished for him. "He makes you shiver like a skinny dog sniffing its behind."

"Watch your tongue, Eva. You have no idea how fast your fortunes can change. You keep spreading accusations about me, and Ulric may lose patience with you, cut you loose. Then I'll be there. He cares more about my reputation than yours, which is already tarnished."

I felt unclean wherever his gaze touched me. "Why would my uncle care about your good name?"

The woman scowled at Randall. "Quiet." To me, she said, "You have what you came for. Go, so we can get back to work."

I really wanted to know what the comment meant. I might have pressed with a few more unwelcome questions, but a shout caught my attention.

"Get her!"

A horde of street thugs barreled toward me. I didn't recognize any individuals, but I recognized the type. This must be Jessup's gang and what was left of Killian's. They were a brazen lot, coming after me in daylight in the heart of the slaver encampment. The war had found me.

"You're right, I should go." I tucked the folded documents into my belt purse and took off in the opposite direction of the pack chasing me.

I had to weave between slave cages, and I stirred up a nest of bogles. The creatures always seemed to lurk around human misery. Their camouflage melted away, and they leapt in all directions to avoid being stepped on. Leathery skin brushed against me. I cringed but kept going.

Thugs were sweeping around the sides of the slaver wagons and getting ahead of me as well as blocking off retreat behind. I ran full speed, hoping to break through before they closed ranks. There was half a dozen of them in my way now, and they had weapons drawn.

No getting past them. I stopped to assess the situation.

Where were my shadows, Grim and Gormless? I'd told them to leave me alone, but they hadn't actually listened had they? This was exactly the sort of thing they were supposed to deal with. Not that I was condoning Duane's actions in sending them to spy on me, but they really weren't doing their job.

Then I spotted them off to the side, surrounded by at least a dozen of Jessup's people. Gormless raised someone over his head, and I stared open mouthed as he threw the man into the mass of thugs, bowling them over. Grim got entangled among them, but I saw his fists moving in a blur as he fought his way clear. Yeah, they were pretty busy.

My attackers converged, and I raised my cane, ready to unsheathe the blade if I had to. I'd never shed blood before, and I didn't want to start now, but unless Grim and Gormless hurried up, I'd be forced to.

I thumped the first one who got within range in the head, but the other four managed to encircle me. A blade flicked. I dodged, but it nicked my elbow. The sting of an open wound in air made me hiss. I pulled off the cover on my cane and revealed the Ashur's vicious-looking serrated steel. A few eyes widened. Maybe they'd be smart and leave before I had to hurt them.

A second later, I realized it wasn't my weapon that made the thugs hesitate. The ground beneath my feet vibrated as the grall thundered down on us.

He threw one man farther than Gormless had. Another one he smashed to the ground with a single blow. I didn't know if the guy was concussed or dead, but he was sure shorter. The others scattered like mice pursued into a wheat field by a saber-toothed cat.

"Leave the nice lady alone," Jorg shouted after them.

Blood trickled warmly over my arm and dripped to the ground. The grall tore a filthy strip of cloth from his already too short pants and wrapped it around the wound. He cinched it tightly, and I gasped.

"Sorry." He loosened the bandage. "You people are so small, it's hard not to hurt you."

"I thought you wanted to be a merchant and didn't like violence?"

"Men who hurt girls and butterflies make me mad," he said. I didn't like being called a girl, but Jorg could call me anything he wanted after saving my life.

"Thank you."

He shuffled his feet with embarrassment. He was so heavy each movement made the pebbles in the grooves of the cobbles bounce around.

Randall hurried over to us, huffing and puffing, and checked the thug on the ground. "Dead."

Jorg's head drooped. Deeply saddened by the pronouncement, a low sound echoed from his throat. He shouldn't blame himself. It was self-defense. Besides, death by grall wasn't considered murder, more like misadventure. No different than stepping in front of an avalanche.

The slaver shook his head. "What do I tell Jessup? He's a business partner, you lout!"

"I was only helping the girl."

"Your loyalty is supposed to be to me. You're fired!

## 13 A GRALL STEPS INTO A BAR...

"And forget picking up your pay," Randall added. "Jessup will want compensation for what you did to his man."

"You can't do that," I said, defending my defender. "They were going to kill me."

"If only they had." Randall turned his back and ambled towards the wagons.

"Don't let him treat you like this," I told Jorg. "Go, demand your pay at least."

The grall spoke as quietly as his deep, booming voice was capable of, "I hated working here anyway."

"I got you fired, didn't I?"

"It's okay, really. But..."

"What?"

"I'll have to go home now. My visa requires I have a patron to stay in the city." He looked north. "It's going to be a long walk."

I didn't know anything about gralls and where they came from, or who in the name of the Three Kingdoms gave out visas to them, but I did know they were considered dangerous creatures, like dragons. The Highcrowne government must require someone to vouch for him. "I'll be your patron. It's the least I can do."

"You have a job for me?"

"Don't I just have to guarantee you won't cause any trouble?"

"I have to be 'gainfully employed' to stay here," he said, morose. "Time to start walking home."

I grabbed hold of his arm; it took both hands to get a grip on him. "I owe you. Follow me, and I'll think of something."

The fracas involving Grim and Gormless was still underway. The two of them were having fun and in no hurry to end it. Only a few of the rival gang's members still stood. I debated about helping, but I didn't want to get any more involved in this war than I already was. It wasn't my problem.

I slipped away with Jorg in tow. I felt fairly safe now with a grall watching my back.

What should I do with him? There certainly wasn't room for another house guest at Viktor's, but I seldom gave up once I got it into my head to do something. I resolved to pay the debt I owed Jorg, somehow.

I let my subconscious work on a solution to this latest puzzle, while I dealt with the old one. I had some slavers to bring down.

I pulled out Kali's forged documents and read them while I walked. I knew the streets in the neighborhood well enough, I didn't have to look up before making a turn. The documents appeared convincing, which explained why the slaver woman was so confident, but I knew they were fake. There had to be some way of proving it.

Magic immediately sprung to mind as the simplest method, but I couldn't afford a mage's fees. Besides, why pay for something I could get for free? Erick seemed to know what he was doing, and he was sure to have some potion or talisman for demonstrating the documents had been forged.

I made my way to the Bowl and Crown Inn and assumed all the passerby were staring at the evil, brother-murdering, pariah called Eva before I remembered the grall. I'd grown used to his booming footsteps behind me, finding it a comforting sound. If I had the money, I'd hire him as a full-time bodyguard and then see what the High Priest's wife and other gossips had to say to me.

The common room hushed as soon as me and my companion entered. Jorg bent double to avoid hitting the top of the door frame. Diners stared, spoons halfway to their mouths. The mélange of lunch time aromas was enticing.

The matron greeted us. "Can I help you?"

"What's good? Ooh, do you have those pastry parcels?"

She couldn't stop looking at Jorg. "...Does it want some too?"

"You should try them," I told him.

"Okay."

"Two pastries," I said.

She pulled out a chair from one of the tables, assessed the grall's size, then put it back. "I'm sorry, there's no place that you both can sit."

"We'll take the food with us."

Relieved we wouldn't be staying, the matron's tense stance relaxed. She hurried to the kitchen.

"Wait here," I told Jorg. He nodded. Since all eyes were on the grall, I followed the matron unobserved.

The kitchen was larger and more organized than Karolyne's, with lots of hanging herbs and shiny pans. I knew shiny was better than blackened and rusted, but that was about all I knew. The cook and matron were both surprised by my entrance. "You can't be here."

"I want to know if Erick Karsten is in. He's the real reason I've come."

The matron frowned, which made me wonder if she guessed something about Erick's illegal activities. "He's not here."

"Can you give him a message then? Tell him Eva needs to see him right away."

"Eva who?"

"He'll know who I am. And thanks for the pastries." I held out a few coppers, not knowing what the price would be, and she took twice as many as I would have liked.

"I'll tell him." She wrapped my food in a thin scrap of cheesecloth and handed them over. "Come again ... but without the grall, if you please."

I narrowed my eyes. "It's not up to me where Jorg goes. He's free to do whatever he wants. After all, who's going to stop him? You?" That ruffled her feathers, which was what I'd intended. I couldn't abide racism or species-ism, whatever.

Admittedly, I didn't like elves or twin sisters, but my opinion was justified from experience.

When we were back on the street, I handed Jorg his pastry parcel. It looked like nothing more than a crumb in his massive hand. He knocked it back and swallowed.

"Mm, good." A moment later, he said, "Food service seems like a rewarding career. It makes people happy. Maybe I should apply for a job here?"

The food was delicious, but the matron's comment about Jorg made it sit poorly in my stomach. "There are better places you can work." And I had just the one.

Karolyne's was terribly busy at midday. I was glad it wasn't my shift. Another girl I only knew in passing was working the kaffe bar.

I spotted utensils flashing in the kitchen and heard pots clanging but couldn't see anyone through the opening, so it must be the dwarf back at work. He was too short to see over the counter and hopped on a step stool every time he needed to put a plate up there.

Karolyne was taking orders as always. She must not require sleep, because she seemed to be here every shift.

Jorg's arrival had the same effect as it had at the Bowl and Crown. Conversation ceased and it went quiet, except for Reginald, unable to see outside the kitchen, who continued to cook noisily.

"A grall," said a goblin, his phlegmy voice full of awe. The mercenaries were back and enjoying a few bottles of fermented milk. Karolyne's new daylight prohibition was not working out very well, especially with the more insistent customers.

Since I had Karolyne's full attention, along with everyone else's, I said, "Guess what? I found you a new busboy!"

When I indicated Jorg, my friend swayed a little. I liked to think my suggestion had been so overwhelmingly brilliant that she was momentarily stunned, but I suspected it was more like the shock induced by sheer terror.

"Order up!" Reginald said.

Karolyne came out of her daze and ran over to me. "What are you doing, Eva?"

"Helping you out."

"Order up!" Reginald bellowed this time.

"You can't bring a grall in here. He'll tear up the place."

Jorg stood, hands at his sides, smiling cheerfully at us.

"He will not. You don't even know him. Let me introduce you."

I did the formals, and when Jorg held out his hand, I was proud of my friend for shaking it. It was awfully dry and scratchy I knew.

"Pleasure to meet you, but you can't work here." Karolyne pointed at the crowded room. "It's too small for one thing. And for another, I'm not hiring."

Jorg's face fell.

I patted his arm. "Listen, I'll convince her."

"Grall!" One of the goblins shouted.

"Stay out of this," Karo told the customer.

"Grall! You think you can smash us? You think you can fight? We're Fierce Brigade and we're not afraid of you!" Raucous laughing among the goblins followed this challenge. Jorg didn't seem to hear them; all his attention was focused on Karolyne.

"I told you to be quiet," she said.

"You're not our master, human!" The goblin swigged back the remainder of his alcohol and shattered the bottle on the table. Dishes clattered everywhere and glass went flying. A few customers looked ready to flee, but Jorg was still blocking the doorway.

"Look what you've done." Karolyne held her hands out to the mercenaries. "Please, sit down. I'll bring you another drink."

"No more drink! Not until we drink blood!" The goblins snickered and cheered, working themselves up to a frenzy with a bunch of warrior chants—then they charged Jorg.

Karolyne and I jumped aside. A wall of teeth headed for us. Only when that deadly mass impacted against the grall's legs did Jorg notice them. He looked down at the teeth buried in his thighs, carefully grabbed a goblin by the neck, and pressed his fingers against the hinges of its jaw until the mouth popped open. He flung the tiny goblin out into the street like a dislodged flea. Snow had begun to fall. The other two goblins were evicted the same way, without a sound from Jorg.

When it was done, he wiped his hands. "Did I miss something?"

Karolyne's mouth hung open. "Amazing." Of course, she hadn't seen him fighting gangsters in the Slave Quarter. I knew Jorg was capable of far more. He'd restrained himself, because he was basically in the middle of a job interview.

Jorg shivered at a draught from the door and pulled it shut. "Goblins are angry, little people."

"Hello? Does anyone care about all this food I'm cooking!?" Reginald called from the kitchen.

"Give me a minute," Karolyne shouted back.

"Oh, give you a minute, eh? Thinks her time is more important, does she? I can't have one nap during the day, but you can take your time and have a little chat during the lunch rush? Why do I even try? No one appreciates when I work hard. All you notice is when I leave. Well, here I go! Goodbye!" He tore off his apron and tossed it on the plates waiting to be collected—I caught a glimpse of his hand—then Reginald marched into the common room.

I stepped in front of him. "What will Gypsum say?"

Reginald frowned. "I'm sick of being held down by women. I'm not listening to them anymore, not to Gypsum and not to you. This time I'm staying quit!" His jaw set, the dwarf walked between the grall's legs and out the front door.

Reginald had quit a few times before, but this time I thought he meant it. Karolyne was stunned. She took in the packed restaurant and tears welled in the corners of her eyes. But this was Karolyne. She quickly pulled herself together, brain whirring away with calculations, and asked Jorg, "Can you cook?"

"Yes, he can," I said with a huge smile. I had no idea if it was true, but I said it anyway.

I helped Jorg find his bearings in the kitchen, and we finished serving the lunch crowd. Surprisingly, a grall cooking didn't scare away the customers; rather, he was an attraction. More and more people from the neighborhood came in under one pretext or another to catch a glimpse of him. There was a lot to look at. Unlike Reginald, Jorg was easy to see over the serving counter.

I couldn't fit in the kitchen, unless I put my back to a wall. There was no room for Jorg to turn around either. But he had only to reach out for something he wanted, like a long-tentacled sea creature wedged in a crevice snatching passing prey. Jorg embraced his new role, cranking out human food as though he'd done it all his life. He wasn't any better at it than the dwarf had been, but at least he had a better work ethic.

In between offering advice on boiling vegetables, I learned that being evicted from the slaver encampment meant Jorg was now homeless as well. My debt was only half repaid. I doubted an inn or boarding house in the entire city would take him in, so I offered a bed at Viktor's. Well, not a bed—since even the one in Viktor's room wasn't large enough—more a pile of bedding.

At the end of his shift, Jorg shook Karolyne's hand again. "Thank for this opportunity. I didn't want to go home to the ice. Expect a visit from an immigration officer in the next few days."

"Elves and their paperwork," she said, knowingly.

I told Karolyne, "I get overtime for helping the new cook get situated, right? My own shift isn't due to start for a few hours yet."

She acted like she hadn't heard.

Jorg followed me home, and, once again, I loved the rumbling in the earth that accompanied us, as well as the shocked expressions of passerby. Let's just say, while holding my Ashur I felt pretty confident, but with Jorg I felt downright cocky. I was almost itching for someone to mess with me.

The flaw in my plan became apparent when we were standing outside Viktor's building, my building now, as I had to keep reminding myself. The doorways were not as large as those found in public houses, like Karolyne's. There was no way to get the grall through the door.

"Follow me." I led him around to the alley in back.

The rear entrance was even smaller. Then, I noticed the trapdoor to the cellar. It was wide enough for crates to be winched down into the storage area beneath the shop. I found the key on my key ring and opened the doors. Rough wooden stairs led into darkness.

"Gralls live in caves, right? A basement is like a cave. You'll feel at home."

"We live in houses," Jorg said. "Big ones. But this will work. Thank you."

Guilty about exiling him to a dungeon, I went down first, swinging my cane in front of me to scare off any bogles and to make sure I didn't run into anything. After cringing from cobwebs and damp wood, damp with what I didn't want to know, I eventually found a lantern.

Using an iron sparker, which I always kept in a pouch, I managed to light it. Ok, I disdained mundane implements, but with my lack of funds and vow to avoid family magic, I didn't have much choice but to adopt a few contraptions.

The cellar wasn't too bad. Old bookshelves lined the walls, and empty crates full of straw packing material were stacked in one corner. Other than that, there was plenty of room for a grall. I found and lit a few more lamps, making the place almost cheery. In the process, I spotted the door to the coal closet beneath the stairs leading up to the bookstore. I'd forgotten to buy coal for my bedroom stove today. Why did I bother with 'to do' lists?

Jorg pointed at the crates. "May I?"

"Go ahead."

With one fist, he smashed them into bits of wood, straw flying, until there was something like a nest on the ground. He smiled. "I like it. Better than my old tent."

"Did you leave any personal items with Randall?"

"A few."

"Well, we are going back there tomorrow to get them. I'll also send Nanny down here with some blankets to help make the place more habitable."

"I like it fine."

"You'll like it better when we're done." I gave him the key to the cellar, so he could come and go as he pleased. "Settle in. I'll be back soon."

I made my way upstairs, formulating my explanation to Nanny on the way. I imagined it might go something like, "Well, I found this stray grall...."

I expected Nanny to be my biggest worry, but I was in for a shock as soon as I stepped into the entry hall—Ilsa was there waiting for me. Behind her, I saw Kali in tears, Nanny grim-faced, and the white armor of three elven guardsmen.

"There she is," Ilsa said, pointing an accusatory finger.

The guards encircled me, and one slapped a pair of manacles around my wrists.

I was too dumbfounded to struggle. "What's going on?"

"Eva Thorne, you are under arrest."

## 14  Innocent

"What for?" Was housing a grall against the law?

The snide elf who fastened my manacles said, "It is a punishable offence to free slaves without permission from the Crowns."

By 'permission' they meant heavy bribe. The tight restrictions on slave ownership in Highcrowne imposed by the other rulers had resulted in the Elf King demanding safeguards to prevent the slave numbers from being depleted. That meant slaves could not be freed, not without significant monetary compensation to the state. The cost was outrageous, so it never happened, even if you did find a kind-hearted slave owner who might consider it in the first place. Kind slave owner was an oxymoron.

"I have no idea what you're talking about." I had watched Duane enough over the years to know it was best to deny everything. I hadn't been the one to free Kali, anyway—it had been Erick—so my innocence was entirely genuine.

"Then why doesn't your slave have a mark?" Ilsa took Kali by the arm and brought her forward so all could see her blemish-free bicep.

Of course, Ilsa was behind this. Getting me arrested was an extreme punishment for ruining her shoes, but I suspected there was more to her evil plan. I should have seen this coming.

I didn't say anything. Ilsa would twist any words that came out of my mouth. One of the soldiers grabbed Kali.

"Stop. What are you doing with her?" I protested.

"She's evidence."

The other two guards manhandled me toward the stairs. I ignored Ilsa and called to Nanny, "Tell Gypsum what's going on. And there's a grall in the basement."

"What?" Nanny's eyes bulged.

"You'll need to look after him until I get this sorted."

Ilsa smiled. "Don't make too many plans, sweet sister. You're going to be stuck in a cage for a long time."

I feared Ilsa would taunt me all the way to the prison, but she only followed us to the street. Her joyful expression made me feel queasy. The last time I'd seen it, she'd been making my deceased pet mouse dance around its cage, her fingers laced with glowing charms and wiggling in time to the creature's movements. I thought her 'cage' reference meant she now considered me her new plaything.

It was because of Ilsa I hated looking in a mirror: I couldn't bear to see her face. Also, they were too easily broken. The risk of bad luck wasn't worth it. I already had my fair share of doom, but my own stupidity was to blame this time. Why hadn't I guessed what Ilsa would do?

Kali sobbed quietly as we were frog marched out of the neighborhood—plenty more gossip would result from this—and to the Watch house in the Market District.

There were elves everywhere, unsympathetic faces, and knowing smirks. I'm sure they didn't care what I'd done, being Solhan was crime enough. Once inside, the guards took my belt pouch and key ring away, locking them in an iron-banded box. Kali's documents were in that bag, my only proof against the slavers.

My mind raced furiously, trying to come up with a way out of this mess. They were leading us to separate cells. I pulled free, the guard holding me shocked I had managed it, and whispered into Kali's ear, saying, "Pretend you can't speak elvish. Don't utter a word."

She nodded, choking back tears. I got a dagger hilt jabbed into the base of my neck for my resistance, knocking me to the ground. I was dragged the last few feet to my cell and tossed inside. A solid iron door slammed behind me.

Whatever story I came up with, I didn't want Kali to contradict it, so I hoped she could keep quiet. Should I claim to be unaware her mark was gone? Play dumb? Or, should I accuse the slavers of selling a non-hereditary slave? The elven guards were unlikely to accept Kali's word she was born free. They could examine the documents and see they were forgeries, but I knew none of these people were on my side. They wouldn't listen, because they wanted me to be guilty.

I felt the walls of my narrow prison. I couldn't extend my arms, and I'd have to curl up into a ball to sleep on the urine-scented straw covering the floor. Jail wasn't what I'd expected. I'd expected barred windows, but there were no windows. I'd also expected awful food, but, as the hours wore on, there was no food either. It was worse than I imagined.

I was missing work, my internal clock told me that much. Karolyne would assume I was blowing her off because I'd helped Jorg earlier in the day. This was Nanny's chance to get rid of me and Kali both. All she had to do was keep quiet, and no one would ever know we were rotting in a cell.

This was only a Watch house, not Northcliff Prison, so if they wanted to keep us for long, they would have to transfer us. There was a slim chance of seeing daylight one more time.

Unless the guards forgot about me. Elves didn't eat or drink as frequently as humans, and I was already parched. I highly doubted they cared.

I gouged my name in the wall with the edge of a manacle. The blocks were limestone, so it didn't take long, but in the darkness, I had to keep feeling my work to make sure the symbols were even. Plenty of past inmates must have had a similar idea, because there were indentations everywhere. I could make out some words with my fingertips, the larger ones were epithets.

One corner had a six-inch hole cut into the stone, an apparent escape attempt, but the budding engineer must have been transferred before he could finish. The walls were at least three feet thick, so it would take ages to dig out. I scraped at the area for a while before I got tired and dozed off.

It had to be morning by now, but there was still no light. This was longer than I had ever sat still in my life. Lady Halcyon had complained of my constant twitching, unable to balance a teacup on my knee for more than a few moments before I had to shift position. Apparently, all it took to settle me down was a night of imprisonment.

It was a relief when I heard the key in the lock. I hadn't been forgotten. The dim light from an oil lamp was blinding, and I put a hand up to shield my eyes.

"Eva Thorne?" the guard asked.

"Yes?" My throat was dry and the word little more than a whisper.

Hands grabbed my elbows and led me down the corridor and into a slightly larger room with hooks hanging from the ceiling. This did not look good.

The chains of my manacles were fastened to one of the hooks, and I was forced to stand with my arms above my head. Where was the stove with the red-hot pokers? My entire prison experience had been disappointing so far, but I fervently hoped people had been even more wrong about the torture part.

A silver-haired elf in white robes circled me. The silver hair wasn't a sign of age but region, likely woodlands. He looked to be about sixty, not quite middle aged for his race.

"Thank you for keeping the slave girl," he said. "We now have proof. Too many of your compatriots evade punishment by spiriting freed slaves out of the country. I am fortunate to have captured someone so idiotic."

"You didn't have anything to do with it. My own sister turned me in, for spite, and you're getting played by her. I didn't do anything. This is a family grudge is all."

"You deny removing the slave mark?"

"I deny everything."

His eyes narrowed. "We have ways of making you talk."

"Red hot pokers?"

"No. Magic."

That was worse. I might be able to endure pain, or pass out and be done with it, but I couldn't resist a truth spell. I rooted myself and said, "I demand an advocate."

"You're not a Citizen."

"I still have rights. I'm not some beaten down servant. I'm a Thorne."

"Is that supposed to mean something to me?"

Apparently, the family reputation was known mainly to humans. This was one time when I would have loved the chance to be hypocritical and use my uncle to my advantage.

"Did you remove the mark yourself? Are you a mage?" he asked.

"No."

"Then a mage was complicit. Give us their name and the consequences to you will be less severe."

"No. I'm not telling you anything about anything, because this is all a mistake."

I recalled a moment when I was eight, chasing after Viktor and Duane in the market. Viktor had been caught with a stolen piece of fruit. Slick and cool as ice, Duane intervened, confidently argued in Viktor's defense, talking so fast he left the disgruntled merchant confused and scratching his head. In the end, Viktor and Duane walked free and kept their stolen treat. What was it Duane had said? I could only recall one bit that had impressed me, and I used it now.

"It wasn't me—I was framed." I smiled. There. That was my story.

The silver-haired elf laughed musically, the other two guards in the room joining in. "How very original."

He gestured to the guard on my right, and a moment later my head was ringing. The soldier had cuffed me with a heavy gauntlet. I shook my head but had no time to recover before a quick succession of slaps forced my chin on my chest. Now I had a headache.

"I thought you were going to use magic to interrogate me?"

White robes swished, a gesture I couldn't see, and a few more slaps made my cheeks sting. They weren't hitting hard enough to injure me seriously, but it was making me mad. "Stop it!"

"None of this will stop until you tell me the truth. I could use a compulsion, but why expend the effort? I know you shall relent."

"You don't know the first thing about me."

"You are a foolhardy child who thinks she is rebellious, courageous even, but you are nothing but a pest in our land. You have no patrons, no protection, nothing to keep you from exile. You think we will house and feed you in prison? No, we will deport you and see how well you fare in your homeland. As I understand it, Solheim is not a very nice place to be."

I'd heard bad things as well, but I wasn't going to let him see how much his threat bothered me. "Well, you're wrong. I do have patrons."

"Are you referring to the imbecilic human they stuck in a Guard uniform?"

"Conrad?"

"Yes, him. He heard of your incarceration and came here pleading on your behalf. I sent him away. There is nothing he can do for you."

I was ashamed to admit I experienced a surge of hope at the thought of being rescued. That hope was dashed before it was fully felt, which was just as well. A lady should never count on being saved. Morgan taught me that when he trained me on my mother's Ashur. He'd showed me the bloodstains in the grooves and said, "None of this is hers."

I wasn't fighting the Dead God's hordes or facing the fall of Solheim—these were policemen with a lot of glamour and very little intelligence. I didn't need Conrad's help. Still, I was glad he had stood up for me. It had taken guts for the new human recruit to confront an elven officer.

"A few slaps and the threat of exile is all you've got?" I had a stupid tendency to taunt those who held power over me. "You know what I think? You haven't hauled out the magic potions or the torture implements, because you know you're wasting your time. You know I'm not guilty, and you're only going through the motions so you can file your reports and say you investigated Ilsa's accusation."

The silver-haired one studied me with lavender eyes. Solhan eyes were pale like that, though usually tinted blue or yellow, so I did not find them unnerving. If that's what he was hoping for, then he would be disappointed.

"You are guilty ... of something."

I swallowed. I'd been right. He knew I wasn't someone with the power to remove a slave mark. Nevertheless, he seemed happy to offer me up as a sacrifice to his superiors. I guessed the emancipationist investigation wasn't going well, and any scapegoat would do.

"Put her back in her cell." The robes swished, and I involuntarily flinched at the gesture, but this time the guards removed my chains from the hook and led me out of the interrogation room.

I was going to rot in here. I only hoped they believed I was innocent and knew nothing about the mage who was freeing slaves. I didn't want to give up Erick. I wasn't being self-sacrificing because I had feelings for him—I wasn't sure what feelings I had for him—rather, I didn't want his work, Viktor's work, to stop. It was what my brother died for. I'd never done anything with my life anyway, so I might as well spend it in prison.

Back in my pitch-black cell, I sat, not fidgeting, for far too long. Having time to think was never good, but this wasn't me. I wasn't the accepting kind. I went over to the pathetic start of an escape tunnel and scratched away with my manacles again. I hoped it was an outside wall.

The ring of metal on stone filled the miniscule room and deafened me to the sound of my own ragged breathing. It helped me ignore the fear that had settled over me like a cold blanket. I fell into a rhythm. Clang, clang, clang, deep breath, clang ... chipping at rock until my wrists were chafed and sore. I immediately heard the discordant note when it occurred: a screech of rusted hinges as the door to my cell opened.

Were they going to question me again? I hadn't changed my mind.

A red glow outlined the dark figure of a man. I couldn't see his face, but I saw my jailer standing in the corridor behind him. The guard was vacant-eyed and drooling.

"Eva," the dark figure said, and I recognized the voice. It sent chills up my spine to see him standing there in an elven Watch house as calmly as though he were standing in his own drawing room. Uncle Ulric.

"What are you doing here?" I looked at the mesmerized guard and added, "How?"

"Ilsa has no secrets from me."

"So, you know she turned me in? Her own sister?"

"Why are you surprised?" He stepped into the room, and the light followed him; it was coming from him. I knew my uncle had magic, but I had never seen such an obvious demonstration of it before.

"How did you get in here?"

"As simple as pulling the strings of puppets. They dance and breathe at my command, what matter opening a door?" He wasn't bragging but stating facts in that sharply precise tone of his.

I was terrified of my uncle. Times like this, I understood my fear was well founded. The silver-haired Guard Captain who had questioned me was a mage, I was certain, yet he had not detected my uncle's presence. Ulric was that powerful.

"Are you busting me out?" He conducted business on both sides of the law, but I had never imagined Ulric committing a crime as direct as a jail break. Too low class for him. Not that I was complaining.

He touched a hand to the roof, which was only a hairsbreadth from the top of his skull. "It's like a tomb," he noted.

"I know. I've been stuck in here for a whole day, and I'm ready to go." I headed for the open door, but my uncle brought his hand down from the roof and blocked my path.

"You are not leaving."

"What? I—"

"I won't have a Thorne living as a fugitive from the Guard," he said.

"You can buy people off. You do it all the time."

"Not for you." Each word was perfectly enunciated in Solhan. He only spoke elvish for business, calling it a degenerate language.

"You bust in here like some Grand Wizard—"

"—I'm not a wizard." He looked at me disapprovingly. I was being imprecise and should know better.

"Whatever you call it, you've gone to the effort of mesmerizing the guards and avoiding the mages, so you can ... what?"

"So, I can pay an unmonitored visit to my niece." He didn't move his arm, and the red light emanating from him made me unwilling to shove him out of the way.

My uncle performed dark magic. I was afraid of it and of him. I'd seen Ilsa and Old Nanny twisting curses to get back at cheating boyfriends or to poison rats, respectively, and they would invariably mention how no one could do it better than Ulric. His reputation preceded him. How many souls had he used up in his life?

"Why won't you let me go?" I reverted to being a scared little girl in his presence.

"You need to learn, Eva. Learn to hate."

"I hate just fine, thank you." I was thinking of my feelings for him and for Ilsa.

He ignored my interruption. "Solhans have enemies. It's time you realized the world is a harsh place. You have been coddled too long."

"Coddled?" I felt like one of his puppet people, repeating everything he said, but I couldn't help it. "I'm living on my own now, Uncle, and I don't need you. Except to get me out of here."

He took my shoulders, and I flinched, expecting to be burned my mage fire, but the red light didn't hurt me. He said, "You have tremendous potential."

"I think you're mistaking me for Ilsa. She's the one who paid attention to your lessons, learned to be a lady, learned your secrets, and she's certainly learned to hate. It's probably time you gave up on me ever becoming a good little monster."

"You are a Thorne. You always will be. You cannot pretend to be something lesser for much longer. Darkness is calling, and you must face it." It seemed his expression softened, but I couldn't be sure in the strange illumination. "Ilsa has embraced her inheritance, but she's not like you—she doesn't question. With Viktor gone, you are more like me than anyone, Eva."

"No. I'm not."

"The path forks before you, my dear. Infinite choices have petrified you, but you must go forward. You remind me of myself at your age. I can't go back, and I wouldn't desire to. Not now. I made the right choices, and so will you."

I shook my head. "You got lost, Uncle."

"The false certainty of youth." He frowned. "You'll learn everything I say is true. In time." He stepped past the open door and began to close it.

"You can't leave me here!"

"I can." He locked the door behind him.

After he had gone, I stood there, mouth agape, as the blackness pressed in. He had abandoned me.

This was one of those times when it would be normal to cry. Because I couldn't, I knew there was something wrong with me, but no matter what he said, it wasn't because I was like Ulric.

# 15   Questions

Hours later, I was covered in limestone dust from my renewed efforts at escape. When the door screeched open again, I foolishly hoped it was my uncle, back to say my lesson was over and I could go home, but it wasn't. It was something better. Food and water, finally! I poured the stale liquid down my throat and looked around for more. The guard smirked.

I scowled at him so hard he made a gesture of protection against the Evil Eye. I didn't know such magic, but he didn't know that. He closed the door and left me to eat in the dark, nothing to see but after-images burnt into my retina. The bread was sour, the apple too soft and mealy, while the cheese was hard and overripe. I ate it all.

I went back to scratching at the wall and daydreamed of white snow melting into rivulets of cool, sweet water. My head ached continually now, either from bruising or dehydration. The shaky control I possessed over my innate anger did not hold up well in such conditions. I wondered if I'd be able to strangle the guard with my chains when he came back. For a moment, I wished I had let Uncle or Nanny teach me a few curses. It would have been nice to watch my captors squirm with an insatiable itch or lose all control over bodily functions.

I sighed, thinking about Ilsa, who was probably sleeping soundly in a soft bed and smiling to herself as she imagined my discomfort. I didn't want to be like my sister, but times like this I forgot why. Everything seemed to work out well for her.

Another day passed where I scratched at the wall and dreamt dark dreams of revenge. I would catch myself feeling angry and focus on the stone instead. This growing fury must be exactly what Ulric wanted me to feel.

The soldier came back with a plate of crusty bread and smelly cheese. He waited for me to guzzle the water and then said, "You have a visitor," and held the door open.

Imprisonment had improved my social calendar.

I squinted and made out a squat figure silhouetted in fire light, a fuzz of hair sticking out from his head at strange angles. He moved closer, and gold-rimmed spectacles glinted above a smiling face with a clean-shaven chin and massive moustache curling up at the ends. It was one of Gypsum's husbands, Markham.

"I'm your advocate." He paused to take in the miniscule cell, before studying my face. His smile broadened. "Is that a bruise on your cheek?"

I put a hand to one of many sore spots. "Probably."

"Wonderful!" He pulled out a stick of charcoal and a piece of parchment from his bag. He turned to my jailer and, in a chillingly professional tone, asked, "How do I spell your name, guardsman?"

His eyes widened. "What's going on?"

"Illegal search, wrongful imprisonment, torture.... We'll have this entire Watch house shut down and the soldiers sent to the Eastern Line by the time I'm done." Gypsum's husband seemed giddy.

Relief flooded over me now that my advocate was here—and competent. I didn't know if Nanny had told Gypsum what was happening as I asked, or if this was Conrad's work, but I was grateful either way. My escape tunnel was progressing too slowly, and I would prefer to leave before I absorbed any more of the 'lesson' my uncle wanted to teach.

The elven guard squirmed as Markham interrogated him. I had always known there was power in the law, though mastering it had never occurred to me. Legal texts and phrasing seemed as impenetrable and arcane as ancient Solhan invocations.

When the dwarf finished, he gestured for me to follow, and the guard did not stop us. Markham knew the way, leading me unerringly out of the cell block and into a common area with a long table. The silver-haired officer in white robes who had questioned me earlier was already seated, rolls of parchment and writing implements on the table before him.

"Miss Thorne. Sir Markham." The elf captain waved us to chairs.

My advocate remained standing. "We won't be here long."

The elf's lavender eyes darkened, but he nodded. "Very well. Miss Thorne is free to go, as soon as she signs the statement."

"What statement? I never said a word. I'm not putting my name on anything."

Markham raised a placating hand and gestured for me to come closer. I bent down so the dwarf could whisper in my ear. "I prepared a statement on your behalf, explaining the Guard's mistake in no uncertain terms. Please, read it if you like, but I suggest you sign."

He passed the parchment scroll to me. I unrolled it and read, my brow furrowed at first, but I soon relaxed when I saw the tact Markham was taking.

"That's right," I said. "Kali is the relative of an old friend. How could anyone have mistaken her for a slave?"

The whole thing was a mass of lies, and no one should believe it, but Gypsum had lent her support to the tale, along with her husband, Sir Markham. I wasn't about to contradict a 'Sir' and neither was the silver-haired Guard captain. I held out my hand for the quill, chains clanking.

As I put the finishing touches on my signature, the door opened. Kali was led in. Right behind her were two faces who made my hand slip, the quill tip cutting into the parchment. It was the half-elf slaver woman who gave me Kali's papers and one of her compatriots. No Randall at least, but I still felt sick. A queasiness settled in my stomach and rooted me to the ground. They knew who Kali was and would prove the false-hood of the paper I had just signed.

The woman smiled as she took a seat, but it didn't reach her eyes. The man watched everyone else in the room warily, not completely putting his weight in the other chair.

"Unchain my client now." Markham's tone was peremptory, and I had the urge to hush him. We were both about to be exposed as liars.

One of the guards obeyed, and the manacles slipped off my wrists, even as I watched the woman with a growing sense of doom. She was sure to give me away any second now. She was half-Solhan as well as being half-elf, a dangerous mix. Both loved little torments.

"Thank you for coming." The elf captain held out two more scrolls for the slavers. "It was I who insisted to Sir Markham you sign your statements with me as witness."

"We understand," the woman said, reaching for the proffered roll of parchment.

"You see..." The elf paused, gripping one end of the scroll while the slaver held the other. He wouldn't hand it over just yet. "...I find it odd the good advocate found two merchants willing to verify someone was *not* a slave. Very peculiar."

The woman's gaze met the captain's, unflinching. "I approached the advocate, not the other way around. Eva's sister told us what happened, and I felt it my duty to correct the situation. The Lallalokan she saw with us is not the same one in this room."

I glanced at Kali. She was stiff with fear, her expression confused, but she kept her lips sealed, still playing the baffled foreigner. Everyone's eyes were on Kali at that moment, which was fortuitous, else people would have noticed my own shocked expression. Why was the slaver saying this? Had Markham bought her off? Gypsum had gone far out on a limb for me. I should have given her a better gift for her last birthday.

The silver-haired elf did not relent. "What, may I ask, did happen to your Lallalokan girl? My informants tell me she was sold at a high price to a Solhan lady." He looked at me.

I frowned. I wasn't a lady. When would people learn that?

"I wouldn't know," the woman said. "Once I have payment, I don't care what happens to them." That sounded like truth.

"And you, Master Harald? Do you concur with your wife's assessment? This Lallalokan and the one you sold are different people?"

The two slavers were married? I would never have guessed. There was no hint of affection in their behavior to one another.

The man, Harald, seemed surprised he'd been addressed. "It's like Jhenna said."

The woman pulled her scroll free of the captain's grip. "You have a quill? I'd like to get back to work."

I gave her mine.

The Guard captain did not look happy, but there was nothing he could do other than pull me aside and whisper a warning. "I'll be watching you, Miss Thorne."

After the statements were signed, the five of us— Kali, Markham, the two slavers and I—were escorted out of the Watch house.

Conrad waited on the street, leaning nonchalantly against a wall. He came over to me and touched a hand to my bruised cheek. "I can't believe this happened. I'm ashamed of this uniform."

"Don't be. It's not your fault," I said.

My dwarf advocate shook the slavers' hands. "Thank you again for coming forward."

"My pleasure," Jhenna said. She called to me as she and her husband were walking away, "I'll be seeing you, Eva."

Harald and Jhenna had saved me when they could easily have left me to rot. What was in it for them? I thought about going after them and asking, but it was bad luck to question good fortune.

I respectfully bobbed my head to the advocate. "I owe you, Sir Markham."

He waved my gratitude away. "It was Gypsum. All I did was draw up a few documents and go around menacing guards until I got in to see you. It was highly enjoyable."

"Still, thank you." I leaned down and whispered so Conrad wouldn't hear. "Will you be in trouble if someone finds out we were lying?"

"I wasn't." I thought he was naïve, until I detected the amusement in his voice. "Gypsum says she knows Kali, and I must believe my wife. The Solhan Circle slavers say she's not theirs, and I am not about to question such credible witnesses. Like I said, I did nothing."

"Harald and Jhenna really did come forward on their own?"

"Yes."

"Did they say why?"

The dwarf shook his head. "Perhaps they like you? You are the same people."

"Solhans sticking together? Not possible."

Markham shrugged and said his goodbyes. I told him I would visit Gypsum soon and thank her in person. After he left, I was thoughtful, wondering what the slavers wanted and when they would ask for it.

Maybe they wanted my heart?

If they had such sinister ulterior motives, I wasn't looking forward to running into them again. I doubted that was their plan, though. What would be so special about my heart? If they needed a soul for dark magic, wouldn't anyone's do? They had plenty of slaves at their mercy already. Perhaps this was some convoluted way of warning me off without risking Ulric's wrath?

"What are you thinking about so earnestly?" Conrad asked.

I hurried to find an appropriate lie, not wanting to share my fears. "...Freedom." The overcast sky, orange and purple in the fading daylight was a welcome sight. "Highcrowne is a lot better looking than a cell."

"And the city is better looking with you in it again." He smiled, showing off those perfect teeth.

I blushed, suddenly self-conscious. The stink of fouled straw clung to me, and I itched from stone dust that had worked its way into every crack. "I need a bath. And I should get Kali home."

"Let me escort you both." Conrad held out an arm to Kali. Startled, she took it. I refused to put a hand on his other arm, wanting both of mine free as full dark approached. "So, you're an old friend of Eva's?"

Kali seemed unsure what to say. Apparently, Conrad had bought the official story. I wasn't surprised; he was too straight and narrow to deliberately participate in a fraud. It was kind of adorable.

"She doesn't speak elvish well," I lied.

"Ah." After that, Conrad more than made up for the lack of conversation on Kali's part. While we walked, he chattered about how the Market District's Watch house was old fashioned and poorly managed, while his own regiment was progressive and served as an example for the future of the Guard.

I stopped listening. My thoughts wandered from the slavers to ways of getting back at Ilsa for what she'd done, but I couldn't think of a retribution satisfying enough it wouldn't end up putting me in prison permanently. Of course, it wasn't the worst thing Ilsa had ever done, so why dwell? It was better to focus on other things.

My personal effects had been returned, and I felt the rolled-up slave documents in my belt pouch. I should try to contact Erick again. If he had come looking for me after I left a message at the Bowl and Crown, he was sure to have heard about my arrest. Maybe he had left town, afraid I would give him up? I hoped not. I needed to talk to him.

I wanted proof Kali's papers were forgeries, although it would be of little help now. I had signed a legal statement swearing Kali was not a slave, and I couldn't haul her out before the authorities later and offer her up as proof. If I did, the Solhan Circle might be fined, kicked out of Highcrowne, or even temporarily imprisoned, but I would also get Gypsum and everyone else who had covered for me in trouble. What good would that do?

Still, I would find Erick, if he could be found, and get those forgeries tested as a first step in establishing the slavers' guilt. The faked documents were a motive, but it wasn't proof they killed Viktor. I wanted to know for certain.

I doubted Kali was the only illegal slave they'd sold. I'd try to access other documents, or their old servant, Olaf, to find the proof I needed. Viktor had died shortly after freeing Olaf. I was certain the slave held the key to more than one secret. He knew where all the bodies were buried, so to speak.

Outside Viktor's house, Conrad stopped and kissed first Kali's hand then mine. "Too much loveliness for one place. This building is undeserving."

"Don't worry," I said, "Nanny balances things out."

I suddenly remembered the grall in the basement and hoped he was all right. He had been left alone with Nanny. "Is everything okay at the cafe? Is Jorg working out?"

"Oh, yes. It's striking to watch him cook. As far as I know, my cousin has no complaints."

"Does Karolyne know where I disappeared to?"

"I told her and swore I would free you, but, shamefully, I'll have to report I only managed an escort."

"You weren't the one who talked to Gypsum and found me an advocate?"

"Gypsum and I are not acquainted, I'm afraid. Perhaps Karo spoke to her?"

Yeah, I doubted it had been Nanny. "Well.... Goodnight, Conrad."

He was reluctant to let me go. Finally, with a furtive glance at the watching Kali, he said, "I'm sorry I failed you, Eva."

"I'm going to bed," Kali said, making a hasty exit. Her elvish was perfect, and I hoped Conrad hadn't noticed.

I sighed, looking at his puppy dog face. He must feel wretched, which explained his nervous monologue on the way here. I thought it was my filthy state keeping his usual flirtatiousness in check, but now I suspected it was his self-imposed guilt at having failed to rescue me from the dungeon. Ego stroking would be required, and I wasn't in the mood.

"There was nothing you could do," I said. "You're a recruit. That elven captain would never have budged. I do appreciate you trying, though."

"It's worse than that." He stared at his feet. "My investigation is at a standstill. Since the docks, I've learned nothing more about your brother's death."

I had plenty of my own leads to pursue, but I had plenty of reasons to keep them from Conrad too. All I said was, "I'm sure you'll get another break."

"What if they're right, and I don't deserve to be a guard? What if I'm so incompetent I never fulfil my promise to you?" He appeared heartbreakingly unsure of himself, so I touched his hand, and he squeezed mine.

"You're not incompetent," I assured him. "And elves are never right."

"I wanted to prove myself to you." His thumb caressed the area at the base of my forefinger, and I shivered. Uh, oh.

Erick had probably left town, I reminded myself. Not that we had an official relationship. Still, did it matter whether Erick had left or not? I thought about that kiss and decided it didn't. Conrad was gorgeous and kind and brave.... Where was I going with this? Oh, yes, but I needed to see how things worked out with Erick first. I wanted to give him an honest chance.

"Conrad..." I began.

"Eva!" Kali came running out the front door. "Come see! Nanny is gone!"

16    SEARCHING

“What do you mean by 'gone'?” I made a throat slitting gesture and raised my eyebrows questioningly. Nothing but Nanny's unexpected demise could get Kali this excited.

“She's vanished! Come on!” Kali ran back up the stairs to the living quarters above the bookstore, expecting me to follow.

Conrad stood straighter, alert, and said, “Let me investigate.” I allowed him to go first this time. The chance to do something guardsman-like seemed to bolster his spirits.

The living room was a mess: the settee torn to shreds, tables overturned, everything fragile broken into little pieces, holes knocked in the walls. The devastation was more thorough than what had happened to the bookshop.

My first thought was Ilsa. She made sure I was sent to jail, so she'd be free to search the place for secret compartments. Viktor had bequeathed silver and gems; perhaps Ilsa figured there was more of the same hidden away and not mentioned in the will? I remembered the way she'd defaced Viktor's portrait and knew she had no scruples.

Still, there was something desperate about this. The broken frames—how much silver could fit inside a painting?—a shattered bud vase, books torn out of their bindings.... Ilsa wasn't interested in anything so small, and if she were bent on vandalism, she had enough self-control to focus on the truly personal items.

"The whole place is like this, and there's no sign of Nanny," Kali said.

Conrad searched with dagger drawn, carefully opening closets and looking behind doors. "You should have come to me right away. The burglar may still be here."

It wasn't a common thief. They all knew Viktor had been Duane's friend. No thief would be suicidal enough to cross The Adder—I meant Duane. Now he had me doing it.

I hurried to the front door and was happy to see my Ashur where I'd left it. Suitably armed, I grabbed an oil lamp and made my way down to the cellar to check on Jorg. He wasn't there, probably at work. I should have realized he was gone, as no one would have dared ransack the house with the grall at home.

Conrad scouted Viktor's old bedroom, and I went to the guest room where I was staying. Clothes were scattered everywhere, but that was how I liked it, and it was hard to tell if anything was disturbed.

Nanny's bedroom was next. It was small and dark, the windows covered with thick drapes smelling of dust and mold. The old woman was a terrible housekeeper, but it was clear the searchers had been in here too. The mattress was torn, feathers piled on the floor. I spotted a door to a small closet on the other side of the room and pulled it open. Clothing toppled around my feet. A really terrible housekeeper.

I was about to leave when I noticed a piece of jewelry on the floor. It was the Eye of the Devourer, two ellipses forged in silver and set with an onyx. Nanny had worn it as long as I'd been alive and never took it off. I carefully picked it up. The tarnished chain was broken, gray hairs tangled around it. Someone had yanked it from her neck.

As often as I'd teasingly wished Nanny harm, the thought of her gone sent me into a panic.

Conrad came in. "I didn't find anyone. The house is empty."

"What about the bookshop?" I put the necklace in the pouch with Kali's documents and set off. Conrad followed as I checked downstairs, the alley, the rest of the house again....

Damn, Nanny still had the only key to the coal cellar. *If there was no other reason to find her,* I thought. Who was I kidding? Nanny was a mother to me, a cold distant mother who doted only on Viktor, but she was a part of my life. I felt shaky inside, almost as bad as the night Viktor died. How could she have vanished? Someone must have seen her taken away?

I went to the neighboring shops and pounded on the doors. Most were closed, but a few of the owners lived on the upper stories as we did. They grumbled about being awoken in the night, but when they saw a Thorne and Conrad's Guard uniform, they were reluctantly polite. No, no one had seen anything. They never did.

I hiked to my uncle's house, winter air burning my lungs. If Ilsa or Ulric had answered, I might have lashed out, but it was Morgan. He hadn't seen her either, and he put a steadying hand on my shoulder as I swayed. He knew me better than anyone, and he knew Nanny.

"I'll tell your uncle," he said. "We'll turn the city upside down."

"Thank you."

I had been through the entire neighborhood, twice, and was weary with defeat. I staggered back to Viktor's house. Conrad and Kali were still following me. I hadn't noticed them the entire time, my gaze focused on each house I checked, every alley I passed. I expected to see Nanny around the next corner.

"I'll find her. I promise," Conrad said.

I nodded. "It's late, and I've got a lot of work to do here. Goodbye."

He frowned at my sudden dismissal. "I understand. You have no reason to believe my promises."

I hadn't meant to insult him. The dead end he'd run into on Viktor's investigation must have made him sensitive. I reminded myself he had no reason to help me at all—the uniform he wore only required him to protect the Central City—so I tried to sound more appreciative.

"It's not like that. I apologize. Thank you for everything, Conrad. If anyone can help, I know it's you." I attempted a smile, and his expression lightened.

He kissed my filthy hand without a moment's hesitation. "I will not sleep, Eva."

He gave my hand another kiss then hurried off into the night, moving as though his armor didn't weigh a ton. He reminded me of a knight on some impossible quest, and he was doing it for me. I closed the door.

Back inside, the wreckage appeared worse than I remembered. I heaved a sigh before setting to work. Kali wanted to help, but I sent her to bed. She'd been sleeping on the straw floor of a prison for the last two days, so she didn't protest too much. I couldn't sleep. I wanted time to absorb what had happened. I also hoped to find some new clue from sifting through the debris.

*Nanny is missing.* The words kept echoing in my head, not really latching on anywhere, just a hollow fact I didn't know how to deal with. Whoever took her had trashed the place, looking for something. Whatever it was, I was certain it had to do with why Viktor was killed.

The slavers, Harald and Jhenna, had to be involved somehow. Viktor stole their bookkeeper and learned something he shouldn't have. I initially thought it was the forged papers and illegal slaves like Kali that he had found out about. Except, the punishment for those crimes would be minor—fines, banning from Highcrowne—unlike the harsh penalties imposed on emancipationists. I didn't see why the slavers would kill over it. Of course, people died for far less. I remembered the street gangs and their never-ending bloodshed. Still, Viktor's heart had been cut out, his soul stolen. It was not random violence: His death had purpose.

When they killed him, they hadn't learned where he'd hidden whatever it was they were searching for. They ransacked the bookshop first and then the house, looking for something small enough to hide inside a book or painting. A document maybe? And Gypsum's brother-in-law, my hired detective, had been killed too, at the docks, where a slave ship was berthed before heading east. I had no idea where that fit in, not to mention the automaton. And why would anyone take Nanny?

Even after hours of work, the house was still in chaos and so were my thoughts. I fell into bed when I couldn't keep my eyes open anymore. My sleep was shallow, and I woke with each unfamiliar sound, imagining the intruders had returned to finish their work. Maybe they would abduct Kali, or me, next?

I got up with the sun and took a bath I couldn't enjoy. Kali was curled up on Little Viktor's old pallet. She was tall and needed a longer bed; something had to be done about that. I peeked in at Jorg too, although I didn't know why I was worried for him. The steps creaked on my way down, and he heard me.

"Eva?" His deep voice sounded like boulders tumbling down a mountainside.

"You're here," I said, relieved.

"So are you! I heard the Guard took you away."

"They let us go." I knew I looked like someone sentenced to hanging rather than set free.

"Everything alright?"

"Have you seen Nanny?"

"The mean old troll who lives upstairs?" That was her all right, and coming from a grall, who must be close cousins with trolls, he would know. "Not for a few days. Is something wrong?"

"...No. Go back to bed." Jorg couldn't do anything to help this time; there was no one to fight. It was like the Devourer had swallowed Nanny whole.

I cleaned up another section of the house, but I didn't find anything worthwhile and didn't feel any satisfaction at the accomplishment. I couldn't bear to stay inside any longer, so I grabbed my coat and my Ashur and headed outside.

Snow had fallen thickly during the night, and the streets were powdered in clean, white flakes. It was hushed, the usual morning bustle of carts and street traffic subdued. The few people I saw kept to cleared paths, but I cut across a lane and looked back to admire my footprints. The only thing better than fresh snow was being the first to step in it.

Karolyne's place was closed; I could hardly believe it. Then I remembered this was Week's End. Explained why the streets were so empty. Everyone was at the temples, giving thanks for another week of life. Karolyne would be at the temple of the Wheel, where they prayed for Fortune's favor and a few more silvers for their coffers. It was almost as popular as the Light Bringer's temple, and some people alternated between the two places.

I didn't have a favorite temple. Perhaps Uncle Ulric had put me off religion, or maybe it was being Solhan. Our god walked the land, and it turned out we didn't like Him very much. I wondered if it would be the same if the Light Bringer came scorching across the heavens, or if Fortune's Wheel decided to roll across the backs of the merchants bowed before it. People might be less thankful if they stared into the demanding faces of their gods.

As I feared, Erick was no longer at the Bowl and Crown. "He left for parts unknown." The matron, who had taken a dislike to me for some reason, was not inclined to tell me anything more than that.

I didn't want to go home, so I kept walking. I sought out a path of fresh snow all the way to the Slave Quarter. The market wouldn't be open today, but the slavers would be in their camp. I was an imbecile, poking a sleeping dragon, but anger burned in my veins like good whisky. I needed to know why Jhenna and Harald had lied for me—and if they had anything to do with Nanny's abduction.

Snow crunched somewhere behind me. I glimpsed Gormless before he hid in a doorway. I hadn't detected him, but Grim must be around as well. Good. Considering my last visit to the quarter, I was not about to begrudge the backup.

Soft blue light reflected off the snow, except near the wagons and slave cages. A series of braziers and campfires encircled the place, keeping the merchandise warm and lighting everything in harsh yellows and reds, like bodily ichor. I strode toward the heat.

Before I made it ten paces, arms encircled me, pinning my Ashur against my side. My assailant was fast and strong. He covered my mouth with a gloved hand and pulled me behind a pile of storage crates.

# 17  OBSERVATIONS

I waited for the first slackening in my captor's grip and struck with the back of my head. I didn't hit anything. The man shifted fluidly, avoiding direct impacts from any of my blows that followed.

Then he let me go.

I spun, gripping my Ashur, but stopped mid swing when I recognized Duane. Why had I held back? I should have hit him.

He put a finger to his lips. "Quiet."

"I was being quiet. What are you doing here?"

"I've been here all night."

"Why would you do that? Looking for a girlfriend?" I glanced at the cages, which contained muscled men, no nubile young girls, but who knew what interested him? I planned to say that out loud and see how he reacted, but my response time was too slow.

"I'm keeping an eye on the slavers. I told you to stay out of this."

"What have I ever done to make you think I would listen?" I was in no mood to hear Duane give me orders, but I was curious. "What have you seen?"

"Plenty of activity since yesterday. Ilsa came and left. Randall and Jhenna argued, then she and her husband left...."

"You could tell they were married? Harald and Jhenna are as unromantic as a pure elven couple."

He smiled. "You're not as observant as you think."

I screwed up my face at him, annoyed.

"They returned around midnight," he continued. "While they were gone, Randall loaded up a wagon with slaves. Bell and Fink followed it to the docks. The loving slaver couple spent a few hours packing up the covered wagons as soon as they got back, before it started snowing. I suspect they will linger no more than a day."

My heart sped up. "No. I need more time. They had something to do with Viktor."

"What did they do?"

"I don't know exactly. You must suspect too, else you wouldn't be watching them so closely."

"I have a feeling," he admitted. "But there is more going on. Tell me what you see."

One of his observation games, was it? He and Viktor were always showing me up. They would glance at the crowd, turn their backs, and describe to me every person there and what they were wearing. I'd practiced whenever they weren't around until I got headaches.

"Wagons," I said acidly, "snow, cages, slaves...."

"How many cages? How many slaves?"

I told him, proud of myself. The practice had paid off.

"Most are empty," he pointed out.

"Well, you did say they had just shipped a wagon load off to the docks, idiot."

He ignored the jibe. "These remaining slaves are all exotics and will be sold tomorrow. The ones they took away were newly acquired here in Highcrowne. I've been keeping a tally of the sales, since this is my territory now."

He'd won the war already? I was disappointed in Jessup, but Grim and Gormless had thoroughly beat up what remained of their gang when I was last here. Who knew how many battles had been fought on dark and snowy nights I wasn't aware of?

"I assume you have a point?" I felt my voice rising and lowered it again. It would be too easy for someone to hear me in the hushed morning with nothing but the sizzle of flames and gentle gusts of wind to cover the noise.

"I do. They sold less than a quarter of the number of slaves they did on their last visit."

"Good. I'd love to see the slave trade come to an end."

"But..." he said, looking me in the eyes to make sure I paid attention. His were a particularly dark green today, I noted, so unlike pale Solhan eyes. "They acquired far more than they sold. Shiploads.

"Demand is up. There's a shortage of slaves in the elven districts and prices are high. Yet, the slavers are selling few and spending too much on the ones they buy from citizens. The slaver's agents outbid everyone else ... except for you. You paid more than any reasonable person would for Kali," he teased.

I didn't like being teased. "Are you saying the slavers aren't selling slaves, only buying them?"

"They sell a few."

"How do you know who the slaver's agents are anyway?" I asked, doubtful of his information.

"They're the ones who buy a slave and, when everyone's gone home, fail to claim their property." He left off calling me the idiot this time, but I sensed the unspoken word.

More bits of the puzzle were bumping together in my head. I had too many pieces of information and no place to put them. I forced my thoughts to slow, and eventually something coherent emerged.

"They bid on their own slaves—the ones they're selling on consignment, I mean, or the ones sold by other merchant cartels—through third parties, so no one knows it's them buying," I said, and he nodded at the accurate summary. "They're keeping up appearances. Why? I don't know much about business, but none of this makes any sense."

"I do know about it, and it is very bad business. Hiking up prices and only buying more? My head hurts trying to comprehend the sheer stupidity. I think you're right—it's all for appearances. They don't want people to know they're taking Highcrowne's slaves away."

"Elves don't like people doing that, believe me. Wait. Did you admit I was right about something again?"

"No. Maybe." He gave me a playful smile, and I hated the thrill that rushed along my nerves. He always had a way of making me feel alive. Sometimes I thought it was the danger he represented, but everyone I knew was dangerous, and they never made my skin tingle when they were near. Whatever it was, I distrusted it.

He gazed in the direction of the river, invisible from here, but I knew it flowed past the base of the mountain on which the city was built. "I'd like to know where their ships are going."

"East," I said. He raised his eyebrows, and I smiled, smug. "I have my sources too."

"You know what you missed when I asked you to look around?" He couldn't let me bask for even a moment.

"I'm sure you'll tell me."

"There are no vagrants, no one creeping close to steal heat from the fires. Your neighborhood is the richest in the Outskirts, and even it has more street people. Look."

I had noticed. He wouldn't believe me if I told him, though. I also knew the slavers could place marks.

They wouldn't.

A poor village in Lallaloka was one thing, but someone would know if the slavers were snatching people in Highcrowne. Wouldn't they?

"Maybe they're disgusted by the bogle infestation," I said, looking for a less disturbing explanation. "I know I wouldn't want to live here."

"When I slept on the streets, I would have hugged bogles for warmth. There's something else happening."

"I'll tell you what's happening: I'm going to have a word with the Circle." I hadn't seen Nanny in any of the cages, not that they would have been stupid enough to put her out in the open like that. I wanted to look in the wagons. If she wasn't there, it meant she was on a ship. They could have smuggled her aboard without Duane's people noticing. I hoped it hadn't left port.

As soon as I moved, he yanked me back to his side, and for a moment our faces were a few inches apart, both of us glaring.

"Let go of me." I enunciated each word, so they were heavy with menace.

"No. You can't walk in there, hurtling accusations. When has that ever worked for you?"

"There's more going on than you know, Duane. That couple, Harald and Jhenna, are the reason I was released from jail. I have a right to ask them why they defended me. And ... Nanny's missing."

"I know." He loosened his grip on my arm. "Nothing happens without me hearing about it. I want to find her too. By the Dead God, Nanny is the one who kept me from starving as a child. She'd feed me stew along with Viktor."

"Her stew is awful. You sure you want to find her?" I managed a fraction of a smile at my own joke.

"It was bad, but better than sewer mushrooms."

I nearly retched at the mental image.

More seriously, he said, "There's no sign of her here. I broke into the covered wagons last night, and she wasn't with the lot who went to the docks. I'm waiting to see where the slavers go next, so I can follow."

I shook my head. "Nanny could be anywhere. I don't know if she was taken yesterday or the day before—I was in prison."

"Never been myself."

"You're joking." I'd seen him commit countless crimes.

"You need to learn to run when you see a Guard uniform. I told your uncle I could bust you out, but he promised to handle it."

Ulric. He left me there. "Why would you offer to help?"

"I was worried about you."

That I didn't believe for a second. "There are more important things to worry about. If Nanny was taken soon after my arrest, she could be on the slavers' ship already."

"Bell is watching the docks. She's waiting for an opportunity to sneak aboard, but the place is teaming with mercenaries."

"I know someone who can get onboard."

Duane looked annoyed now. "Not that guardsman who showed up at Ulric's?"

"Yes. Conrad swore he'd help."

"You know why you've got him twisted so tightly around your finger, Eva? He doesn't have a backbone. He's like some gooey, sickly sweet piece of taffy. How can you stand him?"

"I like good people."

"And what's your definition of good? Not Solhan? You're rebelling, you know. You hate your people so much you're automatically drawn to anything the opposite. I saw Viktor do it too, but he grew up. When will you? When are you going to make your own judgments?"

I rolled my eyes. A typical Duane lecture. He never spoke, saving it all up until it poured out like this. I ignored him, except for the bits I could use.

"I don't like something simply because it's not Solhan. You're not Solhan, and I don't like you." *Besides*, I thought, *I like Erick, and he's the embodiment of all things Solhan—powerful, certain, brilliant, accomplished.*

"Fine. Go to your guardsman. If he helps us find Old Nanny, I don't care how insipid he is."

"Thanks for your blessing." I couldn't breathe without it being sarcastic. I straightened my jacket, rumpled in the tousle with Duane, and set off to find Conrad.

It was colder without the braziers. I glanced back at the flames and saw Duane watching me. He looked away quickly and focused on the slaver's wagons.

I didn't buy his claim he was keeping an eye on the Solhan Circle to investigate Viktor's death and Nanny's abduction. Like he'd said, this was his territory now. He was getting the lay of the land. He pretended to be kind-hearted, doing a good deed now and then, but it was for show. It had worked on Viktor. My brother never let a word be spoken against his friend. I wasn't so naïve. In Duane's heart, this was all business.

The morning services would get out soon, and the streets would fill up. I took advantage of the temporary lull in foot traffic and reached the café quickly. Most businesses were closed all day, but not Karolyne's. The post-prayer crowd was her favorite. People bored and hungry and in no mood to go home and cook would pay extra, especially the Light Bringer's worshippers who were up before dawn and fasting.

The restaurant already had a few customers when I got there, some drinking semi-noxious, yet potent, kaffe, while others examined the menu. Jorg was growling in the kitchen, massive arms swinging about with pans and wooden spoons. He must have left the house right after I talked to him for him to beat me here. The growling had a melody to it, and I realized it was the grall equivalent of humming. It was hard to tell with the tusks, but I thought he was smiling too. Seemed he was satisfied with his new job.

I found Karolyne hunched behind the kaffe bar arranging filled tins on the lower shelves. Without preamble, I said, "Good news is I'm out of jail. Bad news is I need today off too."

"What?" Karolyne stood. "I've been shorthanded all week, Eva. No. You're my friend, and that's the problem. At some point, I need to draw the line. No."

"Nanny is missing. I need to do whatever I can to find her before it's too late." I put on my most sincere expression. I didn't do teary-eyed well. Glares were my strong point, but I tried.

"I thought you hated that old hag?"

"It was more talk than substance. It's a Solhan thing. You treat your enemies bad and your family worse. She raised me."

"Eva...."

"I'm serious. I'm only here to give you the heads up, not to ask your permission. I also need to know if you've seen Conrad. I need to find him."

Karolyne gave a long drawn out sigh, letting me know how exasperated she was. She could fire me; I didn't care. She might not understand it, but some things were more important than money. I wasn't about to take up eating sewer mushrooms, but I was willing to go hungry for a while.

"I really am thinking about hiring somebody else...." I saw her tense posture ease as she relented. "I spotted Conrad talking to people as they left the temples. He seemed pretty intense."

"He's investigating Nanny's disappearance, probably questioning everyone in the neighborhood. He's thorough like that." I felt a warm glow of fondness for him at that moment.

Before setting out to find Conrad, I made a detour to the kitchen. The scents of cinnamon, smoked sausage, and tangy tomato drew me. Jorg was improving.

"Can I ask you something?"

Jorg flipped a flat cake in the air and said, "Of course. Oh, how much coin do you want?"

"For what?"

"Rent." He stood proudly, the top of his head jammed against the roof. "I got paid today. There's no other house that can hold me, so I'd like to stick with your cellar."

"I don't know. Whatever you can spare. It's not important. I was wondering about when you worked in the Slave Quarter. Did you notice anything odd?"

"Like humans kept in cages and sold to the highest bidder?"

Who knew a grall could be so droll?

"I mean, did you notice more slaves shipped down-river than ended up on the block?"

He went quiet, thinking. "They didn't like questions. I asked why we put a girl up for sale only to have the buyer hand her right back, and from the way they looked at me I was afraid to sleep that night. I'm big, but my throat is as vulnerable as anyone's. They had their own buyers, including one of the caravan guards I played dice with. There was a lot of that kind of oddness. So yeah, more slaves were sent to the docks than actually sold."

"You didn't overhear why? Where they were going?"

"No. Randall never spoke except to yell at me, and the other two never talked at all."

"Did you know Harald and Jhenna were married?"

"Sure. They shared a wagon."

"Oh." More observation practice was in order.

I snatched a roast tomato from the grill and blew on it between bites.

"Hey!"

"Thanks, Jorg." I darted away. It would take ages for him to disentangle himself from the kitchen to chase after me, not that I thought he would.

"You're welcome," he said in a laughing rumble.

I searched the temple district. It wasn't the actual 'Temple District' in the heart of the city, with its marbled columns and gigantic arched roofs. This was the human version. It was wedged between my neighborhood and the Spinners and Weavers district, and, while the buildings were more impressive than others in the Outskirts, there wasn't a lot of marble and gold—more like brick and a dash of copper leaf. Still, it was pretty.

I'd often thought about stepping inside one of the big archways of the Light Bringer's temple and admiring the statues up close, out of curiosity, but some part of me felt unwelcome. I trusted my instincts and didn't tempt the god this time either. I checked the other temples first and found Conrad haranguing an elderly man who had emerged from the Hearth Mother's service.

"But your shop is right next door. You must have heard something," Conrad loudly insisted.

"I don't hear anything without my cone," the old man shouted back, before raising the hearing aid, a large funnel made of tin sheets, to his ear to await Conrad's reply.

I laughed. I couldn't help it. Conrad's beleaguered gaze shifted to me, and I immediately fell silent, ashamed of myself.

"Thank you for your time!" he told the deaf man before coming over to me.

"I didn't mean to laugh. I never appreciated how impossible your job can be sometimes."

"At least he was willing to talk, even if it didn't work out." Conrad stood close to me, and I saw how his usually shining armor and golden hair was covered in dust.

"What happened to you?"

"I've been going to places and questioning people I'd rather forget about." There were dark circles under his eyes too.

"You didn't sleep, did you? Conrad..." I wiped a smudge of dirt from his cheek and gave him a wry smile. "I'm taking advantage of your goodness. I'm sorry. But there's something more I need."

I expected him to say, *No. Enough*, like Karolyne, but he nodded wearily. "What is it?"

"There's something strange going on with the Solhan Circle slavers. I can't go into specifics, but I'm worried they're the ones who snatched Nanny. They have a ship full of slaves sitting at the docks, ready to leave anytime, and I want you to search it."

He stared at me expressionlessly for a moment. "You want me to harass the merchants whose testimony helped get you out of jail? What's more, you're accusing them of enslaving a free woman?"

"When you put it that way.... Look, something is going on, and I'm almost certain they were involved with Viktor's death and Nanny's abduction."

He shook his head. He must think me crazy, but all he said was, "I can't do it without a writ."

"Sir Markham and Gypsum can help. The detective I hired, their brother-in-law, was murdered while investigating those slave ships."

"You don't know that."

"It all makes sense. Everything points to the Solhan Circle." As soon as I said it, I doubted the assertion.

I had suspected everyone from Duane to Erick to my own sister. I was bumbling in the dark. Was my hatred of slavery, and Randall in particular, clouding my judgment now? Was I wrong?

"Alright." He was exhausted and unwilling to fight me. "I don't have any other leads. You're sure about this?"

"Yes," I said, strangling my doubts.

"I'll go to Sir Markham." He bowed and turned to leave.

"I'm coming with you."

"No." He'd finally said it. "This is Guard business." His certitude made me hyper aware of the uniform he wore. He was the rightful authority in this city. How dare I question him?

My instinct was to fight for what I wanted, regardless of his rank, but I didn't want to risk alienating him, and his patience had to be running thin. I nodded.

He strode toward the Central City. That uniform would get him through the gates and into see Sir Markham, but not even he would be allowed anywhere near the Crowns. My problems were beneath their notice anyway, unless Duane's suspicions were true. Enslaving free-born humans within Highcrowne might be enough to get the Crowns' attention. Unless they were condoning it. I wouldn't put anything past the Elf King.

I headed back the way I'd come, not sure what I should be doing now. People better suited for the task than me were investigating Nanny's disappearance and the slaver problem. I should go to work, make things easier on Karolyne at least—but I wouldn't.

I kept thinking about the Slave Quarter this morning. That empty square and those lonely fires.

A string of dirigibles passed overhead. More refugees came to the city almost every day by boat, airship, wagon, and on foot, fleeing the wars in the human nations and the encroachments of the Dead God. They shouldn't be here, so no one would notice if they disappeared. I had noticed. Of course, Duane had too, but what mattered was whether or not *I* was going do something about it.

"Eva." The voice whispered from a shadowed doorway.

I turned. "Erick?"

# 18   FADED MEMORY

Erick hadn't left town. He hadn't run, and my estimation of him went up even further. He was cloaked and hooded. His garb wasn't out of place on a winter morning, but it also served to hide his identity.

"They set you free?" His wary gaze darted back and forth between me and the street. "I saw you talking to a guardsman."

"Conrad is a friend."

He was taut and ready to run if needed. I guessed the reason for his agitation.

"Don't worry. I said nothing about Kali. I never mentioned your name."

"Then why did they release you? Your guardsman intervened?"

"No, a dwarf friend backed me up—and the Solhan Circle slavers."

"What?"

"I know. I was pretty surprised myself. They are doing a great many surprising things, like buying up slaves and sending them east. And," I felt a surge of urgency whenever I said it, "Nanny has been abducted."

He tensed. "Madam Olinov is a very dear friend of mine. You think it was the Solhan Circle?"

"Who else?" There was no point in going over my long list of alternative suspects. Conrad would find out soon enough if I was right about the slavers. Yet, now Erick was here, there might be a better way. "Can you find her with magic?"

He eyed the direction Conrad had gone. "Not here."

Erick refused to carry on the conversation in the street. At least, he seemed convinced I wasn't about to turn him over to the Guard, so he agreed to go with me to Viktor's house.

Once inside, he pulled off his hood and stared with dismay at the devastation, which was not as bad as it had been before I started cleaning. "The slavers did this? Why?"

"One of many things I'd like to know. They ransacked the bookshop a few days ago too. I was cleaning it up when...." When I'd kissed him, but this wasn't the time to talk about that. "I think they're looking for something of Viktor's."

Erick glanced at the torn portrait, then bent down and picked up a shattered bit of porcelain. It was the remains of a figurine, a lady in a ball gown with her arms broken off. Nanny, at odds with her nature, had collected delicate, beautiful things.

Had.

I forced myself to stop thinking about her in the past tense. She was alive, and I would find her. "Will you help me?"

He paused, considering. "With a strand of hair or flake of skin, a mage can construct an amulet that allows one to trace the steps of the person. It's expensive and very difficult to produce."

"Can you make one?"

"No." His fingers reached into the pouch at his belt and came up with a flat disc of hemlock hung from a strap of leather. It was engraved with symbols, dark lines and circles where the wood had been scorched.

"What's that?"

"An amulet such as I was describing. This one was constructed from a stray hair left in Viktor's comb."

I felt a shiver. "You had it made?"

"I was able to retrace Viktor's steps from the scene of his death, but nothing came of it."

"I don't care how much it costs. I want one that can find Nanny." My mind raced, thinking of ways to pay for it. I could have the book sale, but if Erick said something was expensive, then it would likely be more than I would make off Viktor's entire inventory.

"There's a brush in her room." I ran for the stairs, not hearing what Erick said behind me, and came back with it a minute later.

He took it, removed the woven mat of silver hair caught between the bristles and placed those reminders of Nanny's existence in his pouch.

"I will have the wizard undertake to produce another amulet," he said. "It takes three days, Eva." From his tone, he thought it a lifetime.

I knew it was too long. In three days, Nanny could be far from Highcrowne, lost among slaves, or dead and burnt. Conrad must search that ship; it was our best chance.

"Do it," I said. "Tell me the price, and I'll get the gold for you." I suspected it would cost gold, not silver.

"Keep your gems and jewels, my lady. I will deal with everything." He was too generous, but I accepted. I had no other way to pay for it.

"You must know I don't have any gems. I don't like being teased."

"You're wrong. In your eyes, I see the finest diamonds." My eyes were pretty pale, the irises almost white. He stepped closer and touched my hair. "These locks of ebony alone would be worth a fortune."

I hated the poetry found on Uncle's bookshelves. 'Thou' and 'art' never made sense to me. This I liked. "Go on," I said.

He raised my knuckles to his lips. "Alabaster skin..." Then he grasped my chin. "Amethyst lips, which I have assayed with my own and know to be genuine. You are wealthy as a queen, my lady."

He continued to look at my mouth, and I wanted him to kiss me already. I leaned in but waited for him to bridge the distance. He didn't disappoint. Sharp stubble pressed against my chin, his comforting scent all around me. His tongue tasted like summer berries, making me want more.

I still felt an urgent need to find Nanny, was aware of Conrad doggedly carrying out my wishes, but at that moment all those things faded in importance, even my guilt over letting them fade. I put my arms and legs around him—riding pants were good for such acrobatics—and he pressed me against the wall.

I glimpsed Viktor's portrait out of the corner of my eye and hesitated for a second, coming up for air. It was then I heard a crunch of glass from across the room. I turned to see what had made the sound.

"Excuse the interruption," Duane said. He didn't look apologetic.

He stood rigidly and looked at us from beneath dark brows. He reminded me of one of the statues in the temple of the Silent God, gaze stern, disappointed in the world and in His subjects. I wasn't one of Duane's subjects, and, as I'd told Jessup's man, I wasn't his girl either.

"What do you want? This is my house now, by the way, and I'd prefer you ask permission before taking a step inside. Not that a burglar like you would understand the concept of knocking."

"I thought you would want my information. If I was mistaken, I'll go." He turned away.

"Wait."

Duane stopped, but kept his back to me.

I told Erick, "Sorry. Give me a moment."

"Who is he?" Erick sounded angry, probably as frustrated as me by the interruption.

"An old and annoying acquaintance. I'll be right back." I stepped on a fragment of broken plate but managed to avoid any more obstacles on my way over. Duane could have moved about the room without making a sound, so he had crunched the piece of glass to get my attention.

"Any sign of Nanny?" I asked.

He and Erick traded glares. "I don't like talking in front of people I don't know."

"Erick is Viktor's friend from the Slave Quarter."

"Is he? Your brother mentioned someone, but we haven't met before. I didn't know he was so old."

"He's not old. He's mature and responsible and a lot of things you're unfamiliar with. You can trust him, not that he'll hear much all the way over there if you keep whispering. Now, speak already." I tapped my foot, a sure sign my patience was about to be exhausted.

"The Circle's wagons are on their way out of the city," he said, steadfastly keeping to a whisper.

"But they still have slaves to sell at market tomorrow. You said they wouldn't leave for another day!"

"I said 'no more than a day'. Your favorite, Randall, has remained behind with a wagon to oversee the sale." Duane's tone was not as friendly as it had been that morning. I hadn't been any ruder to him than usual, so Erick's presence must have annoyed him for some reason.

"And you're sure Nanny wasn't with them?"

"I'm sure."

"Then she must be on that ship. If they've left, then it's not going to be here much longer either."

I hoped Conrad had managed to get a writ to search the boat. I should have insisted on going with him. I could be persuasive when needed, but it was unlikely the magistrate would have listened to a refugee girl from the Outskirts, no matter what I said. Markham and even Conrad had a certain amount of respectability, because of their defined places in Highcrowne society, which I lacked.

At least, I'd learned to negotiate that society without being stepped on too hard. How much worse for a human without wealth or connections? I tried to imagine what it had been like for Duane, surviving here without family, even a hated one. Of course, he had hitched himself to my brother's star the first opportunity he got. I pushed any sympathy for Duane out of my head.

"Bell hasn't been able to get aboard," he said. "I could kill my way past the goblin mercenaries, but it would draw a lot of attention from the Guard."

He was serious. He thought he could take on a brigade of goblins? I knew Jorg was capable of it, but Duane was suffering from delusions.

"Conrad is working on it," I said. "Best if you keep your dagger in your trousers for now."

"I should take care of that matter we discussed," Erick said, interrupting. "If you will excuse me, my lady?" He headed for the door.

"Don't go."

Erick stopped, but he wasn't looking at me. He and Duane were still assessing one another, and the atmosphere was tense.

I dug Kali's documents out of my belt pouch. "I need you to look at these too. They must be forgeries, and I'd like to know how they're doing it. Duane and I think the slavers are taking refugees off the streets, marking them and forging their papers before sending them on an eastbound ship."

"*Duane* thinks so?"

"It's the Adder," Duane corrected him.

"Ah. Now I can put a face to the name. Viktor was very fond of you," Erick said.

"And he hardly mentioned you at all, not without going quiet. I could tell he was keeping secrets." Duane's disappointed statue face was back.

"My secrets," Erick told him. "He was a faithful friend."

"There's something else." I knew I was being annoying, making shameless use of everyone around me, but whatever was happening was bigger than me, and I would take whatever help I could get. "Can I have the amulet?"

Erick drew back slightly. "Why? It will not locate Madam Olinov."

"I know that. The slavers tore this place apart looking for something. It's obviously not here. Perhaps the amulet will help me find what they couldn't."

He reached into his bag and brought out the hemlock pendant again. "It is a dangerous object. If damaged, the power used to create it is released, and it can injure anyone nearby. I don't want you harmed, Eva."

"And I want to find out why Viktor was killed." I snatched it out of his hand. "I'll be careful. Now, tell me how it works."

He took it back from me and said a few words. The wood immediately grew orange, like a coal in a fire, and smelled of smoke.

"It's not going to burst into flame, is it?" I took a step away.

"I invoked it is all. Viktor has been in this spot, which is why it is reacting so strongly. Do not worry, the heat and smell will vanish as soon as you go where Viktor has not been."

"He's been everywhere in this neighborhood," Duane said.

"It might be useless." I was disappointed. How would I be able to tell if Viktor had gone somewhere to buy groceries or to hide something secretly?

"It only shows recent activity. A week at best," Erick said. "That makes it somewhat easier to interpret."

"Viktor has been gone almost a week now," Duane pointed out.

A week? I couldn't believe it. Time was expanding between us. Memories of my brother were still so fresh in my mind. Would they start to fade now, like the amulet's ability to track him? Would I forget where he had been and who he was? I didn't want to forget.

"Then this may be your last chance to discover what he was hiding." Erick carefully placed the amulet on my palm.

It wasn't hot as a coal, but it was warm. I put it in my pouch and felt the heat against my hip bone. "Thank you."

Erick surprised me by taking my face in his hands and kissing me deeply. It was not like a Solhan gentleman to display affection so publicly. He pulled away, leaving me smiling, and cast his eyes triumphantly at Duane. I got it—this was male territory marking. I was no one's territory, but I didn't mind the effort.

"I must go now." He pulled the hood over his head and swept down the steps and out the front door.

When Erick had gone, Duane didn't speak. He leaned against the archway, arms folded, waiting for something. Why didn't he leave already?

Duane could be silent, and it was too quiet in the house without Kali and Nanny arguing. Where was Kali? I felt a flutter of panic, worried she had been taken as well, and hurried up the stairs to look for her, but a glimpse in her room showed she was still sleeping.

I was exhausted and wished I could go back to bed as well, but there was too much to do. I thought about leaving a note so she wouldn't worry when she awoke, but she wouldn't be able to read it. Instead, I grabbed a mealy biscuit from the larder in the kitchen—it gave me warm and fuzzy memories of jail food—and went back down the stairs. Duane was still waiting for me.

"Thanks for the information. You can go now," I told him.

"I don't like Erick. You could do better," he said, butting into my life uninvited, as usual.

"Who? You? You had your chance." Why had I said that? It was stupid.

He gaped. "You were twelve. And Viktor's sister. Your brother would have killed me!"

"Thirteen. And you could have at least kissed me back."

"I thought I did."

I didn't remember it that way. I was embarrassed to remember it at all, but I'd had a crush on Duane once. He was older, and I followed him everywhere, pretending I only wanted to hang out with Viktor. I was so distraught when I found out I would be sent away to boarding school, I spent days planning how to say goodbye. The first time we were alone, I cornered him, confessed my feelings and threw myself at him. My first kiss. It was nice too—before he pushed me away. The humiliation was overwhelming, but I managed to forget all about him by the time I came home again for the end of year holiday.

It wasn't because I'd been spurned at a tender age that I hated Duane. I wasn't that childish. I grew up and learned what he was, saw him working with my uncle, saw him beating up other boys in the street, and the first day Karolyne opened her tavern he swaggered in asking for his cut. I soon realized how fortunate I'd been to get over my crush.

I stared at him coldly.

"I didn't mean to make you angry. I was young too. Oh, forget it." He looked past me, his expression hard, but he still didn't leave.

"What do you want?"

"I want to see where that amulet leads you."

"I'm sure Grim and Gormless will be watching me, so there's no need for you to come along. Besides," I added, "before I spend the rest of the day following a piece of wood all over the neighborhood, I'm going to find Nanny. There's one place left to look, and I bet Conrad is doing it as we speak."

"Why do you put so much faith in that guardsman?"

"I trust my instincts." Actually, it was the opposite of my instincts I trusted, but that would validate Duane's theory I defined 'good' as the opposite of Solhan.

It wasn't my race I rebelled against; it was the Thorne heritage. I never knew my mother or father, but my uncle was an evil force and my sister a sadist. I admired Viktor, and I'd watched him war constantly against his nature. I had no choice but to do the same.

"And Erick? You are quick to trust people you hardly know," Duane said.

"Well, I do know you, and I know I don't trust you. They haven't pissed me off yet."

"Yet," Duane said, emphasizing the word. "I'm coming with you."

"I can find the way to the docks on my own."

"I trust in instincts too, and they tell me to stay close. Why should I shadow you all the way there when I can more easily walk by your side?"

I didn't care what he did. I strode down the stairs and out the door without another word. He followed.

How had I ended up with three men looking out for me? I was becoming like Ilsa, too many admirers, not that I thought Duane's interests were the same as Erick's and Conrad's. He was too pragmatic. What was his stake in this? I didn't believe he loved Nanny's cooking that much. Maybe he planned to take over the docks next? I'd like to see him try.

# 19   Barely Controlled Chaos

The docks were the one place where the Three Kingdoms—Avian, Dwarf and Elf—melded with the outside world and was swept away by it. The orderly, layered and fiercely hierarchal structure of Highcrowne society was visible in the layout of the warehouses, airdock, and the perfectly straight roads cut through the granite of the mountain the city emerged from. But tossed around and over that infrastructure was chaos, like sticks thrown on the riverbank after a flood. People, animals, ships, machines, and every mode of transport available came together in a jumble that made my eyes hurt.

From our vantage point, I could make out the green coils of the Serpent's Ribbon, a broad and slow-moving river that originated in the mountain range Highcrowne was also a part of. The water had cut its way deeply into the rock long before humans ever set eyes on the region. Avians remembered when it was half its size. None but the gods had seen it when it was new.

The gorge cut by The Ribbon was so deep, the highest towers of the palace would fit inside without peeking over the rim. Switchback roads, made passable in winter by buckets of salt and gravel, were crowded with mules, cargo-laden wagons and the coughing, spluttering machines that trundled on metal tracks up and down the slopes, burning foul-smelling black rocks from the human lands. Such monstrosities weren't allowed past the apex of the gorge, for which I was grateful.

Duane of course was smiling like a dog chasing alley rats as he took in all the sights and noxious odors. I'd say this love of chaos and inefficiency must be a human thing, but I was human too, kinda, so I had to blame Duane's inferior upbringing.

He had insisted on accompanying me, despite telling him to go away every few minutes. As good as I was at ignoring Duane's orders, he was better at ignoring mine. All my waspish comments bounced right off his stony exterior.

I didn't share his love of the docks, but I was awed by the massive floating 'clouds' overhead. Zeppelins were like tethered balloons made of silvery cloth and heated air holding cargo aloft. The larger and longer versions, dirigibles, were propelled by engines of magic, steam or simple pedal power. Of course, the more mundane engines depended on people, which meant slaves, and were part of the problem. Despite the stench of oily smoke and awful shriek of metal against metal, perhaps it was better to embrace more of the mechanical contraptions of the South if it meant less demand for slavery?

"Let's hitch a ride on that locomotive," Duane said, pointing to one of the massive machines that had reached the end of its track just a few steps away from us.

"No." While I might think the machine superior to slavery, I still preferred the predictability of my own two feet. "We'll walk."

"That will take forever. How about the wagon then?"

I wanted to hop on and kick back, but the road was so crowded the wagon was moving slower than the people scurrying around it.

"You're going soft, Duane. Just get moving." I set the pace, a punishing one, and weaved my way through the crowds while trying not to get too close to the large locomotives that, frankly, scared the bejeezes out of me. I'd gladly take on knives in dark alleys and curse charms rather than face being crushed inexorably beneath iron wheels or having my skin seared off by a steam explosion. No, I kept well away from those things as I raced down the steep incline.

Duane gasped for breath. He was out of shape. Too much time spent guarding 'his' territory, I supposed, while I'd had a few days of cross city hikes to energize me. Coming back up the hill would be another matter.

I was disappointed when I reached the berth where the slaver's ship was docked. There was no sign of white armor: Conrad wasn't there. Had he failed to get a writ of forced search?

There was plenty of other activity, though. A line of triple-decker riverboats and smaller vessels were moored, stretching around the bend. Cargo was loaded and unloaded, while passengers waiting to go downriver milled around the grimy refreshment kiosks.

"There's Bell," Duane said.

"I don't see her." Of course, I wouldn't. Duane's people were stealthy. It was hard to keep breaking the law if you got caught.

He led me to the other side of the slaver's vessel. I could tell what the ship was meant for from the bars on the windows of what would otherwise have been a passenger ship.

Bell crouched in the lee of webbed and crated cargo. She was decked out in well-worn leather, from short boots to baggy overalls and deep-sleeved jacket. She even wore a leather skull cap, only a few stray blonde locks visible, and skin-tight leather gloves on her delicate fingers, but the gloves were a darker, richer shade of brown than the rest of her outfit. To finish it off, she had some atrocious brass contraption on her head, like a guard's helmet, but brimming with small round lenses attached to jointed mechanical arms. And everything—absolutely everything—was smeared with grease.

I raised my eyebrows.

She looked down at herself and sighed. "I tried to climb a line on the other side of the boat and learned the hull had been freshly tarred."

"I always thought you were the smart one. Maybe I was wrong."

"And I always thought Thornes were too much trouble. Maybe I was right."

"You're still upset about the dynamite."

"We ruined a perfectly good automaton."

"Good isn't a word I'd use in conjunction with any machine. Have you found the evil-er one yet? Maybe we can call that one Ilsa."

"No. Duane's still looking."

"For what?" Duane said, confused.

"He will be ... once I tell him the whole story." Bell positioned one of the lenses over her right eye. She closed the left one and squinted at the boat in the distance through the ocular contraption.

"What in the name of all the gods are you wearing?" I asked.

"It's beyond the comprehension of superstitious primitives still clinging to dark gods and magic."

"Superstitious I admit, but primitive? You're covered in leather hides and shiny bits of rock like some grall just stepped out of the mountains.... And you better not have been referring to Solhans. We're not the only ones with dark gods."

"The only ones with a dark god roaming around conquering things."

"Did you see anything, Bell?" Duane interrupted before a thoroughly enjoyable squabble could start.

"Ship's full," Bell said in her quick, professional, reporting-to-the-boss tone, "but they're waiting on permission from the dock master before they can leave. Several other ships left this morning, and they were ready to edge out behind, when the dock master's office received a report saying they hadn't paid their fees. They were flagged back immediately. They're searching for the paperwork, but I doubt the record will be found."

She pulled out a sheet of vellum from her inner coat, smeared with gooey black liquid like the rest of her. "Completely unreadable now. They may be here a while."

Duane smiled. "Good work."

"Thank you."

Bell was pretty smart after all.

"What do we do now?" I asked.

"We?" Duane said pointedly. "I thought you wanted me to go away and leave you to handle things yourself?"

That was when I thought Conrad would be here with a writ, but I didn't say that out loud. There was no guarantee he would show. I had my Ashur with me—I didn't go anywhere without it these days—and I squeezed my hand around the metal orb at the end.

"You're the one who told me to keep my dagger in my trousers," Duane said. "Those goblin mercs will eat you for lunch if you attack."

"We need to get on board somehow. They'll pay the docking fees again or figure another way to slip out of here. We don't have much time." Why did I keep saying 'we'?

"Have they met the dock master?" I asked Bell.

She shook her head. "He sent underlings."

"Elves?"

"An elf and a human," she said. "Ah. You think we can claim they need a last-minute inspection or something. I'm not really dressed for the part."

I looked at Duane. "*We* are."

"I'm not sure about this," he said.

I too doubted it would work, but I wasn't going to admit it. A dispute over fees was one thing, inspections another. Would they honestly let us examine every slave crammed aboard? If they were stealing free humans, they had to be afraid someone would recognize one of their captives.

Not that I could recall any faces among the street people I'd seen. Except, there was one girl who reminded me of someone I grew up with. It wasn't enough to make me feel like a caring and thoughtful person, though. I knew I was as guilty as anyone of ignoring most of the misery around me. Well, that was about to change.

"Let's go," I insisted.

We would need accessories to look convincing. I went into the dock office and joined the long queue of people there to complain about how their cargo was treated by the longshoremen.

"I lost an entire case of wine!" I shouted. "I bet it's in the dock master's office!" This lent fuel to the general grumbling, and a few short-tempered captains demanded a look around.

With the clerk distracted, I swiped a quill and notebook from the desk.

Duane had been watching. "Not bad. Anyone but me wouldn't have seen a thing."

"Theft is not something to be proud of," I lectured as we made our way back to the ship. Duane seemed to exude an aura of bad influence, but I was doing this for a good cause. "...I was pretty quick, though, wasn't I?" Ok, I couldn't help bragging a bit.

I wanted to do the talking, but he insisted I hold the book and take notes, since there weren't any female dock inspectors. I accused him of perpetuating inequality before I hooked the Ashur through my belt and took up the pen.

The goblin at the top of the gangplank bared his needle-like teeth when he saw us approach. "We pay already! We told you!"

"We're here for something else," I said. Duane glanced back at me, reminding me of my role, and it was difficult to be quiet when he wanted me to.

"I'm here to conduct an inspection," Duane told the mercenary, "to make sure fees and tariffs were adequately assessed."

"We pay!"

"May I speak to your captain?"

"He tell me not to bother him until we ready to leave dock. You let us leave?"

"The sooner we carry out this inspection, the sooner you can go," Duane said.

It had been eerie watching Duane's taut, predatory gait transform into the bored shuffle of a bureaucrat. His vocabulary was different, and his normally commanding tone shifted from the air of personal power to a sense the power of the state was backing him. He had convinced me, but the mercenary was another matter.

"No. Take ropes off boat and go away." The goblin waved his hand dismissively.

"By the Dead God," I cursed. "Let us pass."

"Hey." The goblin squinted at me with beady black eyes and took a sniff with his pug nose. "I know you.

You was with the grall." He fingered his jaw—it popped—and I bet it was still sore.

"I'm moonlighting," I said.

"Tell grall we be back! We'll get him! Now, you go!" He had an iron-tipped spear, which he poked in our direction.

"Hey!" I didn't like weapons being aimed at me. I grabbed the shaft and twisted it out of his grip. Oops.

The goblin was not happy. He opened his mouth wide and lunged. I remembered how those teeth had dug into Jorg's thigh. The grall hadn't noticed the pain, but I would, especially when my head was bitten off. Before the teeth clamped down, I swung the spear I'd taken and stuck the wood into the goblin's mouth. He broke it into splinters, chewed for a moment, and spit the pulp at my feet.

Duane grinned and stifled a laugh. It wasn't funny. Couldn't he see I was under attack? When the goblin's mouth opened again, I threw the notebook into it and reached for my Ashur.

"Not here." Duane clamped a hand around my wrist, preventing me from drawing the weapon. "Witnesses."

I wasn't going to kill the goblin, just give him a knock upside the head so he'd stop trying to eat me.

Duane pulled me a few steps back down the gangplank, opting for retreat instead. The goblin kept coming.

"Halt!" The command made us all stop in our tracks.

Behind us were half a dozen guardsmen. A dwarf had spoken. He wore the yellow-plumed helmet of a sergeant. They were all dwarves, except for the unmistakable human towering over them in white armor.

"Conrad," I said, relieved.

The goblin hid his menacing teeth. "They on my boat! Me innocent."

"What's going on here?" The sergeant strode up the gangplank, the other guards in a double line on the dock behind him. Even with the plume, he was shorter than me.

"Nothing. We were waiting for you." I stood to the side and indicated the guardsman should get on with it.

Duane stood on the opposite side of the gangplank, judging the drop. He was uncomfortable around soldiers and looked like he might retreat over the side now that reinforcements had arrived.

"Miss Thorne is the one I was telling you about, Sergeant. She's Sir Markham's friend," Conrad said.

"Ah," the dwarf bowed. "Thank you for the tip, my lady. The illegal acquisition of slaves will not be tolerated by the Crowns. We will take things from here."

He turned to his troops. "Search every deck."

"What you doing?" The goblin trembled, agitated. He signaled to his compatriots; they had lingered in the background up until this point. "It time for fun, Fierce Brigade!"

Suddenly, eight spears were pointed at the guardsmen and at me. The goblins didn't aim at Duane. He could blend into the scenery when he wanted to.

The white-armored soldiers responded by swinging shields forward and drawing short blades.

The sergeant frowned at the goblins. "Don't be foolish, boys. We have a writ from the magistrate. Stand aside and allow us to conduct our search."

"No," the lead goblin mercenary said with finality.

Duane and I were caught between a mass of little green men with sharp spears and even sharper teeth and a wall of white armor and jutting blades, which was much worse than a rock and a hard place. I was surprised Duane hadn't scuttled away already. I'd go myself, if I wasn't likely to die from falling the twenty feet to the wooden dock below us. Duane was the acrobat, not me.

Instead of fleeing, Duane flicked his hard gaze between Conrad and the spear aimed at my eye, and his muscles tensed, ready to spring into action. He'd decided to fight. I'd seen Duane kill, and I knew the goblins' reputation. This would turn into a blood bath if I didn't do something.

"This is ridiculous," I said. "Listen up, Fierce Brigade. This is the Guard, and they are the law around here. They can have this entire ship impounded and all of you cast in irons. That would not make your captain happy, believe me. Now, go and fetch him."

The goblins cast nervous glances at each other.

"You're not qualified to make this decision," I continued. "Go ... and I'll ask the grall if he's interested in a rematch."

Maybe it was my practiced glare or the enticement of a glorious and hopeless combat against the giant, but their spears were suddenly pointed at the sky, and one of the goblins hurried off to find his master.

"I should put them in irons anyway," the sergeant grumbled. Several spears twitched in response. While the goblins' ability to speak elvish left much to be desired, they understood it fine.

The ship's captain, a plump human from Duane's neck of the woods, was red faced. He swaggered up to us, growling about the incompetence of the city's officials and demanding to see the writ of forced search. When the sergeant showed it to him, he cursed and reluctantly told his mercenaries to stand down.

The squad of guardsmen marched across the main deck and broke up into groups of two for the sweep. The sergeant and Conrad stayed behind and asked to see the manifest and the documentation for every piece of cargo. 'Cargo' was their euphemism for slaves. The captain spit at their feet before obliging them.

Duane slipped away without me noticing.

Typical. I tried to sneak onboard and conduct my own search for Nanny, but Conrad caught me.

"This is Guard business," he said.

"Your people don't know what Nanny looks like!"

"This search has to follow the parameters of the writ, which Sir Markham was kind enough to arrange for me despite the scant justification I was able to provide." He looked more haggard than he had this morning.

"Sorry," I said. "Thank you for doing this."

He nodded and returned to his sergeant's side, going through the paperwork the ship's captain supplied. I felt a tightening around my heart.

Conrad's patience in me was stretched to the breaking point. The least I could do was behave myself for his sake.

I tried sitting, but the fidgets took over, so I paced up and down the gangplank. The search took hours, and the sun was well past its zenith when the glum-faced soldiers were all back on deck.

"We're sorry for the inconvenience," the dwarf told the captain as he handed back the thick sheaf of paperwork. "You are free to go."

"What?" I asked, shoving my way into their midst. "They're stealing people. You can't let them get away with it!"

Conrad took me by the shoulders and led me away from the sergeant, who frowned at my outburst.

"Everything was in order," Conrad told me. "All slaves were marked and documented."

"They can place marks! And they can forge documents!"

"Says who?" He looked at me in such a way I suddenly wondered if he suspected me of being a pathological liar or a hysteric at the very least.

I calmed down, opened my mouth ... and then shut it again. I couldn't tell him the truth about Kali being a slave, her forged documents, or Olaf being re-branded. Erick would inevitably be implicated as an emancipationist. The elven courts would have him quartered and the pieces burned.

"You've made a fool of both of us," Conrad whispered. I winced at his words. "Leave this boat before the captain decides to press charges."

The dwarven squad marched past me. There was a curt, "My lady," from the sergeant. Conrad gave me one last disappointed look and joined them.

I'd done it this time. I didn't have enough friends to afford to abuse them, but I had done just that with Conrad. I doubted Sir Markham, and consequently Gypsum, would be happy either when they discovered how I'd embarrassed him. I'd been lucky to get the Guard to help me at all, and on a 'trust me'. Now, they would probably never help again.

I noted the red-faced captain and the black-eyed goblins all staring at me, and I reluctantly followed the soldiers. Their clomping footsteps vibrated the plank and made my own gait awkward. I reached the relative firmness of the dock and realized I was all alone: No sign of Duane or Bell; Conrad was nearly out of sight; Viktor was dead, and Nanny wasn't home.

I looked up at the steep walls of the gorge, and the long path I'd soon be climbing without even Duane for company, then at the corral of donkeys for hire. I felt my belt purse, but only a few copper knuts remained, along with Nanny's necklace and the amulet Erick had given me. I'd have to walk.

I took a few steps and realized the amulet felt warm. I pulled it out and saw it glowed a deep orange. Viktor had been here. He had stood on this spot in the days before he died.

I shuffled to the side and the glow dimmed, a little further to the other side and it grew brighter.

I must have looked like some mad woman doing a dance on the wharf, but the Docks had a high threshold for strange, and everyone ignored me.

I crisscrossed the entire area until I was sure I had identified Viktor's trail. I followed it to an empty berth with nothing but a numbered marker buoy floating in the spot. Viktor must have visited a ship that was no longer docked. I suspected it was the other slaver vessel Conrad had found on the dock master's log, the one Gypsum's brother-in-law investigated before he was murdered.

I followed Viktor's trail up the crowded road leading out of the gorge. The river dwindled beneath me, and I saw the slavers' ship had oared its way into the center of the current. Its giant paddle wheel began to turn, propelled by Southern steam and slaves shoveling coal. There was a tributary a mile ahead that would take it east and Nanny along with it. I'd failed her.

I dreamed of grabbing the goblins when they were next at Karolyne's, getting Jorg to extract the information on Nanny's whereabouts, and then going after her with Conrad and the rest of the gleaming Guard at my side.

If they'd ever believe me again.

If the goblins even knew where their cargo was bound.

If....

Trying not to feel helpless, I turned away and let the amulet guide me where it would.

# 20 Secrets

Viktor's path was difficult to follow. People, donkeys, carts and miniature locomotives all got in my way, and I had to dodge them while trying to stand in one place and feel the faint heat from the amulet. His trail was growing colder, but I hoped enough of it remained for me to find whatever he'd hidden—whatever had gotten him killed.

I passed near the outer wall under construction. Slaves and laborers levered huge blocks into position. It was massive, made of rough-hewed stone, fifty feet high and ten feet thick: Not a beautification project. Highcrowne had plenty of soldiers and Avian magic to defend it, but the Dead God's rise and the stirrings in the human nations had impelled our far-sighted rulers to begin building the wall over a decade ago. It would enclose the Outskirts as well as add an extra layer of defense to the Central City. Karolyne saw it as a sign the Crowns cared about humans. They could have reinforced the Central City and left us unprotected. I disagreed. This way we were just a more effective buffer zone.

Whatever the reason for building it, the wall was nearly complete. Soon, there would be a gate regulating entry into the Outskirts. Soon, the Guard would have us hemmed in on all sides.

I let the amulet guide me. The place where Viktor died was strongest, the wooden disk a bright orange, but that place held no interest. I'd stood there once before, after they found him, to say goodbye.

I was on the familiar path to Viktor's house and worried this entire approach was pointless. The amulet was leading me in circles. But when the path detoured toward the Slave Quarter, my heart sped up. It wasn't the route home after all. Had Viktor hidden whatever the slavers were looking for under their very noses?

I no longer felt the uneven cobbles beneath my boots or the icy flakes of snow falling on my outthrust arm—all my attention was focused on the amulet dangling from my fingers.

As soon as I stepped into the Quarter, the path turned sharply right. I'd never been this way before. The empty square where wagons camped and the slave block stood was farther south, while the amulet led me west.

I wove through narrow alleys that should have been crammed with refugees hiding from winter winds. There were only a few old men, huddled next to a small fire fed by rotted wood and coal powder, which was disturbing. The slavers were stealing people. Where else could everyone had disappeared to?

I clutched my Ashur in one hand. Duane claimed this territory now, but Jessup's old gang had tried to kill me once already. I wasn't about to forget that.

The wood disk instantly dulled from orange to brown. The trail ended.

I looked to either side of the narrow alley and saw nothing but brick walls. No doors and no place Viktor could have gone. Then I thought to look up. A wooden ladder stretched overhead, connecting the windows of two buildings like a bridge. Quite a few such makeshift bridges and pathways interlaced the upper stories.

I tied the Ashur to my belt, pocketed the amulet and jumped—I was tall enough it was only a hop—and grabbed the ladder, so I was hanging by my arms. Pull ups weren't my forte, but I swung until I got a leg up. A few grunts later, I was on hands and knees. I tried not to fall through the rungs of the ladder and felt the weathered wood digging into my shins.

I scooted towards one window and pulled out the amulet. It was still cold. Wincing and wobbling, I turned around and went to the other window. The amulet warmed again. My brother had been this way.

I clambered through the open casement and into the ruins of an old textile mill. This hadn't always been the Slave Quarter. While Solhans migrated to the Outskirts only fifteen years ago, other humans, like Duane's ancestors and Karolyne's people, had lived outside the Central City for generations. This was one of the older neighborhoods, established when the Crowns still required a killing field around the central wall. Unlike deportment lessons, I had paid attention during history class. The dictate that a killing field exist eventually lapsed, and the areas abutting the wall were filled in with newer neighborhoods, like mine and the temple district.

Wood creaked beneath my feet as I shuffled across the second story floor. The boards were weak, ridden with termite marks, and could collapse at any second. I stuck to the edge next to the brick wall, thinking it less likely to cave in there, and circled the room until I found an old staircase leading down.

There were heaps of broken planks and other debris, places Viktor could have hidden something, but I doubted this area would have supported his weight, so I decided to search the ground floor. I'd spotted looms and spinning wheels down there. The upper story was more like a mezzanine, allowing me to see part of the level below.

The stairs swayed but held together. I breathed easier when I was standing on solid stone.

The doorways and windows on the ground floor had been bricked in when the place was closed, thus the existence of the second-floor entrance, which must have been used by squatters. I spotted piles of straw and ragged bedding, but no street people sleeping in them. It was strangely quiet in the gloomy space. Bits were broken off the looms for firewood, ash marks visible on the floor, but otherwise, the equipment was intact.

Now, where would Viktor have hidden something?

I pulled out the amulet and searched the area, until a warm glow told me I'd found his trail again. It led to the stairs I'd come down and to various corners of the room.

I spotted a series of shallow stone pools, dried out now. One filled with wood ash and another with crystals of rust orange potash. I remembered the automaton at Bell's place and felt my stomach churn. I didn't like gadgets at the best of times, and gadgets combined with necromancy went straight to the top of my scale of wrong.

I took a broken piece of loom and poked at the ashes, but the pools were shallow, and neither I nor the amulet spotted anything there. I turned away and kicked at flagstones and piles of rubble, looking for potential hiding places.

A stone wobbled beneath my foot, and a thrill went up my spine. The amulet was hot, so hot I barely held on to the chain, and its orange light suddenly turned acid green. That was new.

I pried up the loose stone and found a small cavity in the dirt. It was too dark to see, so I reached my hand blindly inside. I felt cold metal and pulled out a scroll canister. This was it.

Hands shaking, I rolled out a stack of vellum sheets.

The top document was a plea to the Crowns, signed by Viktor. I skimmed over it, too excited to alight on any one word for long. The Solhan Circle was mentioned—I'd been right.

I caught sight of a slave certificate for an elf named Fharen and smiled. The bookkeeper, Olaf, had forged documents proving the Elf King was born into slavery. That would get the Crowns' attention.

Viktor had been gathering evidence for some time, but it wasn't only about illegal slaves. There was much more: lists of names, military officers from the look of it, names of ships ... I saw the word 'Solheim', and my breath caught in my throat.

My long-forgotten home lay to the east, the way the slavers' ships had gone. It loomed beyond the river, past the Highcrowne pickets guarding the nation from the Dead God's approach. Solheim was the end of the world—in all ways.

I was so intent, I'd failed to spot the symbol beneath the loose stone. It niggled for my attention. I pulled my gaze away from all the proof I'd dreamed of and examined the glowing rune. It had a nasty, curled shape to it, and a diseased, purple cloud of light emanated from its lines. A booby trap.

The trap did not frighten me. It hadn't gone off, so if I remained still I'd be safe. What bothered me was it being there in the spot Viktor had hidden the documents. He must have been the one to draw it.

I remembered Ulric's and Nanny's lessons, Morgan's too. They all tried to hand down Solhan dark magic for different reasons: family power, tradition, protection. I'd run away to avoid looking into the dark faces of our gods. I swore I'd never be like them ... but I ended up learning more than I wanted.

I cut across the rune with my fingertip, smearing the coal it was drawn with, and a sharp pain revealed the razor hidden beneath. I bled enough to cover the coal marking entirely, which quenched the remaining purple glow. My blood had satisfied it rather than setting it off, and once again I knew this was Viktor's work. Our blood was the same.

The stones in the floor around the now defunct rune shifted like someone in the street moving politely aside. They kept shifting and rumbling until a large opening was revealed, along with a staircase going down. This must have been the mill's basement, and Viktor's spell had hidden the entrance.

I sucked my finger and then held the wound closed.

I didn't want to go down there any more than I had wanted to learn the method of erasing a rune that meant you harm—but I had learned the magic Morgan taught me as a child. And I did climb down into the dark.

My eyes adjusted to the gloom almost instantly; something Solhan eyes were good for. I lit the first candle I found, hoping the flame would make the scene less sickening, but its red light lent a hellish cast. It was a shrine to the Devourer.

Older than the Dead God, the Devourer was the prime creator in Solhan religion. The Devourer had swallowed the old universe to make way for this one. We were fortunate He had not been the god summoned into this world in Old Solheim, else we wouldn't be dealing with an army of undead—we wouldn't have a world to stand on.

Long tables were strewn with scrolls. I had seen their like in Viktor's shop, but alongside them were glass vials and bags of powders, amulets and rune stones, cords and ropes and chains etched with symbols, jars of body parts and tubes percolating with semi-living blood....

There was a photo of Emily, another of Little Viktor, each surrounded by runes for protection and runes meant to conjure wealth—at a heavy price for the wizard's soul—as well as runes I didn't recognize. Which couldn't be good. The only ones I hadn't seen as a child were the ones for Solhan initiates, like Uncle Ulric and Nanny. Very dark spells.

My brother never recovered from his wife's death. Erick had been right: Viktor wanted to die. Why else would he play with such risky magic? And Viktor had been doing much more than that. I half expected to see his heart there on the scale opposite the horse's heart I did spot, its black blood congealed and smeared over the brass. I didn't know what that spell was for, but it was necromancy.

Viktor couldn't have taken his own heart. Seeing this, I wondered if he had invoked other beings who had.

"Viktor..." His name escaped me in a quiet breath. *Not you. You were the good one.* I closed my eyes. *Not you.*

The tears that had failed to come for years suddenly gushed from beneath my eyelids and washed down my face and neck.

I'd lied when I said I liked ponies. I'd met a girl once who adored them. She'd been sunshine and fresh air and everything I wasn't. I'd wanted to love them, if it meant I could be like her.

I could never be.

Seeing the rune trap, seeing this place.... While my stomach heaved with disgust, beneath everything was a flutter of excitement. Energy tingled along my nerves, dying to burst through my skin. It itched to reach out to the scrolls and implements on the table, to connect with power.

The truth was the dark called to me, just as Ulric said, maybe even more than it called to Ilsa. It was irresistible. I knew if I gave myself to it for a moment, to cast a curse or wield a spell, I'd be gone forever. The dark would have me. I couldn't give it anything, else it would take all of me.

"No," I said to the room, to what it represented. "Turn around, Eva. Walk away."

I thought I was winning, but then I heard metal scrape against stone. I whipped around, not because of willpower but because of survival instinct. The automaton stood on the stairs, looking at me with those bronze eyes. It raised an arm and pointed at Viktor's workstation.

"...Me." The automaton's voice didn't sound like it came from a machine. It came from a place far away, like someone shouting across a windy forest where the susurration of leaves made the sound blend in with the voice of the trees.

"You?"

"...I am ... me." It pointed at the photos, and I suddenly understood.

"Emily," I said. "You're Emily."

Of course. Viktor would do anything to bring her back. And now he was gone, so what was the point? This thing could not be a mother to Little Viktor. It was barely Emily at all. But it kept pointing at the photos.

"Your son is safe. Duane and Ulric are looking after him." Everyone knew I was not the mothering type, or even slightly organized, so it would be no comfort to add I also checked in on Little Viktor, despite risking run-ins with Ilsa.

"...dead. Viktor..." the machine Emily said.

I nodded.

"...me ... dead?"

"Yes, you're dead too."

"...no ... more." She held her bronze hand before her blank eyes and watched the fingers move with the whirring sound of tiny clockwork parts. "...not ... me."

She dropped her arm and stepped toward me. I wanted to run away, but now I knew this was Emily, and I couldn't. She pulled open the metal plate covering her chest to show me the pulsing flesh inside. "...make ... end."

She wanted to die. I couldn't live like that either. My soul bound to a machine powered by dark magic? She should be with Viktor now.

"Goodbye," I told her.

She just looked at me with those blank eyes.

I reached into her chest and smudged out each of the charcoal runes inscribed on animal parts. I had to wipe my hand on my pants after that. Then I took a small blade from Viktor's worktable and scratched out the symbols etched inside the automaton's casing.

Emily slumped forward, before toppling to the ground with a clang of metal. I dropped the knife. Its metallic sound merged with the echo from her ghostly shell.

I could have done that at Bell's place, but I didn't want anything to do with magic. I didn't want to confirm Bell's assumptions. And I didn't want bloody organ goop on my fingers. The dynamite would have been better, if it had worked.

I knew it was only a machine, but a part of Emily had dwelled inside it for a time. I took a moment to mourn her passing—again. She'd been the one who took my big brother away from me, but I never hated her. She'd also been the one who made Viktor smile.

A door creaked open above me, and I froze. The place had turned into a thoroughfare. Carefully, I rolled up the sheets half-forgotten in my left hand and returned them to the scroll case. I placed the case in my belt, exchanging it for the Ashur. Footsteps were loud on the stones above me, and the person seemed to notice as well, suddenly stopping to wait and listen.

I clenched my hands on my weapon, afraid the Ashur would slip out of my sweaty grasp. Keeping my breathing shallow when my heart was racing made me crave more air. I wanted to take a big gulp of it, and my lungs ached, but I held still.

It might only be Grim and Gormless following me around like lost puppy dogs; except them I would never have heard coming.

Floorboards creaked elsewhere in the old mill, and I knew there were at least two people. Abandoning stealth, I hurried up the stairs and drew my blade. I didn't want to hurt anyone, but if I was outnumbered it was best to be prepared.

I dashed into the shadows beneath the mezzanine. One figure, bundled against the cold, faced the other way. He turned around, and I recognized Harald the slaver. Jhenna the half-elf joined him from the level above, taking the creaking old steps as slowly and quietly as she could.

"I thought you two had left town?" I said, startling them. Their gazes swept the room until they spotted me in the gloom beneath the stairs.

"Did you find it?" Jhenna asked me.

"Find what?" Always play dumb, let them do the revealing; that was my motto. Besides, I didn't know if they meant the papers or the dead automaton.

Harald whispered a few words beneath his breath, and I felt the answer unwillingly roll off my tongue: "Yes, I have them."

Must be the documents they were searching for, and Harald must be the mage who could place slave marks. He also had the ability to make me say things I didn't want to.

"Give it to me," He held out a hand for the scroll case.

At least he couldn't make me do things I didn't want to. I levelled the sword at him. "No."

His gaze focused on me. A few more mumbled words preceded a comical waving of hands. I was unsure what the spell was meant to do, but I felt nothing, and Harald frowned.

"It is a sacred blade," Jhenna told him. "It protects her."

I looked at the Ashur. I'd never known what the carvings in its surface meant, but I was suddenly grateful they were there. My mother's weapon evidently granted some magical protection.

Emboldened, I asked, "What have you done with Nanny?"

"Nothing," Jhenna said.

"The same 'nothing' you have planned for me?"

"We don't want to hurt you. Give us the documents and you can go."

Harald was too quiet. I glanced his way and saw he held a leather thong dotted with bone charms, feathers, and dried bits of flesh, including the shriveled remains of an eye. He was trying to curse me.

"Put that down. Now." I raised the serrated blade threateningly.

I caught movement out of the corner of my eye, but Jhenna was so fast I barely had time to step back, my hair rustled by the breeze made by something passing next to my ear.

She had an Ashur as well. Hers was bone like mine, but where I had a silvery orb at one end, she had the gold figurine of an owl. It was that bit of metal that had nearly crashed into the side of my head.

Angry, I lunged, hoping to push her back so I'd have a little more space to think. She drew her own blade and came after me, using the bone sheath to knock my weapon aside. I struggled to block her attack and return to the offensive, but she pressed forward, fast and sure. She was well trained. My own lessons had been sporadic over the years.

I didn't like being in a fight with someone who was clearly my match, while worrying about a mage in the corner casting curses.

I tried to go between them, wanting to escape up the stairs and out the window, but I was penned in. I needed to get the documents to safety ... and me too. I didn't think the current situation boded well for my health.

Harald began casting another spell. I didn't want him to do that.

I backed up, putting a wooden support beam between Jhenna and me, and circled in his direction. Jhenna was too good for me to devote more than a fraction of my attention to Harald. I swung the sheath of my Ashur at him, felt a glancing blow against something soft, perhaps his forearm. He gasped and took a step away. I hoped I had distracted him enough to break the spell.

Unfortunately, it had distracted me too.

Jhenna closed in. She hooked her blade against mine and twisted, trying to pull the Ashur out of my grip. I felt my weapon slipping away, so I brought the sheath back around to stop her. She blocked it with her own. My blade went flying. I backed up, so she couldn't get in a killing blow. I had only the sheath to defend with now.

Jhenna came in with a low swing using her own sheath. I sidestepped enough to allow it to glance off my thigh—it would leave a bruise—but reserved my block for her follow up strike with the blade. I was sweating now.

Dust rained down from the floorboards above, and I squinted to avoid getting dirt in my eyes. Great, like I needed another handicap.

Jhenna squinted too and glanced up. Someone was coming. I took advantage of her brief loss of concentration and lunged for my blade, which lay on the ground beneath the crumbling staircase. I rolled and came up crouched and ready, armed once more.

Planks bowed and creaked overhead but didn't break, although someone heavy was moving across them. As he came down the steps, I realized I could hamstring him, but I didn't. The tiny feet following the big ones convinced me I'd chosen correctly, especially when one of the small feet caught between two rungs, sending Grim falling face first with a loud smack. Gormless quickly extracted him. My backup had arrived.

Once again, I was grateful Duane didn't listen to me. Of course, I would never tell him that.

Jhenna was on guard, watching me and watching the new arrivals.

"You okay, Eva?" Gormless popped his knuckles.

I relaxed my stance. "Fine, once you break this cow's arms."

Jhenna scowled. "You're making me angry."

"You're outnumbered," I told her. "Put the Ashur down."

She assessed Gormless, who, if not grall-sized, was still impressive. "Please. I was a bit bored with you, and I see nothing yet to make me fear." She dropped the sheath but held the sword two-handed. "Come."

Grim drew a dagger and threw it. Jhenna dodged and, in a blur, sliced the air between me on one side of her and Gormless on the other, forcing both of us back. She was fast. She hadn't been bluffing, she had been holding back before.

Perhaps the three of us would eventually wear Jhenna down, but there was no chance to find out. We'd all ignored the unarmed Harald for too long. Big mistake.

"*Kharvu!*" the mage said, waving his necklace of horrors in the direction of the two men.

A rotting odor, like meat left in the sun to liquefy and attract flies, filled the room, and I gagged. Grim collapsed, screaming, as black sores formed all over his body.

Gormless avoided the brunt of the curse, but he rubbed at a disintegrating patch on the back of his hand. He frowned like a child ready to burst into tears over a scrape. "That hurts!" The thug rushed Harald.

Jhenna moved to intervene, but I swung, aiming the silver orb on the hilt of my sword for the section of skull above her left ear. My full strength wasn't behind it, because I wanted her alive to answer my questions. She turned in time to avoid the blow and knocked the wind out of me with her fist. I braced for another blow, but Jhenna ignored me and went after Gormless.

"Stay away from him," she said. The slaver was concerned enough for her husband to leave me at her back. Of course, she didn't need to see me to kill me.

I regained my feet and stumbled forward, ignoring the cramp in my gut. Gormless was focused on Harald, inching painfully toward him as the putrefaction of his flesh worsened, oblivious to Jhenna's raised sword.

"Watch out!" I said.

If it weren't for Gormless's famous luck, he would have been crippled. Jhenna aimed the blade for his spine. He turned in time to catch the blow on a rib and kept turning, so the blade bounced off bone rather than embedding itself in his chest. He clutched a hand to his bleeding side.

Jhenna look poised to spin around with another strike. I assumed a two-handed grip and caught her blade against mine.

I smiled as I saw Gormless raise a massive fist, ready to smash her from behind. The slaver noted my expression and kicked backwards, slamming her heel into the big man's groin. With a surprised look, he slumped.

What had happened to Gormless's luck? It had never failed him before now.

Harald was whispering more curses, and I realized he was the real problem. Not that Jhenna skewering me wasn't high on my list of worries, but the mage was very effectively negating my three-to-two advantage. I couldn't get past the other woman's swinging blade to reach him, however, so I backed toward Grim.

"Are you okay?" I asked, hoping Grim had recovered enough to help me out.

He gave a high-pitched keen and, frightened, I glanced down at him. "I can see the bone," he said through clenched teeth. That didn't sound good. It didn't smell good either, and it was spreading.

My knowledge of magic was patchy, due to my concerted efforts to stay away from it, but a spell that could rot living flesh fell under the Dead God's purview. Such practices had been forbidden along with his worship. 'Forbidden', meaning the penalty for disobeying the law was decapitation or burning at the stake. Harald wasn't playing nice, and he wasn't afraid of the consequences.

I dodged another swipe of Jhenna's sword, but my muscles ached. I was tiring, and my backup wasn't helping. I was in the same prickly situation I'd been in before they arrived, trying to deal with a mage and a master swordswoman.

I couldn't afford to look down to be sure of my footing, but I took a big step backward, putting Grim's prone body between me and Jhenna. She tried to circle around, but Grim finally did something useful and grabbed her ankle. She couldn't jab at him for fear of opening herself to my attacks, but her footwork was hampered as she tried to pull loose. I came at her in a flurry, expending a last burst of energy to finish things.

There was a moment when she was off balance, and I was certain I could slip the blade into her throat, but I sensed the nearness of her death and pulled back. I disarmed her instead. Triumphant, I stood there with my blade pointed at her right eye. It was the formal signal demanding surrender.

She sighed and looked down. I looked down too, because I was on fire. The scroll case wedged in my belt was consumed in an unnatural green flame. More of Harald's magic.

I yelped, undid my belt, dropped the pouches on the ground and stamped on them and the scroll case to smother the fire. The canister bounced and rolled across the stone floor, flames swirling around it as it turned. Eventually, it slowed and became a molten heap, before flattening into a shiny puddle of liquefied metal.

The proof Viktor had gathered against the slavers, what he had died for, was now gone. I glared at Harald. He had a satisfied smile on his face.

The mage began to weave another spell. I clutched my Ashur and moved toward him. "I'm going to cut off your hands if you try anything else," I warned.

"And if you do, I will kill you," Jhenna said. She had retrieved her weapon.

But she'd surrendered! There were supposed to be rules. I dodged reflexively, and the tip of her blade only grazed my wrist, giving me a deep scratch but leaving my limb intact. I had to stop giving the bad guys ideas.

I decided on a new tactic, one I should have adopted much sooner, and ran toward the mage, leaping over Gormless, who was now unconscious—I hoped, and not dead—from Harald's curse. The slaver was unarmed, the Ashur protecting me from his magic, so I pointed my blade at his eye.

"Give it up, Jhenna, or I'll do worse than remove his ability to cast spells."

My ultimatum might have worked with a reasonable human being. I could cut down her husband before she reached me. She had to capitulate or lose him. Problem was, Jhenna was half-Solhan as well as half-elf. I'd fought my own nature for so long I'd forgotten most of my people did not. They despised weakness and an instant of fear turned quickly to fury.

"Kill him then," she said. "I'll be sending your soul after his, and you can serve as his handmaiden in the Dead God's realm for all eternity." Solhan threats could send shivers to your marrow.

Harald's wide eyes pleaded for his life, even if his wife wouldn't, and I knew I couldn't cut him down in cold blood. Swearing under my breath, I turned to face Jhenna. She came at me steadily, relaxed and confident. She was tougher than me and she knew it. Her blade streaked forward, and I almost didn't block in time.

"What are you doing?" Harald said. "You can't kill her."

"She threatened you," Jhenna answered, never taking her eyes off me.

"The documents are gone. We can go," he argued.

Was the slaver trying to spare my life? After everything I'd learned? It didn't make sense. Of course, I had no proof of what they'd done, and I'd burnt my bridges with Conrad and the Guard. Come to think of it, I wasn't much of a threat.

Jhenna didn't seem to care. I had awakened her ire. I saw the glint of enjoyment in her cream-colored eyes and knew a thousand arguments wouldn't convince her to spare me. She craved my death like I'd learned to crave a heavily sweetened cup of kaffe. She would bleed me dry and sigh with satisfaction when she was done.

"Tell them it was unavoidable," she said, smiling.

In the flurry of sharpened iron that followed, I struggled to stay alive for one more second. I was reacting rather than taking the offensive. Part of me knew it wasn't smart, but no coherent thoughts had time to reach my brain. I lived on reflex now. The drills Morgan had made me do twice a day, which had slacked off to once a day, when I remembered, were the only thing keeping my flesh on my bones.

Those were the same reflexes that allowed me to see the one chink in Jhenna's guard. She was a great fighter, but she wasn't perfect. She dropped her elbow occasionally, and right there, visible in the bend between forearm and bicep was her heart. I had parried and was in the right position for once to continue the swing and come up into a lunge. I braced the Ashur's long handle against my wrist and aimed for the gap in her defense. I pushed with my legs and felt the blade slip underneath her sternum.

I'd struck on instinct, but the result was the same as if I'd meticulously planned her murder. Jhenna stiffened, and her sword arm dropped. Her eyes bulged with the effort to raise it again, but her body failed her, and she crumpled.

She stared up at me accusingly, before her gaze turned to infinity. I had killed her.

# 21    ALL I NEVER WANTED

I wanted proof the Solhan Circle had murdered my brother. That way I could see to it they were punished, lawfully, whether it was by a Highcrowne magistrate or the makeshift council of merchants who ruled the Outskirts. My uncle was an influential force on that council, and whatever he willed would be done, so it wasn't entirely fair, but at least things would have been conducted properly, in a civilized way. I worried about being civilized and good, because I knew my own heart. I knew I was a Thorne.

Sweet rage coursed through my blood whenever I thought of finding Viktor's killers and having them under my power, the satisfaction it would bring me. What would be so wrong with doling out justice? It's what Ulric and Duane did. It's how they ruled the neighborhood. But I fought that reasoning.

At some point, the Thorne name had come to represent everything I hated. Maybe it was the shame I experienced hearing the histories of Solheim as told by others. Only Gypsum and Karolyne had cared to be my friends; everyone else shuddered at my white eyes and easy frown. I liked to think it was something different inside me, the same thing I had thought present in Viktor, a spark, which told me to fight against my nature. I had always wanted to be like Viktor. I didn't want power over others; I wanted power over the taint inside me. Solhans embraced that darkness, reveled in it. They saw strength in cruelty, while I saw loss of control. And it was too easy to lose control. Not even Viktor had managed to avoid it in the end.

It would be so easy to kill for Viktor's sake, but then something overwhelming would be unleashed. There would be little left that was recognizable as 'me'. I knew it would happen, which was why I had tried so hard to get proof, to ask others for aid, to keep my blade sheathed. Had that been my first mistake? Unsheathing my blade?

When I killed Jhenna, I felt her soul brush against mine. I felt the power of it. And I felt the darkness pushing against my insides, felt its triumph. I knew she was guilty. It didn't matter that my proof had burned in mage fire. She had stolen my brother from me. So, when she exhaled her last, delight coursed over me, and it was difficult to understand why I should feel remorse.

Why had I feared this? In that instant, I was gone. I was someone else, someone I never wanted to be. If I accepted it, this would be who I was forever. I would finally stop drifting aimlessly, searching for my identity: I would know I was a joyful killer, and I would never fear anyone again or let anything stand in my way.

The only thing that saved 'me' was the knowledge I didn't intend to kill her. I had not given in. My mind was still mine, even if the instincts of my body and muscles had betrayed me. Those muscles were trained by a Solhan; what else did I expect them to do? It wasn't my choice. And the darkness receded slightly, enough for me to breathe again and look up from Jhenna's corpse to see the expression on her husband's face.

Harald was calm, pitiless, and he hated me. I didn't need to see the sheath of her Ashur, which he had picked up, didn't need to see it descend, didn't need to feel my skull rattle and blackness envelop my vision, to know he wanted me dead. He did not wrestle with his conscience like I did. He chose to kill me.

When I woke, I expected to find myself in the Dead God's realm. Instead, I lay on a hard bed, crammed between iron-banded chests and scattered pillows. The wooden ceiling was low, and the only light came from a barred window in the wall above me. I was in a slaver's wagon.

Jhenna's body lay next to me on the bed, dressed in flower-patterned silk and glass beads. This cramped space must have been her home, and her husband had returned her to it. But, why was I here?

The unlit lanterns and decorative circles of stained glass hanging from the roof swayed, rattling like bones. The wagon was moving. A jolt bounced me a few inches into the air, and Jhenna's arm flopped next to mine. It was cold. How long since she'd died, and why hadn't she been burned?

Panic sent me into full alert. I jumped to my feet and tried the door. Of course, it was locked. The wagon was solid wood—walls, floor, roof, everything— and there were no windows except for the tiny one above the bed. It was a secure slave transport converted for private use. How could Jhenna have endured living here? Maybe they still used it for slaves when the other wagons were full?

I climbed on the bed, trying not to step on the body, and stuck my nose between the narrow bars. A single driver held the reins to a set of oxen.

"Help!" I shouted.

Harald looked back at me, and his expression was almost as lifeless as Jhenna's. He quickly returned his attention to the oxen.

"You can't leave me in here with her!"

"I want you dead," he said distantly. "I will allow my beloved the pleasure. It's the last gift I can give her."

"This is insane." No one in their right mind would let him do this. "There's a dead woman in here!" I called to anyone within earshot.

Harald closed the shutter. Now, I had no light. I fumbled for my sparker, but my belt was gone. I had dropped it in the textile mill when the scroll case caught fire.

What had I seen before Harald shut me in darkness?

I found one of the lanterns and felt my way across shelves, which were lipped to keep items from rolling off, until I reached the fire runestone and a sheaf of dried rushes. All I had to do was think about fire to get the magic to work. Still, my fingers trembled so much it was hard to light the taper. When the lantern was alight and I could see, I exhaled with relief. I had fire. I could burn Jhenna's corpse.

Unfortunately, I would burn along with it.

Harald had left me a choice, knowing I would die either way. I preferred to wait, but not too long.

Jhenna would rise three days from the moment her heart stopped. She would kill her way to the Dead

God's side, never resting until she reached Solheim, and she would let nothing stand in her way, not barred windows or a stupid, Solhan girl like me.

I kicked the door, trying to bash it open. It was reinforced from the outside. I heard the metal bar stretched across it clang hollowly each time I struck. My skeleton would break before the door did. I kept at it, desperate. Panting and sweating, I shouted at the shuttered window. "Harald! She'll kill you too!"

He didn't answer. He must know he would die. He was probably counting on it. He'd loved Jhenna a lot more than I'd guessed, and he wanted to join her.

I was a terrible observer of human nature. I hadn't guessed they were married, hadn't guessed he was a mage, and I hadn't guessed he would plan such an extravagant revenge. Oh, and I hadn't guessed the wagons leaving town had been only a ploy, so I wouldn't know they were tracking me. Harald and Jhenna must have hoped all along I would lead them to Viktor's hidden documents.

What other information had the scroll case contained? There hadn't been time to examine all the papers, but, in addition to Viktor's plea to the Crowns, I'd seen a signed statement from Olaf, a list of people, including soldiers, who had been paid off by the slavers, and several pages written in Solhan I hadn't deciphered.

It was my native language, but I'd first learned to read and write elvish, the dominant language in

Highcrowne; even dwarves spoke it. There was something about Solheim, I remembered. Was that where we were headed? Was Harald that suicidal? He was keeping a dead woman in the back of his wagon, so he probably was.

I dug through wooden chests and tore through the junk stowed beneath the bed. When I was done, the place was as trashed as Viktor's house, but I failed to find any sort of weapon. Harald had cleared the place of anything I might use to break free.

Once again, I thought of burning, seeing no other way out of this. But it was my last resort. I couldn't have been unconscious for long. There was still time.

Exhausted, I sat on the narrow floor, unwilling to lie on the bed next to the body. The fidgets had me up again in no time.

I banged on the shuttered window to get Harald's attention and tried not to scream at him this time. "I'm thirsty. I need water and food. Please."

If he opened the door to give me supplies, I'd have a chance. Harald ignored me. I pleaded and scratched at the wood like a mewling kitten until my voice went hoarse. No one listened to the pleas of someone locked inside a slaver's cage.

Hours later, the wagon stopped, and the window opened. I'd been slumped beneath it, half asleep, and I jerked awake at the sound. "Harald?"

I saw sky, orange clouds reflecting the sunset, but the sun was behind us, and a break in the mountains lay ahead. We were going east.

Harald's face pressed against the bars, surprising me.

"I'm thirsty," I said for the millionth time. By now, it was true.

"Another day is gone," he said. "You have less than two remaining." He began to close the window, and I thought furiously.

"You want to watch her kill me, don't you? It will be disappointing if I'm weak from starvation or dead from thirst."

He thought for a moment then shut the window. I stared at it, waiting for him to come back, wanting more than anything to hear the bar on the door pulled aside. Agonizing minutes later, the window opened again, and he splashed a cup of water in my face.

"I don't want you dead too soon, but I don't care how weak you are." He closed the shutter.

I darted my tongue out to catch the rivulets running beside my mouth, and then I sucked on the wet patches where my shirt was soaked. I wanted to live as long as I could. The two days he'd given me weren't enough.

I don't know how many more desperate searches I made of the wagon. I found nothing to help me escape or defend myself. Jhenna's flesh had already grown unnaturally solid, like an eggshell. I could press into it, but the resistance grew with each passing minute. Her skin would continue to harden, and by the time she rose she would be almost impossible to kill.

It was easy to see why the Dead God was winning. His armies were fed by our deaths, and His creations were unstoppable. If a human corpse was burnt to ashes right away, the curse could be controlled. Once risen, only a mage could destroy it, or a mass of soldiers with sharp swords, but the corpse always took a few soldiers down with it.

Jhenna wasn't invulnerable. If I had a weapon, I could dismember her, but I didn't have my weapon anymore, and I didn't practice magic. I was tempted at that moment, but I didn't know any useful spells.

The Avians, the founders of Highcrowne, had magic enough to keep their borders safe. Human refugees flocked there to take advantage of that protection, but the generosity of the Crowns was growing thin. They had tolerated human settlements within their borders for centuries, and elves relied on human slaves, but the arrival of the Dead God had changed attitudes. While never citizens in this land, humans had been downgraded to an infestation.

Now, those troublesome refugees living on the streets had been taken away by slavers. Had the

Crowns sanctioned it? It would eliminate many problems for them.

I didn't think it was true, though. The elves needed us. Besides, the slavers had worried Viktor's evidence would receive attention from the government, so their activities weren't approved of. Even if there wasn't a conspiracy involving the Crowns, something more was going on, I was sure of it, but I couldn't think very well with Jhenna's vacant eyes staring at me.

I tried once again to break down the walls of my cage, which might soon be my casket. The light dimmed and went out. I fumbled in blackness to find more fuel, but things were scattered everywhere.

I felt moisture on my skin and licked a salty droplet. I was crying again. I gasped, and the tears stopped, but there had been a few. I shook as pent up emotions battered their way out of me. I had killed. But I could still feel—shame, fear, regret—and I could still cry. After too many years, I could cry.

The shutter creaked open. Night and stars were visible.

"Harald?"

There was no sound. Now, ashamed to be seen in this state, I wiped my face and licked the moisture from my hands. There was not enough water to waste.

The shutter remained open, so I went over to it. "What do you want?"

I put my hands around the bars, and my fingers brushed something leathery. I pulled back. It was a bogle, camouflaged and invisible in the semi-dark.

# 22  SACRIFICES

Had the bogle opened the window?

"Can you unbar the door?" I was being whimsical and never expected an answer. There were a few slithery dry sounds as it scampered off. At least it had left me fresh air and a view of something besides this box.

Surprisingly, I heard more rustlings against the door. I hurried over and put my ear to it. There were tiny grunts then a frustrated curse, "Yeck!"

A moment later, it was back at the window, no longer camouflaged. Ugly eyes and large, hairy ears pointed my way. "Sorry," it said in a twitter. "Too little."

I knew bogles could say a few words, like parrots, but I had no idea they were so intelligent. Real hope rose in me. It hadn't been able to get the door open, but it might still be able to help.

"Do you know where Highcrowne is?"

It looked around then pointed west.

"Yes! Can you take a message to someone there?" I wasn't sure if anyone would listen to a bogle. People's first reaction was to kick them. But I had to try.

"A lot of someones there. Big, big, many peoples," the creature said.

"Yes, but I want you to find just one."

"...Sounds like work. What you give me?"

I looked around, assessing my situation. "I don't even have food and water."

"I like food," it said, licking its lips.

"Well, I don't have any."

"Oh. Bye, bye."

"Wait!" I said, panicked. The creature stopped. A bogle showing up was the only piece of luck I'd had. I needed to figure a way to make use of it. "What if I promise to give you food later, when I get out of here?"

"You want a bargain?" it asked, raising one bushy eyebrow.

"If that's what it takes."

"A bargain cannot be broken. A bargain is serious. You sure?"

"Yes!"

It hesitated. "Ok. Message now, food later. Who get message?"

Good question. Uncle came to mind. He would tear Harald apart, if he didn't consider this another test of my ability. What use was a Thorne who couldn't survive a walker raised by the Dead God's necromancy? Uncle only cared for survivors. And would Conrad even want to hear my name again after I embarrassed him in front of his sergeant? There was Duane, but he wasn't the heroic type. Why would he try to rescue me?

"Can you find Erick?" I asked. He was the only one I could count on. "He's Solhan, like me, wears a hooded cloak and carries pouches full of magic...."

What was I doing? I had no idea where Erick could be found. There was no way I'd be able to direct the bogle to him. "I've changed my mind. Go to Karolyne. She runs a cafe in the Outskirts. Tell her where I am and that I need help. Please."

"Confused." He—I had decided the bogle was male—shook his head, and a large black bug was almost dislodged, but it scurried behind one hairy ear. Out of politeness, I repressed a shudder.

"Find Karolyne. There's a grall with her that you can't miss. He cooks food." The bogle should be able to locate the one grall in town.

"Food?" He licked his lips.

"Yes, but tell her about me first. Otherwise, you won't get food." She'd likely smash him with a broom if she caught him in her larder. The little guy had better talk fast.

"Me go."

"Hurry!"

After a few more mutters of, "Food!", the bogle was gone. Did it even understand what I'd asked?

The next morning, Harald closed the shutter without a word to me. He was likely used to bogles messing with things.

My thirst was agonizing, my head ached, and there was nothing to distract me from it but hunger. I scavenged through the contents of the wagon one more time, looking for anything edible. I had a mental inventory of it by now. I found an old wineskin, the residue at the bottom practically vinegar, but I drank it anyway. I briefly wondered if lamp oil was drinkable, but I didn't want to use up that supply. I had the lantern relit and sat, holding it against my gurgling stomach, staring at Jhenna.

At times, my agony faded, and I felt light, floating, unbothered by my predicament. I liked those moments, but they were too few.

The wagon was on the move again. When it stopped for the night, I begged Harald and received another splash of precious water. With a smile, he told me there was only one more day left.

The bogle was nothing but a wistful dream. The creature was too stupid to carry a message, and, even if it managed to find Karolyne and tell her I was in danger, how would anyone reach me before it was too late? The oxen were slow, but a bogle's tiny legs made them even slower. There was no help coming.

I spent my last day of life kicking at a side wall, hoping to break through the wood there since it wasn't reinforced. I was weak, my efforts useless, but I had nothing better to do.

Jhenna moved.

I stopped pounding on the wagon and held my breath, all attention focused on her, wondering if this was it. There it was again: the fingers on her left hand twitched. I had run out of time.

I jumped to my feet and grabbed the flask of lamp oil I'd kept in reserve. I was terrified of stepping within her reach, but in a moment, it would be too late, so I sprinkled the fuel over her.

The liquid ran off marble skin and glass beads but pooled in the silken dress. Would she even burn now? Was it too late? If I'd done it right away, I might have saved Harald, but I would have burned too. I would have missed out on these last days of life, of gnawing hunger, of tortuous waiting.... At least bargaining with a bogle had been interesting. I didn't care about saving

Harald anyway. Still, I wished I could have saved myself.

She sat up, and I was surprised to see how graceful she moved. I had expected something monstrous, but Jhenna was lovelier than she'd been in life.

I'd heard that when the Dead God's power first animated them, they were filled with it, brimming with holy energy. This was when they were most dangerous. Over time, the god's power withdrew, and the corpse began to rot. Survivors of the wars in the human lands reported near skeletons throwing themselves at city walls. They were ineffectual in that state, but I couldn't wait the months or years it would take for Jhenna to weaken.

She looked at me, and I felt cold settle in my bones, the yawning chasm of death falling away before me. It was not her eyes that gazed into mine but the eyes of my god. He had murdered nations.

I wanted to beg for my life, plead to be the one exception to His wrath, but there was no point. I stood straighter and raised the flaming lantern in my hand, defiant.

She darted forward, quicker than I could blink, and took my wrist in her hard grip. My joints ground together, and I gritted my teeth against the pain.

This wouldn't stop me. I smiled and relaxed my fingers, letting the lamp clatter to the ground. I smashed the glass cover with my boot, and the escaped fire raced up Jhenna's dress. It licked at my leg. Instinct told me to run, but I couldn't move.

Jhenna's mouth opened in a silent scream. A hollow voice issued from the darkness of her throat. It said, "Come to me, Eva."

The fire was only inches away, but I shivered at the god's words. He had spoken, and He knew my name.

"Your blood and your heart and your soul are mine," He said. Jhenna released my wrist and held out a hand, inviting me to take it. "Come home."

Flaming liquid ran off her hard skin and fell as golden droplets. She resisted the fire, but the floor of the wagon blackened as the wood began to burn. The heat was now worse than my hunger. Smoke filled the claustrophobic chamber and scoured my throat.

"You can't have me." My voice trembled, betraying my fear. "And you can't have Jhenna either. There'll be nothing left but ashes."

"There is no escape." The mouth shut with a clack of teeth.

I felt a sickening sensation in my gut, like the world had tried to shake me loose. I'd never heard of a corpse speaking. Yet, it had spoken to me. Why? Why did the Dead God know my name?

Maybe He knew everyone's.

A wild look suddenly twisted Jhenna's features. That chasm behind her eyes closed, the god's awareness was gone, leaving a vacant dead thing in its place.

This was what I had expected. A risen corpse was insane; it tore everything around it to shreds until it tasted blood. Life was needed to satisfy it, to sustain it on its journey to Solheim. Or maybe it hated the living and simply wanted to kill, who knew? I had hoped the fire would have finished me before this. The hand once held out invitingly was now hooked, ready to strip the flesh from my bones. She charged.

I dodged. I wanted to die quickly, but I couldn't fight the reflex.

She hit the wall, making the wood crack. I jumped on the bed, and she tore the mattress apart trying to reach me. Feathers drifted through the smoke.

The pillows and bedding burned; soon the whole wagon would be engulfed. When her outstretched arms tried to encircle me, I rolled away, and she punched through the wall in frustration. Screaming, she tore a few planks to splinters. The wagon jerked forward, the oxen reacting with fear.

There was now a narrow hole in the front of the wagon, a way out. But to reach it, I'd have to get past a burning dead woman.

I stood by the door. "I'm here, Jhenna."

She screamed and rushed toward me again.

I threw myself beneath her arms. I heard more wood crack, the metal bar across the door clang loose and bounce on the ground. She'd made another exit, but I wouldn't attempt to go past her again. I rolled across the bedding. The sleeve of my jacket caught fire.

I kept going and climbed through the first hole Jhenna had made.

The wagon bumped over the rutted dirt road, the oxen out of control and running as fast as they could with a burning pile of wood strapped to them. I hopped to the ground and felt my ankle jam.

I rolled, trying to extinguish my clothes before my hair caught fire. The white fur was my favorite jacket, and it was ruined. I lay on my back and sucked in a lungful of air. Smoke billowed from the wagon, but the wind blew it away from me, so each breath was wonderfully fresh.

Harald was on the side of the road, open mouthed, staring at me. He must have abandoned the reins when Jhenna smashed through the wall. His reflex for living was as strong as mine, no matter how much he acted like he wanted to die.

Jhenna screamed, and I sat up.

The wagon was a pyre, and she was still kicking around inside it. A wheel splintered on the left side and sagged. The oxen, white-eyed and confused, their burden dragging strangely, circled around.

I stood, shaking with exhaustion, as Jhenna tore through the back door. She was on the road now, crouched and looking for me. I could run, but I was injured and too weak to get far. She would be upon me in seconds; only the wagon stood between us. I had a desperate idea.

I hissed, enduring the pain in my ankle, and ran toward the wagon, toward Jhenna, but really toward the moaning oxen.

The god demanded a sacrifice—it didn't have to be human. I veered to the side to avoid being run over but stayed abreast of the animals. The broken wagon dug a furrow in the frozen earth. The oxen were tired, moving slow enough for me to keep up.

Jhenna was a marble nude polished by fire. She saw me and smiled with mad hunger. She didn't run but took great strides, reaching me in the space of a few heartbeats.

I held the bridle of an ox, and when she swiped at my face, I threw myself over the animal's back and stood on the wooden neck of what remained of the wagon. She missed and struck the ox instead. Her blow was like a sledgehammer. The animal screamed as bone splintered, and its legs buckled. She reached for me.

I leaned back too far and fell. The hoof of a terrified ox loomed next to my face. I flinched away, and it bruised my cheek. I expected its weight to sink into my gut or crush a limb at any moment, and I forgot all about Jhenna as I tried to stand.

She caught the sleeve of my jacket and tore it away. Her empty eyes were so close I thought they would swallow me. Better to risk being trampled.

I ducked down and scrambled beneath the legs of the second ox. He—from my position it was easy to tell—kicked my thigh, but I made it out the other side with my flesh intact. The animal wasn't so lucky.

She tore into its neck with hooked fingers, and blood sprayed across her skin. Her gaze turned feverish as life pulsed beneath her fingertips. She put her mouth over the wound, gulping fresh blood from the squirming animal's neck. I shuddered. That's what she had wanted to do to me.

I hoped the animals would make her forget about me, but there was no guarantee. I felt the urge to pray, but this was the Dead God's domain, and He was the one who wanted me. Fearing a strike from the heavens, I whispered the Light Bringer's name instead. Who knew if He listened to prayers ... or would ever help a Solhan?

Jhenna looked up, and my breath caught. Was I next? She didn't appear to see me, however. The corpse turned and walked toward the Eastern Pass. I wasn't about to stop her.

When she kept going, and her form shrunk with distance, I exhaled. I was alive. The animals were dead. I turned away from their mangled remains, feeling like a monster for getting the helpless creatures killed, but glad that it was them and not me.

Harald was on his feet, staring daggers. "Why didn't she kill you?"

I didn't know. Perhaps the animals appeased her hunger, or perhaps it had something to do with the cold voice that issued from her throat. I hoped it had simply been the blood. The alternative was more frightening. It was never good to be noticed by gods.

Harald took a menacing step toward me. I tried to move but felt shaky. My head swam, and I fell over. I'd survived immolation and a walking corpse, but a pasty-faced mage and an embarrassing swoon were going to finish me off?

Lying with my cheek against the frozen scrub grass, I heard hoof beats. My head felt like a lead ball attached to my neck, but I managed to lift it and saw a horse and rider silhouetted against the sun. They headed towards us, the flaming wagon acting as a beacon.

Harald searched his belt pouch for spell ingredients. He probably planned to deal with this too-curious traveler before finishing me. As weary as I felt, I had to move, if not for myself then for the stranger. No one else should die.

I crawled to the shattered remains of the traces that held the dead oxen and found a scrap of wood. I faced Harald, holding it like a dagger. I was too far away, and I hadn't yet managed to find my feet, but when I saw him making hand gestures, I threw the wood, striking him across the knuckles. He dropped the charm he held and swore.

The ground shook as a black warhorse rushed toward me, a cloaked figure leaning against its neck. I rolled aside, but he wasn't after me. The stallion's massive chest bashed Harald, who collapsed. The horse went after Jhenna next.

"Stop!" I warned the newcomer.

Jhenna's walking corpse shouldn't be messed with. I watched with stunned horror as the rider circled her. She would tear him apart.

The cloaked figure dismounted. The wind blew his hood back, and I recognized Erick. No.

I staggered to my feet and stumbled after him, knowing there was nothing I could do to save him.

I saw his mouth move. Jhenna stopped in her tracks and faced him. The fire that had spent itself after having burnt up her clothes and hair, but which had left the rest of her untouched, suddenly revived itself.

Or had Erick conjured it?

It ate away at her body. The heat grew intense; I felt it where I stood. Erick was nearer but didn't back away. Jhenna did not fight the flames, and soon she crumbled into a pile of blackened ash, like a burnt building collapsing under its own weight. By the time I reached them, the fire was out, and the pile of ash was unrecognizable as a person.

"Erick." Amazement filled my voice, amazement that Erick had found me—almost in time—and that he had destroyed Jhenna.

He reached me in three strides and put his arms around me. "Eva. Thank the gods you're alive." His mouth was on mine, and I felt more tears cut through the soot caked in the corners of my eyes. This time they were tears of relief.

"Are you alright?"

I nodded. "Well ... thirsty."

He took a water skin and rations from his saddle-bags. I drank until my stomach felt ready to burst, but when I saw the dried cakes, I swallowed one of those as well. I gagged and tried to eat more slowly.

Erick stared across the frozen plain to the gap in the Eastern Mountains. "You were going to Solheim?"

"Harald was headed that way." I coughed. "But I don't think he expected Jhenna to let either one of us live long enough to get there."

"It's fortunate that Solheim's pull is strong here. The walker would indeed have killed you if left to rampage."

"Oh, she did plenty of rampaging."

"Then it is a miracle you live. It's time we discovered the meaning behind this. I will speak to Harald."

"I want the satisfaction of 'speaking' to him myself. Help me walk." As the adrenaline that fueled me dissipated, my sore ankle clamored to be acknowledged.

I held out an arm and Erick took my weight. Then he surprised me by swinging me onto his saddle. The horse was well trained and didn't stir from munching yellow grass. Erick led me and the animal back towards the shattered remains of the slaver wagon.

Harald was on the ground, stunned from the horse's charge. Erick bound his wrists with leather cord, raided the cache of magical ingredients in his belt pouch, and shook the slaver into alertness.

"Where were you destined?" Erick demanded to know. "Tell me where you've been sending slaves and why."

Harald was rigid with fury, but he kept quiet.

"You will speak." Erick felt in his bags for a spell to use. I hoped mages weren't immune to others' magic. From the way Harald fought from tasting the herbs Erick shoved into his mouth, I doubted even he could resist.

Falling snow sizzled as it hit the embers of the wagon. I felt sorry for the oxen, bound to it for so long, and then killed for being in the way. I stared at the debris while Erick struggled with Harald. I wanted desperately to hear what the slaver had to say, but I didn't want to look at him. He made me angry, and I liked the feeling more than I should.

I climbed down from the horse and looked around. Beneath the driver's seat were a few items that hadn't burned: a small barrel of water, part of a bedroll, and a small strongbox. I recognized it, the casket from Viktor's bank vault, which I'd thrown in Randall's face when I bought Kali. I kicked it out of the ashes and used a twig to lift the metal clasp, which was still hot from the fire. My silver with the foreign markings was inside. There were gems and Highcrowne coins as well.

When the strongbox cooled enough for me to lift it, I transferred it to the satchel of dried travel cakes Erick had given me. Slaver money was tainted, but why should I let someone else find this? Most of it was mine anyway. Besides, I felt better knowing the money wouldn't be used to buy more slaves.

When I returned my attention to the slaver, I noted the sick on the ground. Harald had tried to vomit up the herbs, but it was too late. He looked feverish and swayed.

"Now," Erick said, "answer me."

"I was headed for death. My Jhenna should have killed us all."

"You at least," I said.

Erick raised a hand, warning me not to interrupt his questioning. I bristled, but there was probably a good magical reason that Harald should hear only one voice. Of course, Erick could just be bossing me around, which I didn't like. He had come all this way to help me, though, so I gave him the benefit of the doubt.

"Where were you sending the slaves?" Erick asked again.

Harald strained against the compulsion, his mouth clamped shut, jaw grinding.

"Stop trying to bite your tongue off," Erick ordered.

Harald obeyed, the fight suddenly leaving him like a gust of wind through an open door. Blood edged the slaver's mouth.

"Were you sending slaves to Solheim?" Erick seemed to dread the answer.

After a long moment, Harald said, "To the fort on the border of it."

"Why?"

Harald turned and looked at me with the vacant gaze Erick's magic had given him, as though his soul had stepped out, leaving nothing but the shell behind. "Ask your sister."

I stiffened. "Ilsa?" I didn't want to believe she was a part of this. It meant ... I wasn't ready to think about what it meant.

"You know more. Tell us," Erick said.

"Jhenna." A flicker of life returned to the slaver's eyes then vanished again. "Jhenna played message runner. To the Central City. She could pass into the elf court."

"The Elf King is involved?" I said. I knew he hated humans, but to round up all those people and sell them into slavery? And Ilsa? How could Ilsa possibly be a part of that? She was human too. "Why?"

But Harald would not obey me, and Erick had to repeat everything. "What does the Elf King want with refugees?"

"The Compact of course. The agreement that ended the war," Harald said.

"Which war?" I gave Erick a contrite look. Curiosity always took over no matter what other orders I gave my brain.

Harald continued as if I hadn't interrupted. "The Compact keeps the Dead God from advancing. This whole world would be his if not for what we do."

What was he talking about? The Dead God had taken Solheim and all the kingdoms near it. Highcrowne, protected by ancient magic, was the closest unconquered nation. Even now, lesser human kingdoms on the Dead God's border fell. That war hadn't ended as far as I knew.

Oh.

Now that I thought about it, it was strange how Highcrowne remained free. I'd always assumed Avian magic kept it safe. Maybe it was really this Compact. It was human sacrifice.

I felt sick, thinking of the street girl whose name I didn't know, all those slaves on the ship, Nanny....

"You sent them to die?" I was shocked and angered by the enormity of it. I itched to hold my Ashur again. Harald deserved to join his wife.

Erick shook his head. "I have seen wagons bring offerings to Solheim. I have watched from a distance as the victims were bound, begging for their lives, and thrown over the wall to the hordes below. But only two each month, in honor of the moon gods who brokered the deal. The Solhan Circle and the Elf King have sent thousands. The Compact has never demanded so many. More offerings will only feed the Dead God's power."

So even Erick knew about it? Who else was in on this atrocity?

"Tell me everything," Erick ordered. I wanted to say the same thing, but my fury kept my tongue firmly planted against the top of my mouth for the moment.

"I thought it was for the Compact," Harald repeated. "But something Jhenna said makes me think the Elf King is up to something."

"What do you mean? What is the Elf King's plan?" Erick growled.

"How would I know the plans of a king? I only heard Jhenna say King Fharen did not want to pay the Compact forever."

"Tell me what he intends!" I'd never seen Erick so angry, his lips raised in a snarl. He fingered the dagger at his belt, and I thought he might murder Harald then and there.

Erick was Solhan too. He must find it as difficult to deny his nature as I did. But we needed the slaver alive as proof. This was bigger than the Outskirts and the merchant council. This was why Viktor had been drafting a plea to the other two Crowns, gathering testimony from the slaver's bookkeeper, lists of names and military officers involved.... This was a matter for kings.

I put a hand on Erick's, keeping it away from his weapon. "We should take him back to Highcrowne."

"There is no defeating Solheim," Erick told Harald, seemingly unable to hear me. "None of us can stand against the god."

Harald smiled a bloody smile and shrugged. "If a god can be raised, maybe He can be laid to rest again."

# 23   Highcrowne Justice

I didn't know about armies or facing down gods. I couldn't even comprehend a conspiracy so large it involved one of the Crowns, the Solhan Circle ... my sister. It was all too big for me, so I focused on the one thing that had kept me going. I could finally ask the question that had been haunting me for so long.

"Why did you kill my brother?"

No response.

"Answer all her questions," Erick ordered.

"I didn't kill him," Harald said.

"Don't lie to me." Fury burned through my veins. Before I realized it, I'd slapped Harald's face.

"He can't lie," Erick said.

It couldn't be. I had finally gotten justice for Viktor, or so I thought. Had I killed Jhenna for nothing?

No. Harald may not be able to lie, but he could be very precise with his answers. "Did Jhenna kill him then?" I asked more calmly. "Did Ilsa?"

"I don't know," he said, unrepentant. "I hope so. He was an annoying bastard."

I moved to slap him again, but I stopped myself this time. My control was too thin to allow anything past it. I had to battle that sweet anger. "What would she have needed his heart for? Jhenna or Ilsa?"

He shrugged. "The most potent magic is fed by souls."

"What about Nanny. Why did you take her?"

"We searched your brother's house, but we never saw the old woman. Perhaps Jhenna took her later without telling me? She made most of the decisions." Unexpectedly, the life returned to him, and he hung his head, tears falling to the grass. Erick's spell of compulsion must have worn off. "What will I do without her?"

"You won't have long to be alone," I soothed. "The hangman will stretch your neck for what you've done."

"Good. Good."

He disgusted me. I went to the horse and stroked the animal's mane to calm myself. Erick came up beside me.

"Why didn't you tell me about the Compact?" I said.

"Few who know about it are allowed to live. I chose not to endanger you." Erick put his arms around me. "In any event, a greater evil has been perpetuated by King Fharen. His abduction of so many humans, whatever his plans for them, not only risks those people's lives but also the Compact and the thin hope Highcrowne has of survival."

This was way too big for me. "All I know is I want Nanny back, and I want Viktor's killer brought to justice." Whether it was Jhenna or Ilsa, I would find out.

"Harald will reveal every one of his compatriots," Erick said. "I will hunt them down. I promise. Someone must know what became of Madam Olinov."

I wanted more than a promise. I wanted this to be over. The ache left in my chest by Viktor's death had not dulled with time but continued to grow stronger.

Erick tended my burns. The salve he used cooled the reddened skin on my arms and legs and enabled me to ride the horse without discomfort. I ate to replenish my strength, while Erick walked beside Harald.

The slaver was bound and tied to a short tether. Erick held the leash and questioned him more as we travelled.

The horse was faster than oxen, but there was no way it could carry three people. The burned-out wagon was beyond repair, even if I could bring myself to step inside one again, which meant the trip back to Highcrowne would be a long one. I almost wished for one of those frightening locomotives to speed things up.

Along the way, we learned Randall was still in town and within reach. I was eager to see him put in irons too.

The Solhan Circle's other wagons were encamped farther east, near the pass leading to the fort and the Solhan border. Olaf the accountant was with that caravan. I hoped the slave my brother had once tried to help would finally be freed for good. The Guard would have to go after him, however, because it was the opposite direction from where I wanted to go.

I needed to find Ilsa. My sister might be the only one who knew where Nanny was and what had really happened to Viktor.

I dozed with my head resting on the horse's neck. When we camped for the evening, I was fresh with questions for Erick. "I sent a bogle to fetch Karolyne, but you came instead. Not that I'm complaining. Did the creature find you?"

"Yes. I have spoken to them before, and they know me. Bogles see much and are useful for avoiding trouble. I employed a few as lookouts whenever Viktor and I set a slave free."

"You employ them?"

"They dislike the scraps they're forced to eat and prefer proper food if it's available." He took a bite from one of the travel cakes and chewed slowly, his expression making it clear he preferred proper food as well. "They have no use for currency, but they also appreciate a few copper knuts in payment."

"Huh," I said, fascinated. "I'll have to remember that about them." If I found the bogle who helped me, I'd reward him with a platter of food, as promised, bought with my newly recovered silver.

I tried to ignore the slaver trussed up on the other side of the fire and put my head on Erick's shoulder. "I may have forgotten to say it earlier ... Thank you."

"Thank you for living," he said, stroking my cheek. Gently, he whispered, "I need you."

I smiled. "You need trouble, do you? I come with a lot of baggage, tagged with the name of 'Thorne'."

"I know, but I'm still here." He kissed me, and, even this far outside fortified city walls, I felt safe.

I snuggled closer, tired enough to fall asleep after all. As I drifted off, I saw Jhenna's burning form, silent and stone-like, and started awake again.

"What is it?"

"Nothing." I shook my head, trying to clear it. "How did you stop her? Jhenna was immune to fire until you came along."

"The means to destroy the Dead God's minions is a simple magic to learn. All it takes is the right knowledge."

"It looked to me like you commanded her to stop, and she did. She obeyed you." I tried to keep the awe I felt out of my voice. Power like that frightened me a little, but I couldn't help being impressed by it.

"There is still consciousness inside them, a soul trapped, but the compulsion driving them makes them do whatever unspeakable things are necessary to reach the god's side. The god is not the only one who can compel, however." He smiled and smoothed my hair. "Sleep."

We reached Highcrowne in a little over four days. It was sunset, the entire mountain above us and the massive stone buildings of the Central City all glowed orange. I was excited when we rode into the Outskirts, ready to fight with the Crowns themselves, whatever it took to see the slaver's dealings stopped.

After we stabled the horse, we dropped the saddlebags, including my strongbox of coins, at Viktor's. The place looked the same as I'd left it—a mess.

Kali ran down the stairs and stopped just short of hugging me. "Jorg and I've been looking for you everywhere. You vanished like Nanny, but I like you. I didn't know what to do." She caught sight of Harald and went quiet, cowed by the presence of her old slave master.

"Don't worry about him. He's not going to be here much longer." I filled Kali in on my adventures over the last week, leaving out many details I wanted to forget. "This isn't over yet," I told her, heading to the front door. "We'll be back soon."

Erick suggested I stay home and rest, but I didn't like those kinds of suggestions. After I put on my one good dress—I know I was stupid. Who I was I trying to impress?—I took hold of Harald, raised my weary chin high, and started walking.

Erick followed with an amused expression. I think he was starting to realize that damsel in distress wasn't my usual state, and I preferred to be in charge.

Before we left the Outskirts, Erick raised his hood and said, "This is where I must take my leave, Darling Eva. I wish you luck with your crusade."

"Where are you going?"

"Not far. I will find you later when the excitement has died down."

"I can't picture my excitement dying anytime soon."

He slipped into the sparse shadows beside the columns of the Light Bringer temple.

I kept walking, Harald trailing behind thanks to a renewed compulsion left on him by Erick, one that placed the slaver under my command. Not that Harald had much fight left in him. After I dealt with him, I'd face Ilsa. She, I was certain, would put up a fight.

I strode up to the Guardhouse in the Goldsmith's Quarter, Conrad's Guardhouse, looking as high class and authoritative as I could. I had to erase his memory of my past idiocy. But Conrad wasn't there. Only dwarves, with their brusque voices and inscrutable, hairy faces, answered when I knocked and told my story.

It started sounding ridiculous, so I kept to the salient points, such as slavers stealing refugees off the streets and shipping them to the front, presumably under the Elf King's orders but against all Highcrowne laws.

"I see," the dwarf captain said. I still hadn't gotten his name, but he remembered me. I could tell by the dubious expression and the arch to his bushy eyebrows that seemed to say, 'Another wild yarn. This woman is crazy.'

I didn't let go of Harald's leash, even as soldiers surrounded us and marched us uphill. I hoped we were headed for the Central City, but they stopped outside the prison in the Market District. I hadn't enjoyed my stay there, but being locked in the wagon with Jhenna had been worse, so my memory of it was almost fond in comparison.

"No," I told the dwarf captain. "This isn't good enough. Didn't you hear me? King Fharen is involved."

The dwarf snorted. I must have really amused him this time.

The gate creaked open before I could come up with a better argument. I recognized the silver-haired mage who had questioned me on my last visit.

"No," I repeated. "You can't trust Harald to an elf."

"Miss Thorne," the elven mage said. "You've changed. I didn't hear you complaining about my race before, and now you seem to have your friend on a leash. As impenetrable as human behavior often is to me, I find that part particularly perplexing."

"This slaver is not my friend. He has a confession to make." While Viktor had been gathering suspicious documents, I had proof positive to offer. I commanded Harald to speak and tell his story again.

The elf cut Harald off before he could finish. "We do not concern ourselves with human affairs."

"This should concern you. It should concern the Elf King himself, since he's been caught out. Maybe you shouldn't have bothered so much with emancipationists when there are far greater problems to deal with."

"Miss Thorne..." he began condescendingly.

"Harald here," I said, yanking the slaver's tether to make him look up, "has been stealing people off the streets and shipping them to Solheim. That is against Avian law. Highcrowne law."

"Miss Thorne, I do not care what he says. A human has no right to accuse a Citizen of anything, let alone a Crown."

I had forgotten I was in Highcrowne.

"What about the law? No new slaves can be created in the Three Kingdoms."

"Ah yes, there is that. We may have to investigate the activities of the Solhan Circle further."

"So, we humans can't testify against a Citizen, but we're still subject to Highcrowne's laws?"

"Yes, that about sums it up." The elf's smile indicated he had no remorse for the obvious inequality.

Their investigation could continue for weeks or months, with the bureaucracy's glacial pace, so I reminded them of a few crucial details.

"You need to send guards after the caravan in the Eastern Pass. They have more illegal slaves there, and in the ships on the river. They must be stopped before they reach the border with Solheim. And don't send a lowly messenger to alert the soldiers at The Wall. Slaves could not have been taken through the pass without the officers there knowing. You need to send someone reliable."

"Of course." The elf mage gestured for his own men to step forward.

The dwarves made a gap, and an elf guard reached for the leather leash I held. I let go—what else could I do? I was surrounded by the Guard. They were supposed to be the good guys.

When Harald was theirs, all I got was a dismissive wave. "You may go now," the elven captain said. "Be assured the Crowns will enforce the law."

"I'll be more assured when I see a few more people on the streets again."

His frown made me wonder how many of those refugees would be diverted down the southern fork of the Serpent's Ribbon and wind up in the war-torn human nations rather than returned to Highcrowne.

I'd been so stupid. Again.

I turned to go but stopped with my back to them. "One more question, Harald." I'd forgotten to ask the slaver everything. I blamed my oversight on exhaustion and not wanting to look at his hated face any more than I had to. "You deny killing Viktor, but what about the private detective I hired, Oberon? Do you blame his death on Jhenna as well?"

"No. I killed him," he said matter of fact. "Oberon recognized some of the refugees we'd branded as slaves, and it was easier to dispose of him. He was only a dwarf."

The dwarf guardsmen grumbled loudly. That would ensure they dealt with the slaver. Seemed Harald was as racist as my uncle. Solhans, elves, humans, dwarves, would none of us ever just get along?

"Goodbye, Harald."

"See you by the Dead God's side," he said, cheerily.

According to some Solhan beliefs, we would all end up serving Him once this life was over. Harald was reminding me how pointless my efforts were: we were going to the same place.

I'd had enough for one day. I wanted to go home, but there was still Nanny.

I asked after Ilsa until the moon was high. I visited all her friends and favorite shops, but not even Morgan had seen her. Maybe she knew something, maybe she didn't, but she'd managed to avoid me very effectively. I would look for her in the morning.

At least, I could show Gypsum my face again, tell her we'd captured the man who killed her brother-in-law, even if it was my fault the detective had gotten involved in the slavers' business to begin with. One mystery solved.

Maybe she would be more inclined to forgive me for abusing her friendship of late? I didn't have a peace offering for Karolyne, but I'd think of something. Showing up for work might be a start.

But I passed by Karolyne's café without going in. I didn't have the strength to face the crowd inside. They were loud and settling in for the evening. I saw merchants and mercenaries through warped glass panes, clustered round the hearth.

As I stepped onto the deserted cobblestone street, oil lamps switched on, thanks to pure and simple

Avian magic. Their orange glow reflected off icicles hanging from the eaves of nearby houses.

Conrad was waiting for me, like he'd been after I was arrested, so quiet the lights hadn't sensed him. I had a moment of déjà vu. He stood straight as a guard fresh out of training, which he really was. I had demanded too much from him.

"Are you all right, Eva?" He took my hands, and they trembled in his strong grip.

"Yeah. I'm sorry about the way I embarrassed you at the docks."

"I'm more ashamed of not believing you. When you were missing, I went crazy, looking all over the city. I feared you were dead."

"I was there to save her." Erick stepped out of the dark and put an arm on my shoulder.

Conrad jumped. I wondered how long he'd been waiting, not realizing Erick was there too.

I stiffened, not enjoying the male posturing. "I'd dealt with Jhenna. I'm sure I could have handled Harald." Irritation always made my tongue get away from me, so I added, "But, I'm glad you came along, Erick."

"I think everyone's forgetting my contribution." Duane smiled as he emerged from the shadows, a different set than the ones Erick must have been hiding in.

Erick started, which made me smile. What goes around comes around: you can't out stealth a master thief.

I didn't feel like crossing swords with Duane now, but I cocked a hip and said, "Just what do you think you did?"

"Mister Adder told me that you'd been taken," Conrad said. "Everyone was looking for you."

"His name isn't Adder," I said automatically. I thought of the fight in the old textile mill and felt a twitch of sympathy for Duane. "Did you find Grim and Gormless?"

Duane nodded. "They were in bad shape. If not for your uncle...."

"They're alive?"

"Yes, Ulric reversed the spell used against them. It was awful before that, terrible." He held out my Ashur and belt pouch. "I found these. I can't believe someone managed to disarm you."

"It has happened from time to time." I looked at the blood dried on the Ashur, outlining the carvings in deep brown, and thought that I wouldn't be disarmed by Jhenna ever again.

Inside the soft leather bag, I found the amulet that led me to Viktor's workshop and revealed the dark magic it seemed no Thorne could escape. After I refastened my belt pouch, I hung the amulet around my neck as a souvenir of my brother and a reminder of where I was headed if I didn't watch myself.

"You disappeared at the docks," I chided Duane. I straightened the amulet on my chest.

"I knew the Guard was incompetent." He didn't care that Conrad was standing right beside him. "So, I searched the ship for Old Nanny myself. She wasn't onboard."

"Then how did Jhenna get her out of the city?"

"Another boat?" Duane suggested. "I've kept up the search, for both of you, but no one has seen her and there is no place she can be. She must have been taken out of the city another way. I will find her, Eva."

I gave a noncommittal nod. I had hoped the Guard would discover Nanny when they seized the ship on the river, but Duane's information dashed that hope. I put my lips against Erick's ear. "We have to find Ilsa and Nanny ourselves."

Duane must have heard my whisper, because he tensed. He had to be peeved by my lack of faith in him—I tried hard to annoy whenever the opportunity arose—but he didn't say anything.

"Tomorrow," Erick whispered back. "I will do whatever it takes to reunite you."

I sighed, weary and aching for a real bed, even if it was the guest room. "You're right."

To Duane, I said, "Tell Grim and Gormless thanks for helping me."

"And me?" He shot me an insouciant smile. Duane was being uncharacteristically flirty, and it made Erick's hand tighten on my shoulder. I was certain baiting Erick was Duane's sole objective. Conrad looked miserable. I thought it best to put an end to the torture all around.

"Thank you. All of you," I said. "But I'm tired. Goodnight." I took Erick's hand and led him toward my house.

I felt the other two watching me, like an itch between my shoulder blades. But, by the time I reached the door and Erick kissed me, I managed to forget all about them.

"I'm used to camping beside you now. I'm not sure I can sleep in a bed alone," I said.

Erick smiled. "I must admit that I cannot bear to leave you alone, not when you are hunted by someone so ruthless."

"Harald is in prison."

"Yes, but someone else wants your heart."

"You're jealous of Conrad? He's a friend."

"I was thinking of the Adder."

"Even more ridiculous." I kissed Erick in such a way he could not doubt my feelings for him. Another crush? I was notorious for them, but I didn't care. "Now, do you want to come inside or not?"

"I could not forgive myself for abandoning you now." He carried me across the obstacle-cluttered floor and up the stairs, kissing me the entire time.

Kali peeked her head out of Little Viktor's old room. "Eva?"

I came up for air. "Hello."

"What did they do to Harald?" she asked.

"Can I tell you the whole story tomorrow?" Erick looked ready to set me down, but I clutched his neck tighter. I wasn't going to let him get away.

"Of course," she said with a knowing look. "See you in the morning." She ducked inside and bolted the door behind her.

Although Erick had managed to evade the fragmented furniture and broken glassware downstairs, he tripped over the clothes scattered on my bedroom floor. The bed caught us both.

There was enough light from the streetlamps filtering through the window for me to see his smile and the glint of desire in his eyes.

"Now," I said, "I've heard that Kells are skilled in the arts of the bedchamber. You once mentioned passing through their land during your travels."

"Yes."

"You pick up any local lore?"

"Some. Shall I show you?"

"Please." My troubles weren't over, but, when Erick looked down at me, I felt happier than I had in a long time.

Hours later, I dozed, satiated. Erick had learned a lot from the Kells, and I was jealous, thinking of the girls he must have met there. How was I going to hold his interest? Still, it seemed I was managing. Every time I opened my eyes, he was looking at me with a faint smile on his lips.

"Shouldn't you sleep?" I asked. "We have work to do in the morning, remember? More detective work."

"I want to fix this moment in my memory. I want to always remember you like this."

"Sleepy and messy haired?"

"Beautiful, happy ... and in love with me."

"You think I'm in love with you?" The arrogance of the man.

"I know you are." He held up a stone. It resembled a raw emerald, but one that glowed with inner fire. More magic. "This tells me what you're feeling."

"Cheater."

"I'm a bad man."

"You're Solhan; you can't help it," I said, only half in jest.

His smile faded. "I mean it. I don't want to do this. Forgive me."

I was still half asleep, but something about his tone made my heart speed up.

"What?"

"Forgive me," he repeated.

Then I noticed he held more than the glowing gem in his hand. There was a vial suspended above me. A silver drop fell as I watched. I was transfixed and didn't move away in time. As soon as the liquid touched my lips, the cold sensation spread across the surface of my skin, encasing me in what felt like solid ice. It was like the privacy potion Erick had used before, except I couldn't say a word or move a muscle. I was paralyzed.

He said, "Time to meet your destiny, Eva."

# 24 BARGAINS

I experienced one of those horrible moments on the edge of sleep where terror flutters in your chest and you want to wake up but can't. I was already awake. The potion Erick gave me trapped me in a nightmarish limbo, where I was aware of the danger and able to think clearly but unable to do anything to save myself.

"Preparations are necessary. Do not fear, Eva. I will return shortly," he whispered into my ear, before quietly exiting the room. It was him returning I feared.

I fought to gain control of my body. I couldn't even open my mouth to cry for help.

The potion hadn't worn off by the time Erick slunk back in, half an hour later. He wrapped me in the blanket from the bed, leaving my face uncovered, and slung me easily over one shoulder. He carried me through the kitchen, down the back stairs and to the alley, where a two-wheeled cart waited.

This must have been how Nanny was taken without anyone hearing or seeing anything. The slavers weren't responsible for her abduction. It had been Erick all along. Was this how he'd removed Viktor's heart without a struggle? Would he do the same to me?

It was after midnight, the streets quiet except for the creak of wood and rustle of cloth as the cart's movement shifted me from side to side. I couldn't see where he was taking me, but it couldn't be far. Erick pulled the cart himself, and I heard his labored breathing as we went uphill. It would be impossible to get me out of the city this way. He was likely only searching for a good spot to leave my body.

Should I have guessed it was Erick? I'd had my suspicions at first, but then again, I'd suspected everybody, and he'd done so much to allay my fears. He hated slavery, and he'd risked his life to set people free. Had it all been a ruse to ingratiate himself with first Viktor and then me? Was I that bad a judge of character? He even saved me from Harald ... because he wanted to kill me himself.

I was stupid, and weak, just as Ilsa said. I'd fallen in love with him. Briefly. Those feelings were well and truly gone now, but they hadn't yet turned to hatred. I hated myself too much to leave room for anything else.

The cart stopped. This was it then: a stupid end to a stupid life. When Erick picked me up, his expression held such pity I couldn't believe he was doing this voluntarily. He could be under some sort of compulsion. I felt a surge of hope. Perhaps he would break free and release me? Perhaps I hadn't misjudged him?

It was false hope. He unlocked a metal door and carried me down a narrow tunnel into a cave excavated from the mountain on which Highcrowne was built. It was a deserted dwarf structure. The place must be structurally unsafe for them to have abandoned such a large chamber. Light from a circle of braziers did not reach the farthest walls.

The first thing I noticed was the heart. It rested inside a white circle painted on the stone floor, magic symbols smeared across the flesh with black charcoal. It looked fresh, but I sensed it was Viktor's.

Erick placed me in another small circle of my own. The white paint was tacky. I felt it against the bare flesh of my leg. I could feel again. The potion was wearing off, but I couldn't move yet. He held out his hand, and a bogle ran out of the shadows carrying a wooden mortar and pestle.

"Here, Master," it said.

The bogles were working with Erick, and not simply as lookouts. It hadn't been luck that a bogle found me in the slaver's wagon. Erick must have ordered it to watch me. He couldn't let anything happen to his human sacrifice.

He took the mortar. "Thank you. You have done well with the preparations." He was always polite.

The bogle rubbed his hands at the praise and backed away. It paused briefly beside the circle containing Viktor's remains. "Must not eat the heart," it muttered, "must not...." It scurried into the shadows.

I slumped like a sack of grain, while Erick smeared the black paste the bogle had brought in the hollow between my breasts, just below the amulet I'd used to track Viktor. The amulet felt hot against my skin with Viktor's living heart so near. It warmed the paste, which stunk of soot and animal fat. At least I hoped it was animal. The symbols he drew were the same as those on the heart.

He bound my hands and feet and tied them to a metal loop anchored into the stone between my knees. I was in a prayer position, legs trapped beneath me, head bowed forward, hands squeezed tightly together. While I gave passing respects to the household gods, I hadn't prayed in years. Probably too late to start.

"Where's Uncle 'Ane?" a child sobbed.

No.

"Little Viktor?" I could speak.

"Eva?" I recognized Nanny's scratchy voice. More surprising than finding her in this dungeon was the fact she'd remembered my name.

I could move my eyes but nothing more. Straining until I was afraid an eyeball would pop out, I finally caught sight of her on the opposite side of the chamber. I sensed Little Viktor somewhere in the darkness to my right, but I couldn't see him, and his sniffles were muffled.

"If Erick hurt you, Vikky...."

"You'll do what?" Nanny asked. "Call the Guard?"

"I shall leave you to your reunion," Erick said. "There is one crucial component missing. When he arrives, we can begin."

"I'm going to kill you, Erick!" That was my voice, but I hadn't said it. I'd been thinking it. Ilsa was here too. She had the same voice as me when she shouted. Wonderful. Weren't things bad enough already?

"You don't mean that, my love." Erick's words made my stomach twist. They sounded so intimate. I suddenly knew he had been with Ilsa as well.

"Farewell, Ladies and Young Gentleman. I will return soon enough." His footsteps echoed over Ilsa's curses. She kept it up until the metal door screeched open and clanged shut again.

Only when Erick was long gone did my twin stop screaming, panting for breath.

"Not so special without your charms," Nanny mocked her.

"You didn't fare any better," Ilsa retorted.

"He's one of the Nine," Nanny said. "We never had a chance."

"Ulric will stop him." I couldn't see her, but I knew Ilsa's nose was in the air. She put a lot of faith in our uncle.

Nanny cackled. "Not with five of us here now. If Ulric is smart, he'll put the world between himself and Erick and leave us to die."

It was becoming clear now. Viktor hadn't been killed because of his activities against the slave trade—he'd died because he was Ulric's nephew. Everyone in this chamber had a connection to my uncle, either through blood, or in Nanny's case, through affection, having raised him from an infant.

This had nothing to do with anything Viktor or I had done and everything to do with being a Thorne.

It took several more minutes for the paralysis to pass. When I could raise my head, I saw Nanny and Ilsa restrained as I was. They were on the opposite side of the chamber from me and Viktor's heart. Little Viktor was between the heart and Ilsa, and he'd been trussed up too. That made me extra angry.

Together, we formed five corners of a large pentagram. The painted circles around us were connected by straight, white lines that intersected in the center of the pentagram. It was a magical arrangement, but I had no clue as to its purpose.

"What does Erick want from us?" I wriggled my wrists, hoping to loosen the fastenings.

"Other than our love?" Nanny asked.

I had a thought that made me cringe. "You and Erick didn't...?"

Nanny cackled again. I wondered if she was enjoying this. A theatrical Solhan sacrifice might be just the way she dreamed of ending her days.

When her hilarity subsided, she said, "No. Only you and Ilsa tumbled into his bed. But we were all fools for him. He used a glamour to convince the child he was Mister Adder come to take him for ice cream. At least that's what I've gathered between sobs."

"Mister Adder? You remember Duane's current street name but forget my real name half the time?"

"Some people are more memorable than others. Like Erick."

"He was charming," I said, defending my earlier stupidity.

"He was ruthless," Ilsa said, admiringly. She must have been shown a different side than I was. "But I can't believe he betrayed me."

Ilsa had stolen another one of my boyfriends. It had always been her favorite summer pastime. She'd swoop in and take any boy I showed the slightest interest in. She must not have known about my old crush on Duane, because he was the only one she stayed away from.

Wait. I'd spent the last five days alone with Erick and only last night did we become intimate. That meant I'd stolen her man for once. One side of my mouth came up in a self-satisfied smirk.

I'd been regretting my weakness of late, wondering what good trying to be good had ever done me. Naively falling for Erick was my crowning ignominy, but Ilsa had the same weakness. She'd fallen for him too. She wasn't any stronger than me. Of course, being in the same boat as my sister—a sinking one—didn't make me feel superior either.

"What part did you have to play in all this, Ilsa?" I knew she was guilty, and I wanted her to admit it.

"Don't try your detective tone with me, Sugar. You're no elf. We're sisters. I know you better than you know yourself."

"I don't know you very well, because Harald the slaver fingered you."

"Like I said, you should stop playing detective. You're not very good at it."

"I learned the Elf King or someone high up in his court was sending instructions through Jhenna and organizing a roundup of refugees and street people by Solhan Circle slavers. I learned those people were sent to the border of Solheim."

"Old news," Ilsa said dismissively. "I've known about that for ages."

"I was afraid of that."

"If only you'd stayed home, Sugar, you wouldn't be so hopelessly in the dark. Jhenna came to see Uncle, but I stepped in and offered to take some responsibility for the family businesses."

"What do they plan to do with the refugees they stole?"

"I don't know and don't care. Simply winning the gratitude of the Elf King will go a long way to getting citizenship for humans."

"Except for the humans you shipped to Solheim."

"For the humans that matter, like Thornes. Real Thornes, I mean. You and Viktor both disowned your heritage."

"Viktor not so much," I said, remembering the shrine to the Devourer I'd found and the abomination he'd created with Emily's soul. I quickly changed the topic. "But you didn't know Erick was freeing slaves, did you? You were surprised to find Kali in my house."

"Viktor's house," Nanny interjected.

"Erick? He'd never ... Of course. I see. His ruse reeled in our poor, naive brother and you. Believe me, he was first and foremost a mage dedicated to Solhan dominance of the Outskirts and Highcrowne itself one day. 'We will need a new Solheim,' he said."

"That's the crap he fed you?" I was truly dismayed by Ilsa's gullibility. "Who could have possibly believed such nonsense?"

"And freeing slaves out of the goodness of his Solhan heart was more believable?"

"Enough," Nanny said. I could suddenly picture the woman who had once dragged Ulric around by his ear and raised generations of ruthless Thornes. "Erick is a liar. All that matters is getting out of here alive."

"Whatever Erick has planned, we have to stop him," I said.

"Oh, we hadn't thought of that." Ilsa snorted, one of the unladylike behaviors she only shared with me. This ordeal was really bringing us together as a family.

I ignored her. "Nanny, what do you know about this ritual? What are these symbols for?" If I understood what was going on, I'd have a better chance of figuring my way out of it.

"It's beyond my ken," Nanny said. "Erick is one of the Nine. Only Ulric would know what he's doing."

"What does that mean?" I asked. "Erick being 'one of the Nine'?"

Ilsa snorted again. "Is this your plan? Will you try talking him to death? Or is it only us you wish to kill with boredom?"

I truly disliked my sister. "Well, Nanny?"

"The Nine ruled Solheim. Few knew their identities, which is why I failed to recognize Erick. When I figured it out, it was too late. The Nine were the most powerful, the most learned. And they summoned Our Lord."

I swallowed. "The Dead God? I knew Solhans brought him, but I never knew who. Erick was responsible?"

"He wasn't the only one."

She hadn't said it, but Ulric had to be one of the Nine. I'd always known my uncle was no shoe peddler.

Everyone in the neighborhood deferred to him—and feared him.

"So, Erick has a score to settle with Uncle?" I guessed.

"Ask Viktor what he thinks." Nanny nodded toward the heart, and another cackle wracked her body. I worried for her sanity.

"Viktor's gone, but we're still here. Well, hopefully not 'here' for much longer." I bent forward and dug my teeth into the thick rope that fastened me to the ground. I'd chew my way out if I had to.

A handful of bogles dropped their camouflage and ran at me, the patter of tiny feet echoing in the chamber. "Stops that!" One jumped on my head and put his hands over my eyes.

"Get off." I shook my head but couldn't dislodge him, even as I kept gnawing at the rope.

Small, leathery fingers pinched my nose shut. More tiny fingers, smelling of rotten vegetables, pulled my lips back. I spit out the foul taste and bent forward again. My teeth hit leathery skin. One had thrown itself across the bindings, blocking my escape with its body.

"Ouch!" the bogle screamed. "Stop biting, or me bites you!"

Nanny laughed.

"We tried that too," Ilsa said. "Keep at it and those filthy creatures will gag you. They won't remove it again until you're starving and agreeable." She seemed to speak from experience.

"I can't picture you ever being agreeable," I said. More awful tasting hands were shoved into my mouth, so I surrendered. "I give up."

The bogles dropped to the ground. The one I'd accidentally bit rubbed at his side and gave me a reproachful look. "I not food. I thought you was nice."

I couldn't tell one creature from another, but I'd only ever spoken to one bogle before. "Are you the one from the wagon?"

"I carried message like you asked ... sort of."

"What does that mean?"

"Nothing." He pressed his ears to the side of his head. I couldn't be sure, but he looked guilty.

"I thought we had a bargain," I said. That made him even more nervous. "You haven't asked for pay-ment. Did Karolyne give you food?" I knew he'd gone to Erick and not to the cafe as I'd asked.

He trembled so violently I thought he'd rattle apart. "You know! I break bargain. Food lady screamed and kicked me then had grall toss me across street."

"It's not your fault." I didn't know why I felt sorry for the creature who was helping to keep me captive, but I did. All he wanted was food. I didn't believe he realized what he was doing.

He struck his small fists against the ground again. "Yeck! You too nice. I lied. Grall threw me different day, when I was spying. I didn't go to your friend at all. I tell Master, and he said he go save you. He forbade me to tell anyone else about you. We have old bargain, but...."

"What?" I pressed.

He was silent.

"What is your bargain with Erick?"

"We obey Master, help him, and he gives us food. But he never said we can't make new bargains. I made bargain with you, but he told me to break bargain. I thinks Master should not have told me that. It was wrong. I'm confused. Which bargain do I obey?"

Yes! A bogle with a moral dilemma. I didn't think they had much in the way of morals, helping Erick do his dirty work, keeping women and children imprisoned for a dark ritual, but they had a personal code. Personal codes often made you do things you didn't think were wise. I knew that only too well, but in this case, I could use it to my advantage.

"You're the one who told me a bargain was serious."

"I know, I know." He wrung his hands.

"But I can see how it would be difficult to disobey your Master. He told you not to go to Karolyne, so you can't do that now, to finish honoring our deal." I didn't want to wait around for a rescue anyway.

"I can't?"

"No. I don't want to get you in trouble, but you gave your word to me also. How about we modify our bargain?"

"Change it?"

"Yes. Instead of sending a message, how about you untie me?"

He blinked. "Master said—"

"—What did he order you to do, exactly?"

"He says we is not to let you break free."

"Perfect. He didn't say you couldn't untie me. I wouldn't have broken free then." I lifted my wrists as far as they would go, indicating he should cut the rope. In the periphery of my vision, I noted Nanny and Ilsa's rapt attention. They were wise enough to keep quiet and not interrupt the negotiations.

The bogle's shriveled red eyes bulged out of their sockets, and he trembled. "I don't know...."

"This is the new bargain," I said. "Otherwise, what happens if you break your word?"

Some of the other bogles watched the exchange, heads swinging back and forth between me and the one with teeth marks on his belly. One of them answered, "He be cursed. He never find food, never find warm place to hide, never make another bargain."

Didn't sound much different from the existence bogles already endured, but the speaker shuddered. Were there worse things than living on garbage and sleeping in slave cages? "Even the Void will turn him out," the creature added.

Bitten Belly put his face in his hands. "Me no break bargain. Me no break...."

The outer door clanged against stone. Erick was back. The bogles scattered into the shadows.

"Kek!" Ilsa cursed. "You should have talked faster, Eva. Now we're lost."

"I didn't see you doing anything," I shot back.

"Well, I don't associate with filth like you do. How was I supposed to know they could be reasoned with?"

Nanny shushed us. "He's coming."

Erick removed his cloak and dropped it. Bogles scurried to catch it, and it took three of them to hold it off the ground. There didn't seem to be anyplace for them to put it, so they stood there waiting like a horizontal, living coat rack.

He smiled, flashing his blue eyes at each of us, though the smile vanished when he looked at me. He couldn't hold my gaze for long. He quickly turned to Nanny. "What have you ladies been discussing, Madam Olinov? I feel my ears burning."

"It's your cols I'd like to see burning," Ilsa said.

Erick winced and made a protective gesture. "You have a nasty imagination, my love."

"I never loved you." She spat. It almost reached him. Who knew a lady of Ilsa's caliber had mastered such a skill?

Erick held up the raw emerald. It didn't glow now, but that's how he'd known my feelings. Ilsa scowled.

"Why is it so important?" I asked. "Why the games? Why not simply murder us as you did Viktor?"

"I did not want to kill Viktor, but he fought...."

Erick stiffened as a high-pitched sound tore through the silence and echoed off the walls of the cavern. This was followed by the disembodied voice of my uncle: "Message received. Let us end this, Asheen Erick."

When the sound had faded, Erick said, "Ulric has answered my challenge." He sounded surprised. He gestured to one of the bogles holding his cloak. It was Bitten Belly. "The blood. Now."

The bogle hesitated to drop his end of the cloak, but he did and scampered into the shadows. He returned with a wineskin. Erick wasn't going to drink blood, was he? I cringed as he un-stoppered the container and held it to his mouth, but he didn't drink. He whispered a few words instead. He went to the center of the pentagram and poured a red circle just large enough to hold one more person.

While Erick worked, I tried to catch the bogle's attention. I wiggled my fingers and raised my eyebrows until he noticed. I pointed my chin at the bindings, reminding him that there was still a bargain being discussed.

Bitten Belly shook his head and trembled, waiting at Erick's elbow for the next command. Coward.

When Erick finished, he tossed the skin at the bogle—who quickly vanished with it—then backed away from the circle he'd made. Erick's retreat brought him closer to me. "It was not a game, Eva. It was necessary."

"And you're sorry." I recalled his body pressed against mine, the soft words in my ear, before he let the drop of potion fall upon my lips. I should stop falling in love, I mean lust, so easily. One of these days it was going to kill me—or today. "You should never have hurt my family."

He looked ready to say something else, but the high-pitched sound returned. Erick snapped his attention back to the red circle. A column of bloody light filled the center of it. It wasn't bright; I could look directly at it, but it was disturbing.

A fever swept over me. Droplets of perspiration covered my skin, and I felt weak, like something was being drained from my veins. The bloody light came from me. Somehow, I was feeding it. When the light vanished, I gasped, feeling some of the strain diminish.

The circle was no longer empty. Ulric stood inside it.

Wow. Teleportation. I'd never seen that before. It would be handy for avoiding Highcrowne's notorious hills. Too bad it required blood sacrifice and evil soul magic, but that explained why it wasn't a common mode of transport.

My uncle slowly looked from Erick to me, to the others, tied and bowed down, and then to the white lines and arcane symbols painted across the floor. A grim expression set across his features, as though he were readying to do truly terrible things. "Asheen Erick, I command you to set them free."

Erick shook his head. "No more commands, Ulric. I have the advantage here."

"Then, you will learn it is unwise to tangle with Thornes," Ulric rumbled, his voice like thunder.

# 25   You Tangled With the Wrong Thorne

efore Ulric's words finished echoing, he raised his hands and pressed against the air around him, making it shimmer and ripple like a heatwave in summer. The line of bright red blood on the floor that encircled him began to boil.

In response, Erick placed one foot on the white line connected to my circle, and I felt a tug on my heart. My pulse increased. The charcoal symbols on my chest writhed like serpents. I panted for breath, sure my chest would crack open from the strain, but Erick stepped away and put a foot on the line extending to Viktor's disembodied heart next. It beat faster. Erick continued around the chamber, playing on Nanny's and Ilsa's lines. Even Little Viktor was not spared; he cried and begged with baby words. Erick was draining us all to fuel his spell.

Nanny's face turned red and sweat poured from her. This would kill her first. I looked at Viktor's heart and wondered if even death would free us. Erick had chained us together, entwined our hearts and souls into a macabre construction. But what was its purpose?

Uncle pulled back from the edge of his invisible cage, and the shimmering air dissipated. "Let me go," he repeated.

"The Nine scattered across the world, but I found three other Asheens. Their power is now mine, and yours will be too," Erick said.

"Is that all this is?" Ulric asked, a derisive note in his voice. "A power-hungry boy looking for comfort in the dark?"

"No, and I do not seek comfort. I do not hide behind walls of Avian magic like you, nor lose myself in the pleasures of Kells like the others. I plan to finish what was started."

"We failed," Ulric told him.

"You failed," Erick said. "We were on the brink and you shied away. The god did not completely cross over."

"I wish I'd stopped it sooner. We thought we could make the Dead God our servant? We were powerful but unwise, Erick. I came to my senses in time to save my soul."

"You shouldn't have bothered, for I have come for it. Freely give yourself to us, and your loved ones will be saved. But you won't, will you? You will force me to consume them to compel the power from you, because you love no one."

"I'm not forcing you to do anything," Ulric said. "Go now and leave us be. I will forgive what you've done."

"I killed your heir. There is no going back and no forgiveness."

While the argument was illuminating, I was less concerned with Erick and Uncle's past disagreements and more concerned with escape in the present, so I began to gnaw on my ropes again.

Bitten Belly appeared beside me. "No."

I glared, and the creature trembled from my practiced menace. "You broke your bargain."

Erick glanced at us, and the bogle vanished with a yelp, quickly blending with stone and darkness.

"There is no going back, so let it be done. Eva!" As Erick said my name, he stepped on the line connected to my circle, and my heart began its frenzied dance again.

Ulric's brow furrowed. He pressed at the invisible barrier that Erick had trapped him with, but the more he fought, the faster my palpitations. I couldn't get enough air. I looked into Erick's sad eyes and knew he would show no mercy. He was a better Solhan than me.

"Stop this," Ulric demanded.

"You're the one who's killing her. Surrender, and she lives."

"I see past your lies," my uncle said. "You desire my power, but you need her soul."

In a few moments, I would be dead and then Erick would move on to the others. I slumped forward, unable to hold myself up anymore.

My hair parted for an invisible form. The bogle was next to my face. I couldn't see him, but I could feel him and hear him. "I no break bargain," he said. He grunted and wiggled in closer. Small claws and dry hands rubbed at the charcoal marks across my breast. "Play dead."

When the symbols were destroyed, I felt my connection to the spell severed. It stopped pulling at my heart and emptying my veins of energy, but I remained flaccid and lifeless looking.

Nanny gasped. At least someone mourned me. Hearing footsteps on stone, I knew Erick now stood near Viktor's heart. My uncle moaned.

"It hurts?" Erick asked. "Good. It hurt Eva more, but her sacrifice was inevitable. She is a part of us now, and I feel your power slipping away, following hers. You will soon be finished, Ulric, whether you surrender or not. Why not spare the child and your remaining niece? Or Madam Olinov at least? The woman nursed you and taught you your first spells. How can you be so ... heartless?"

"You cannot control a god," Uncle argued. "We were arrogant to believe we could. We summoned but a piece of Him, and He nearly destroyed us. I thought it best to close the seal to the Void and sever His power."

"Your indecisiveness is what destroyed Solheim. I am not as hesitant as you." Erick's voice was full of scorn. It was the same tone Ilsa used to criticize my weakness. How could anyone think my uncle weak?

"Even with all the power of the Asheens, even with mine, you will be unable to command Him," Ulric said. "You will fail. And if you bring the god over, He will be unstoppable. There will be no hope of controlling him. Everyone will die."

"You are mistaken. I do not wish to command Him anymore. Why do you think it took me so long to find you? While you and the others ran, I stayed. I kept up my role until the last, as did Lili. The Dead God asked me to be His servant, and I accepted. We all go to Him in the end, why not bring the end for all a little sooner?"

Ulric gasped, but it wasn't in response to Erick's story or the mention of my mother's name. He was in pain. I wanted to know what had happened to my mother and father in Solheim. Were they alive, like Erick? But now was not the time to interrupt.

Why had my uncle allowed himself to be captured? Was he arrogant enough to believe Erick couldn't hurt him? Or had he simply underestimated the necromancer like the rest of us?

My hands shook as the bogle sawed at my bonds with a broken blade. Threads of rope frayed and split apart. I felt numb, a passive observer, and as freedom loomed, I wondered what I could do to stop Erick when had Ulric failed.

"As a servant of Our Lord," Erick continued. "I have seen many things, and I know how futile it is to run. He is coming for everyone. You especially, my old friend."

"Why?" Ulric asked, a hint of hope in his voice. "Why have you hunted down the Nine? Does your lord want revenge for our loss of faith? Or does He fear what we can do?"

"Surrender your soul," Erick insisted, ignoring Ulric's torrent of questions.

My hands were free, and the bogle slipped behind me to work on my ankles. I reached out to brace myself, and my fingers brushed the white circle enclosing me. I felt life within it: Erick's, Ilsa's, everyone connected to the spell ... and mine. That's where it had gone. I needed it back if I was to survive.

I had little knowledge of necromancy. Turned out I didn't need it. Erick had drawn my soul into his cage, but it knew where it belonged, and it trickled back into my body on its own.

I reached out for more, trying to hurry it along, and touched my twin's soul, so similar to mine. I didn't like that we were identical at this level as well, but it made it easy to draw on Ilsa's power. I sensed the darkness in the charms around her neck and wrists, the pent-up energy, but I didn't want that kind of power.

I tugged on her soul through the white lines drawn on the floor, just as Erick had tugged on mine, and she screamed.

Ilsa must have sensed our connection, because when I relented, she glared at me. It didn't matter if she was pissed off. What mattered was that I—the only one loose—be strong enough to face Erick. I had my doubts about that, but at least now I felt whole again. More than whole. With my soul returned and some of Ilsa's thrown in as well, I felt stronger than ever.

The change in the flow of energy did not go unnoticed. Erick's eyes slit with fury.

I wobbled to my feet, the bogle still sawing at the ropes that bound them. I snatched the makeshift dagger from him. It was so tiny I had to hold it between thumb and forefinger, but I made the last cuts quicker than his small hands could manage.

"Stop her," Erick ordered.

More bogles appeared from the shadows and ran toward me. Even Bitten Belly wrapped himself around my ankle in a half-hearted attempt to restrain me. He had to obey his master.

I ignored the small creatures clawing at me and lunged for Viktor's heart. It beat erratically, almost exhausted. I cringed at the feel of the living flesh beneath my fingers, but I stifled my revulsion and threw it into the nearest brazier. It sizzled and pulsed in the flames. Fire would set my brother's soul free and prevent Erick from stealing any more of his power.

"Stop!" Erick sounded desperate.

My uncle threw himself at the magical barrier, taking advantage of the shift in power. The air shimmered, and Erick seemed torn between going after me and stopping Ulric.

He retreated to Ilsa's line, renewing his connection to the spell trap. Ilsa cried out again as her life fed Erick's spell. I had cut into Erick's power source, but he still had more lives left to burn, and he kept Ulric caged.

I threw off a bogle who went for my face and saw Erick pull a charm from his belt pouch as he readied a curse. I went for him with my minuscule blade. He dropped the charm and grabbed my wrist, pushing the weapon away. I tried to twist loose, but he caught my other arm and drew me closer to him.

"Why are you trying to save Ulric? You despise him."

"I hate you more." I kneed him in the groin and slashed with the small blade.

I barely penetrated the clothing, managing only a shallow wound from collarbone to the bottom of his ribs, but it must have hurt, because he hissed and loosened his grip. I tore one of the largest pouches from his belt, scattering the contents across the floor, and stepped back. I'd disarmed him of his ability to cast curses.

I thought he was frightened of another scratch from my blade, because he retreated a few steps, but he wasn't running. He planted both feet on one of the white lines. Potions, charms, and amulets were a fraction of the magic he could wield. Erick reached out a hand, and my heart clenched, as if held in his fist.

"I've touched your soul, Eva. I can call it back to me from anywhere now."

I took an involuntary step toward him, trying to follow the life force he was stealing from me. He was doing it without me being connected to the pentagram on the floor and without the markings on my skin. I was impressed. I hadn't known such a thing was possible. I was getting quite the education today.

I gripped the bogle knife tighter. I wouldn't be able to drive it deep, but some areas were more vulnerable than others. I shuffled toward Erick, trying to look resistant. When I was close enough, I lunged, aiming for the artery in his neck, and put all my weight behind the blow.

Blood everywhere. On my hands, across my face. A red mist and the smell of iron surrounded me.

Erick took a step toward me, and in that step, he transformed from the man I had known into a creature like nothing I had ever seen before. It was shadow and death, and it reached out for me.

"You are mine, Eva," he said, but it was not Erick. It was the voice that had echoed from Jhenna's mouth, the voice of the Dead God.

The creature stretched out a smoke-like arm that grew longer and longer, until it touched the circle of white paint surrounding Little Viktor. The boy screamed.

"No!" I ran to shield him, rubbing out the painted markings with my boot as I did it. "Take me instead."

"You are already mine." The creature wrapped its shadow arms around me so tight I couldn't move.

I squirmed, but the shadow was harder than flesh, harder than steel left in the snow, yet just as cold. I'd never felt so trapped. It was more than physical restraint; it was the presence of the god. It engulfed me, heart, soul and mind. I was lost in it, as though I were in a vast, dark room, feeling about for something I recognized.

Then I smelled cinnamon. It was like fire in the night. One of my oldest memories was the scent of cinnamon smoke, incense like that used in the temples. I moved toward the aroma. I knew I was still in the dungeon with my family, still caught in the shadow creature's arms, but my mind was elsewhere and trying to escape a strange new prison.

The darkness was so thick it had never known light. Was this the Void? Was this death? It was empty and went on forever. I breathed in cinnamon, letting its sweetness fill me and push back the cold. Only the cinnamon made me know I was alive. Or was I? Had the creature's touch killed me in an instant?

"No. You are alive," a rich voice said. It was masculine and reminded me of the cinnamon, warming and full of excitement. I still couldn't see, but arms enfolded me, a man's arms.

"Erick?" I asked.

"No." Lips found mine, and they knew me better than Erick's ever could.

I was drawn into the kiss, pulled so sweetly away from the darkness and deeper into clouds of cinnamon smoke. The tingle of it seemed to coil beneath my skin, pulling at me, making me long to be in this moment forever.

"Come to me," the man said.

"I am with you," I answered, as I would in a dream.

This had to be a dream with its strange logic. I wouldn't normally kiss an unknown man in the dark. Well, probably not. There was something familiar and alluring about him. Maybe I'd dreamt him before? His voice sounded like long-lost memory.

"It is beautiful, here. If you only knew." With that, he breathed out more cinnamon smoke. It glowed, first gray and then amber.

Smoke billowed, growing larger and larger until I saw shapes moving within. People danced. Laughs filled a high chamber and echoed off marble walls. I was there with them, surrounded by ethereal shapes like the shadows of people just out of reach.

As the images cleared, I saw beautiful young couples smiling at one another, a little girl twirling in a new dress, an old couple whispering lovingly into each other's ears. They all had white skin and pale eyes. They were all Solhan.

"Where is this?" I asked. The man was still invisible to me, hidden in the darkness that lurked at the edge of the vision.

"Solheim, of course."

"Solheim is a ruin. Everyone's dead."

"You know nothing of death. But I will teach you. Touch their souls."

Now that I knew what I was seeing, I felt them. Souls. There were vast legions trapped in Solheim. The darkness was filled with them and not empty at all.

A face appeared in the smoke just inches from me: Jhenna. She hissed, her clothes on fire. Erick stood beside her, blood still spraying from his neck.

I gasped and took a step back.

"Forget them." The man's arms held me tight. "You were promised to me, and their ghosts cannot claim vengeance. You are mine." His voice became the cold, distant susurration of the Dead God.

Suddenly, I was back in the dungeon, and it was the shadow creature who had me in its arms, its cold lips next to mine.

I wanted to ignore the image it had shown me of Solheim and its ghostly denizens, call it a mere dream, but I knew it spoke truth. I felt a pull toward that place that could only be called longing. Aching.

The cinnamon darkness that was the Dead God touched me again, and I felt that touch stretching all the way to far off Solheim and the legion of souls contained there. But it was a connection that went both ways.

I pulled back.

It wasn't like holding something with my hands; more a connection to the center of my chest, as though an invisible rope were tied around my sternum. With each heartbeat, the connection throbbed. There were other, smaller, frayed lines hanging from the main rope, connecting me to Nanny, Little Viktor, Ulric, Ilsa.... Strands stretching everywhere to everyone I knew.

Sharpest was the strand connected to Erick. Not the shadow creature standing in his place, but Erick's soul, which had fled his body after my knife found his neck. Because I'd taken his life, the connection was strong.

I focused on that strand, instead of the main rope connected to the god. I imagined 'pulling' on the frayed thread of Erick's life, and I felt him draw closer. Soon, he was within the chamber with us. I tugged again, and his soul merged with the shadow creature, which still held me in its chill grasp.

The shadow's white, Solhan-like eyes widened in surprise. I tugged harder, and suddenly the eyes changed to pale blue—Erick's eyes.

"Eva," Erick's voice said, replacing the distant echo of the god's.

The shadow demon vanished, leaving only Erick behind. He crumpled, dead eyes staring sightless into the depths of the cave above us. But I felt a spark within him. The soul I had found in Solheim was now trapped in the flesh.

Erick's soul was still mine to play with. I had its thread so tightly in my grasp, I knew I could take his power, including all the power he had stolen from the other Asheens, and bend it to my will. Of course, I hadn't a clue what to do with it. Ilsa would know. As would Ulric. I'm sure they had dreams of glory, while my dreams were filled with the cinnamon god and forgotten in the morning.

I never realized how alluring holding power over a soul could be, but I didn't want power. I didn't want to go to Solheim, dead or alive. I didn't want the god to have me, and He would if I stepped down that path. I knew it.

I let go of Erick's soul and allowed it to rest inside his corpse. The thread stretching from me to him suddenly grew bright green and then vanished.

I didn't know what the others had seen when the shadow held me, but they must have seen me let go of the connection to Erick, because Ilsa and Nanny gasped.

I stepped over to the blood circle that imprisoned my uncle and wiped across it with my fingertip. The circle stayed intact, but blood stained my finger. Somehow, I knew it was Erick's: The blood of an Asheen to contain another Asheen. I knew enough from watching Nanny perform her spells when I was growing up that a blood circle formed by another couldn't be broken unless you made it your own. This was going to be gross.

I smeared the blood across my lips, washing away the taste of cinnamon—and licked. As soon as I swallowed the iron tasting blood, the remainder of Uncle's circle boiled away, adding another layer to the scent of death in the air.

Ulric was free. He checked Erick's body, noted my blood-smeared face, and then nodded with approval.

I cut Little Viktor loose with the bogle knife and held him tight. He was fast asleep but breathing. I hoped he passed out before seeing what I did to Erick, or the shadow of the Dead God inhabiting him.

I wished no one had seen that creature, which was like my most intimate secrets exposed. I wanted to pretend I had not felt what I felt or seen what I'd seen when connected to Him. Ignoring it all helped the pull of Solheim fade. A nightmare forgotten.

I gently laid Vikky on the floor and then freed my sister.

"Give it back," she said, her tone frigid and her glare as good as mine, if not better. She was referring to the part of her soul I'd taken.

"I don't know how."

She was gaunt and hollow-eyed, her skin pasty. Apparently, the soul had influence over the health of the body. I was learning more about necromancy than I ever wanted to. I was willing to learn more, if it meant finding a way to give Ilsa her soul back. I didn't want her taint inside me.

"Do you know how to fix this?" I asked, wary.

"You can steal another's soul to empower your own—when you kill them." I didn't like how she looked at me.

"Well, I'm not opening a vein for you. I'll find another way." Ulric had to know what to do, and he seemed pleased enough with me now to help, but I didn't relish talking to him.

I'd rescued my uncle—and Ilsa. How had that happened?

The metal door at the exit clanged open, and I whirled in time to see wide-eyed bogles scurry for the shadows. They were fast. White armor came into view: Conrad. The company had improved. Slightly.

Duane was with him. He nodded to acknowledge my uncle, and then stopped to check Erick for any sign of life. He wouldn't have gone near if he'd seen Erick's earlier form. A smile turned up the edges of his mouth, but then he gave me a disapproving look. Duane must know I was the one responsible; I was covered in blood. I had thought he'd be pleased: I was a killer like him now. Maybe it was the ritualistic way of it he didn't like? The symbols painted across the floor were a sure sign this was nothing like his street war.

I could picture Duane and Bell discussing me, clucking their tongues and saying, "We knew it. She was destined for that dark, evil necromancy stuff."

"Are you all right?" Conrad asked. I was unsure how long I'd been staring past him.

"I am," Ilsa cut in.

Conrad did a double take when he saw her.

"My sister," I explained.

Ilsa had a glorious smile when she used it, despite her now pasty complexion. "Hello there."

Conrad wasn't my boyfriend, but she was already showing an interest. Not good. Although, this did mean she would act charming and behave like a decent human being while the guardsman was around.

Uncle untied Nanny. She was limp, splayed on the ground. Erick must have drained her more severely than I thought.

"Nanny?" I went to her and took her hand. "Can you hear me?"

Her yellow-tinged eyes registered the crowd leaning over her, and she frowned. "All alive I see. Even you, Ilsa."

"It's Eva," I corrected automatically. "She's okay," I announced, not sounding as relieved as I felt. To admit affection for Nanny would be to admit weakness, and the old woman would not hesitate to use it against me in future.

Nanny sat up, swatting my hands aside when I tried to help. She looked Conrad up and down. "What's a human doing dressed as a guardsman?"

"He is a guardsman," I said.

"Well, where was he when we needed him?"

"Conrad has helped more than you know."

"Kali did not see you rise in the morning, Eva," Conrad said. "I went to the docks to discover whether you'd hired a boat, but...."

"Long story short," Duane interrupted, "this fool was wandering around like a lost hatchling when I ran into him. One of my lookouts saw a wagon leaving Viktor's house last night. We tracked it to this cavern." He glanced at Erick's corpse. "I never liked him."

"I did," I said.

"It is best we burn the body soon," Uncle told us. "The god will desire such a powerful servant returned to his side. Can you make the arrangements?"

Duane nodded and backed toward the door, giving me one last accusing look before departing.

I was worried too. What had I done? I'd murdered two people, kissed the God of Death and ripped a soul from His grasp. I was going deeper into the black than Duane or anyone had ever taken me. All by myself.

# Epilogue

The funeral pyre blackened the white sky and scattered ash on the snow around us. My uncle's normally severe expression relaxed briefly when the last of Erick was dust.

Had Ulric known someone would come calling from old Solheim, asking him to pay for past sins? Had he lived in fear? I wondered about my uncle, but it was like the fascination one had with an ice viper, trying to understand how such a creature functioned. I didn't sympathize with either one.

A crowd gathered for the cremation. There were always spectators at human funerals, some hoping to see a body burnt too late to rise. I never wanted to see it again.

Soot-covered workers used long, iron poles to contain the embers as they collapsed. Forests had been cut down to tend our dead. Refugees usually huddled nearby, stealing heat from the pyre. I'd always ignored them before, but now that they were gone, I felt their absence.

While Duane had been arranging the funeral, Conrad and I had checked in with the elven captain at the Market Guardhouse. I wanted to know what was happening with the enslaved refugees. I saw no reason to tell him I had found my brother's murderer, or that I had killed him. The elf wouldn't care, and it was safer if he didn't know my uncle was one of the Nine.

Even after so many years, those directly responsible for the Dead God's rise would be hunted down if anyone knew who they were. There was no law to cover summoning a god, but plenty would want retribution, and the Crowns would mete it out. I couldn't condemn my uncle to death, and the Thorne name didn't need to be marred any further.

The elf guardsman would not tell me what had been done with Harald. I asked if Randall had been arrested at least, and I learned he'd been cleared of the charges under torture.

"What?" I'd asked.

"He knew nothing about the other slavers' activities, and my spells confirmed it. We let him go," the captain said.

I was incredulous. All those slaves could not have been shipped to Solheim without Randall's involvement. The elf was disinclined to listen to my epithets, however, so I was escorted out of the Guard-house and asked, once again, not to bother him with human business in future. There was no mention of the refugees on the boats. The authorities hoped the whole affair would soon be forgotten.

Conrad kept me from doing something I would have been arrested for. When we reached the street, he let go of my shoulders, and I punched a wall in frustration. My knuckles bled.

"This isn't over," Conrad said. "I will discover what became of those people. But for now, I must report to my unit or be expelled from the Guard."

Still angry at the elf captain, I couldn't stop frowning. "No. I'll find out what happened to the refugees."

"I'm not leaving this alone either," he promised, before hurrying off to his posting in the Red Precinct.

There was nothing to gain by turning Ilsa in. Her crime was stupidity—with evil intent. She liked to think she had orchestrated the enslavement of the refugees, but it was all the Elf King's doing. She was a pawn.

I looked at her now from across Erick's pyre. She seemed none the worse for wear. While Conrad and I had been talking to the Guard, she'd bathed and changed clothes. Her purple dress had a matching coat and was set off by white, diamond-studded gloves. It was easy to see where her priorities lay.

What bothered me was there was no sign of the hollows under her eyes or the pasty complexion she'd had earlier. What had she done?

She seemed to regret nothing and had gone back to business as usual. I thought that included ignoring me, but I caught her looking my way with a predatory gleam in her eye.

I'd replaced Little Viktor at the top of her blacklist. She wanted the rest of her soul back, no matter what she must have done before the funeral to 'replenish' herself already. What was I doing, thinking in euphemisms? If sweet little me could be a murderer, Ilsa had to have done far worse.

I noted Randall, battered from his interrogation, watching from the edge of the crowd. At least the elf captain had interrogated him. Part of me thought the elf had been lying. I was getting cynical.

I wanted a few harsh words with Randall myself. I needed to learn everything he knew about the deal between the Elf King and the Solhan Circle. As much as Randall disgusted me, it would be easier to question him than Ilsa. I took a step in his direction, but a hand pressed on my shoulder.

"Eva," my uncle said.

I twitched out of his grip and gave Randall a glare before I said, "What?"

"In the cave, you did not hesitate to do what must be done, and you showed the strength I've known all along you possessed."

"I don't want your praise." I was disgusted by it.

"Very well." Ulric took his hand away. "Still, I can help you. I have much to teach. Come by the house later."

"No." I might go there to see Little Viktor, but never for him. Randall was inching away, and I was impatient to go after him.

Ulric touched my shoulder again, and for a moment I was paralyzed. Magic, without charms or a word uttered. Better than Erick. "You will come," he commanded.

The paralysis didn't last long, but when I could move, Ulric was across the square. Randall fell into step behind him, the slaver giving me a knowing smile that made me want to punch something again.

All the time I'd been looking for Viktor's killers, I'd merely been disrupting Uncle's business. That's why he left me in jail, certain the slavers, who he controlled, would testify on my behalf. I bet Ulric had used magic to guarantee Randall's silence when questioned by the Guard. I bet everyone in his employ was so bound by magical compulsion they had no choice but to obey him.

Not me. Whatever spell he'd just tried to cast hadn't worked. I wouldn't be visiting my uncle's house any time soon. I never wanted to see him again.

In the days following the funeral, I questioned everyone I knew and they knew about the slavers' ships. I made a stop at every Guardhouse in every precinct humans had access to, generally causing trouble and doing what I could to give the enslaved refugees a voice. I pestered Gypsum and Sir Markham endlessly, and they promised to do all they could.

The extra energy I stole from Ilsa helped, but I could only do so much before my body gave out. I eventually went home to Viktor's and collapsed, exhausted.

I slept a whole day. When I woke, my frantic, guilty urgency had passed, and I'd resigned myself to the long road ahead. First priority was the boats, but the bigger problem was the unjust treatment of humans ... and the war of course. I felt so small compared to that.

Yet, the Dead God had known me. And, somehow, I'd known Him.

I was at Viktor's. My home now, I reminded myself. I felt the cold amulet around my neck. There was no trace of my brother anymore.

Nanny was resting in her bed, well not resting, since she was screeching at Kali.

"Bring me a warm rag this time, you cur!" The old woman tossed the washcloth she'd used to wipe her face into the bowl on the nightstand. "You have to put the water over the fire to boil it. You do know how to make fire?"

"Why did you rescue her?" Kali asked me.

"Sorry. I can take care of this." I reached for the cloth, but Kali tore it away from me.

"No, the kitchen is the opposite end of the house, and I'll wait there as long as it takes for the water to boil. I think the fire needs fuel. It may take a while."

When Nanny and I were alone, the old woman smiled and patted the bed beside her. I got goosebumps. Had she seen Viktor's shade? Was that what she was smiling at? She gestured again. "Sit beside me, Eva."

Nanny with a kind face and soothing voice? This was the most definitive evidence I'd had of her senility.

"Are you okay?" I asked.

"You're a woman now. There are things you should know."

She wasn't going to try to tell me about sex, was she? That talk was a few years too late. "I've been a woman for a while, and I know about men."

Nanny chuckled. It was healthier sounding than the mad cackle that had seized her in the cave. "I mean you're a Solhan woman. Adulthood is not recognized, your life is not respected, until you take the life of an enemy.”

“What are you talking about?”

“It’s our custom, but it is never spoken of with children or to outsiders. While it’s good to have enemies, Solhans have enough don’t you think? No need to make others fear us more.”

I feared us. “You mean you’re being kind to me because of what I did to Erick?”

She frowned. “I’ve always liked you, Eva, even though you look like *her*. I’m trying to fulfil my duty as an elder. I must give you formal recognition with this.” She spread her fingers, revealing a small scar in the shape of a star in the webbing between her thumb and forefinger.

“I’ve seen that mark before,” I said. “It means they all...?” I was surrounded by death. I felt it suffocating me. Just about every Solhan I’d ever known had that scar—even Viktor. Ilsa had it when we were children. I shuddered. No one told me what it meant.

“Bring me my bag from beside the mirror.”

Stunned, I recovered enough volition to obey. She retrieved a silver knife from the leather bag. It reminded me of the one I got from the bogle, but this weapon was finely crafted, polished to a brilliant sheen, and sharp.

“Give me your hand.”

“Erick wasn’t the first,” I said. “I killed Jhenna too.”

"You only get one mark." She smiled, like I was a child asking for extra sweets.

"I never wanted either of them to die. It was necessary. I didn't want it."

"We all want our enemies to die, whether we admit it or not. It's a good thing. It is good to be the one who survives."

"No." I hid my hands behind me. "I don't want a trophy."

Nanny scowled, but I turned my back on her and went downstairs to help Kali.

Later, I walked to Karolyne's unmolested. The Solhan Circle business had made its way into the gossip whispered on street corners. More people said hello to me. Even the head priest of the Light Bringer temple and his wife smiled on their way to the funeral grounds. While the details were unclear, people knew Erick was Viktor's murderer. In the court of public opinion, I'd been exonerated.

In my own mind, I knew better. While Jhenna and Erick had been self-defense, and no merchant magistrate would hang me for killing them, no one knew how much I'd enjoyed it. I'd touched their souls. Power called to me. All the lost souls in Solheim, in the Void itself, called like the endless, crashing thunder of ocean waves.

I longed for one more cinnamon kiss.

I fought my desires until they faded. And distractions helped. I wanted to forget about my conversation with Nanny, about Ulric and Ilsa's schemes, about Erick. I went to Karolyne's intending to find normality, to go back to the way things were before.

I hadn't seen Karo at Erick's funeral. Conrad had told her everything, how I'd found justice, but she wasn't the sort to leave work for any reason. She'd even taken to sleeping on a pallet in the office. I'd worried about my obsession over Viktor's murder, but Karolyne had problems of her own.

"I'm back," I said, throwing out my arms and making a grand entrance.

Jorg was tossing a salad in the kitchen. He waved with a set of tongs made of small shovels. They looked mostly clean. "Eva!"

I didn't recognize the dwarf behind the bar. Another one of Gypsum's troublesome relatives perhaps?

Karolyne's hands were full of dirty dishes. She swung by on her way to the kitchen. "What are you doing here?"

"I work here."

"Not anymore."

"But ... I was kidnapped. There was a risen corpse, a fight with mages, more kidnapping.... You can't fire me."

"I can't afford to pay you and Gypsum's cousin too." She indicated the dwarf spiking a cup of kaffe with brandy. Karolyne had decided to mix her two most potent drinks into an even more addictive combination.

"But I was here first."

"Well, he's here more often." Her features softened. "Sorry, Eva. You must have realized this wasn't working out. Sit down and Bert will give you a drink on the house."

That was my severance pay? A drink that was likely to keep me coming back for more? Sometimes, I wondered about our friendship. I didn't blame her for firing me—I was a terrible employee—but she could have done it with more sensitivity. Of course, sensitivity wasn't my specialty either.

"Fine." I sighed and slumped into an empty seat. I put my chin on my hand and took a few minutes to indulge in feeling sorry for myself. The new server, Bert, came by with my drink.

"You look like you can use this," he said.

"I could use my old job more."

He patted my shoulder sympathetically. "I've only worked here a few days, but you're probably better off finding something else. I'd move on too, but Gypsum isn't giving me a choice. She says I need to learn about hard work. It's better than the mines at least."

"You *have* only been here a few days then." I smiled wanly. "I'll be okay. It's not your fault. Thanks for the kaffe."

"I don't think you can call it that anymore."

I took a sip and felt it burn down my throat and eat a hole in my stomach. He was right.

I leaned back in my chair and enjoyed being a customer. I'd recovered my silver from the slaver's wagon, plus a bit extra. Jorg was self-sufficient—he even paid a few coins rent for the basement—so I only had Kali and Nanny to take care of. I'd be all right, if I didn't do anything stupid with my money again. There weren't any slaves in Highcrowne left to buy anyway.

Why did I feel like such a failure then?

I paid for my next, fortified kaffe, enjoying the way the room began to sway around me. It also eased the lingering pain in my shins from too much walking up and down hills, which was a bonus.

A few hours later, Gypsum found me sloppy drunk. She put her hands on her hips and clucked in the disapproving way only dwarven mothers could. A small swarm of her offspring buzzed around me, but my senses were so sluggish, I barely saw them.

"How could you let her get like this?" Was Gypsum talking to me?

"She's a grown woman. I can't keep her from doing anything." Karolyne clanked some cutlery loudly against a plate and slipped away.

"Bert," Gypsum said, "get Eva some plain kaffe. Now."

When the strong, sugarless drink had jolted me into full consciousness, Gypsum's disapproving expression came into focus.

"Are you still mad about the docks?" I asked. "Sir Markham backed up Conrad, and then I embarrassed them both, and you. I'm sorry."

"Pish posh." Gypsum waved away my apology. "It's the government who's embarrassed. Someone must have known refugees were being taken off the streets, but they looked the other way. When you rubbed their noses in it, there were a lot of red faces around the palace, believe me."

"It's a human problem, I was told. They're not going to help those people." I felt as bitter as the taste on my tongue at that moment.

"I may not be one of the courtiers with direct access to the Crowns, but, for one of such lowly birth as me, I can be a nuisance."

"Your mother was a baroness or something," I said. Gypsum was hardly as low born as she behaved.

"My sister got the title." She squeezed my cheek when my eyes began to droop. "Pay attention now. The point is, something is being done. Those ships were intercepted, and after a brief detour south, they were pointed in the right direction. Those people will be back. They'll be home soon."

"They're saved?" I felt lighter.

"Yes. More than that, your information was deemed invaluable, and the government saw fit to give you a reward." She held out a small bag embroidered with silver thread. "There won't be any sort of formal presentation or anything. And no one is mentioning Fharen's name, so you shouldn't say anything more about the Elf King either. Those kinds of accusations will get you into trouble. But they told me to pass this along."

Open mouthed, I took the bag, and a quick peek inside revealed ten gold coins. Whoever 'they' were they were rich. This was a fortune. The freshly minted shine suggested they came straight from the Crowns Treasury, a payoff to keep me quiet. It was never going to work. I almost handed the bag back to Gypsum but stopped. That would be stupid. I could cause more trouble with their money, so I stuffed the pouch down my bodice.

With this I could afford to buy a new jacket. Some coal for all the stoves in the house would be helpful too. Oh, and some proper furnishings for Jorg's room.... Staggering drunk or not, I had to get this to the Merchant's Bank before it closed. The bank would keep me from spending it all on useless baubles. I was bad with money.

"This too." Gypsum handed me a downy feather.

I raised an eyebrow as I took it.

"From the Avians. The writing on the shaft says 'Truthspeaker' and 'Protector of Hatchlings' I think. I don't read Avian well, so don't ask me what it means. It came with the gold," she said.

Maybe it was Avian currency? I'd heard they valued funny shaped sticks and other odd things. It was elves and dwarfs who insisted Highcrowne have a coin system. 'Truthspeaker' didn't sound too good though. Could mean a black mark on my record, or more trouble. Still, I tucked it away with the gold.

"Thank you, Gypsum. But why the reward? I didn't do anything."

"That's not what Conrad told Markham. He relayed the whole story as he understood it. You uncovered an agent of the Dead God and risked your life in the process. Your investigation illustrated how blind and stupid the Guard has become. More reforms are in the works."

"Wonderful!" Karolyne had been listening in. "I hope that means a promotion for Conrad. If anyone deserves...." She was off serving the next table, not even waiting to finish her comment.

I felt a surge of joy so strong I gave Gypsum a hug. I wasn't usually so demonstrative, and she blanched. "What was that for?"

"Giving me my first good day in a long while." I'd stopped the slavers, helped people, and I'd found Viktor's killer. The last bit was the only thing that gave me mixed feelings. In the process, I'd become a killer myself—and a good Solhan.

But Gypsum's words made me feel I'd done something right. I wasn't worthless. I'd figured out what was going on when no one else had, I'd faced death, and now I'd been paid for it. Butting my nose in where it didn't belong came natural. Maybe I could make a living out of it?

*Maybe Stanley the elf detective wants a partner?* I smiled to myself. *Ah hell, what did I need him for?*

A few weeks later, I fastened a new sign on the metal pole overhanging Viktor's shop. It read: *Kali's Books & Thorne Investigations (enquire within)*

Kali nodded approvingly. She still couldn't read the sign, but we were working on that. She learned quickly, and, using the symbols in Viktor's ledgers, she had already managed to operate the shop on her own for weeks. She was enamored with the leather-bound volumes and vellum scrolls. I was glad Viktor's work would continue.

I only wished I'd learned how to remove slave marks, so his secret work could have continued as well.

The mercantile life wasn't for me. I was glad to let Kali manage the shop. She enjoyed it. As for me, I preferred to lounge behind my desk and wait for someone to come in with a problem. Kali would have to tell them to find me at Karolyne's—because my desk was a table close to the kaffe. The normal kind. After recovering from a two-day hangover, I wasn't touching the spiked form ever again. I could have worked from the bookshop, but Nanny, who was all alone in the house, tended to visit every hour for a screeching match with Kali. It was quieter elsewhere.

I headed for Karolyne's but glanced back and saw Nanny's sour face peeking from an upper window. She let the curtain slide back, and I got a chill. She had been upset ever since I refused to accept the star-shaped mark between my fingers. She grumbled about ingratitude, forsaking tradition, being a traitor to my people, etcetera. That was another reason I hid at the cafe.

Also, being near Nanny's household spells and charms gave me a strange tingle in my hands. Even this far away, I could feel her doing some minor necromancy, and my hands glowed with sympathetic green light, like they were trying to join in on their own. The taint of Ilsa most likely.

Of course, it could be my own magic. The 'potential' Uncle Ulric was always talking about. It didn't matter. Ignoring everything I didn't like worked most days. I clenched my hands into fists to smother the glow and kept walking.

I ran into Conrad going the other way.

"Hi." I blushed. Since he was no longer working double shifts to deal with my problems, Conrad had time to get his beauty sleep, and it had done its job. He was gorgeous.

"I like the new sign," he said.

"Thanks. What are you doing here?"

"I wanted to buy a book. And ask if you wanted to do something sometime?"

"Besides track down missing people and slavers?"

"Exactly. I'd like to ... be friends."

"Buy your book. I'll be at Karolyne's having kaffe if you want some."

He looked at the bookshop, clearly reluctant. The shopping excursion was obviously an excuse to ask me on a date, but he wouldn't admit it. "Right. I'll see you there."

I smiled as he went over. Kali stood tautly behind the counter, poised to pounce on her new customer as soon as he stepped inside. I'd leave the big strong guardsman to get out of this one himself.

I crossed the street and dropped a coin into the bowl held out by a beggar. There was a whole family of refugees crouched in the alley behind him. He must be the bread winner. I added a few more coins. "What's your name?" I asked.

He seemed surprised by my direct look. "Henry, My Lady."

"I'm not a lady. Is this your family?" I let him introduce his wife and two daughters. I tickled the toes of the infant boy. They slowly relaxed in my presence, and I tried to remember their faces. Every single one.

I spotted Grim and Gormless. Spotting them was usually an accomplishment, but they weren't hiding. They'd recovered from the flesh-eating curse and were back to being imposing. Gormless smiled, and I smiled back.

Duane dropped from his perch on a second story landing. I jumped and quickly tried to cover my surprise. I hadn't known he was there. He flashed mischievous green eyes my way and took out a few apples from the bag he held. He juggled them, managing six pieces of fruit with fluid grace. It irked me that he looked good whenever he did anything.

Refugee girls darted out to watch. They giggled as he threw an apple to each of them. He tossed a few more behind his back, then caught them in the burlap bag. He bowed and gave the sack to the girls.

"Thank you, Mister Adder," they said before running back to their parents.

The bell over the bookshop door rang. Conrad was back. He and Duane glared at each other across the street.

I put a hand to my mouth to smother my grin. Their competitive antics helped me forget about blood circles and cinnamon dreams. I needed all the help I could to forget.

I strutted down the cobblestoned road, headed for Karolyne's, swinging my Ashur and my hips. I walked a little more sexily than normal, but I couldn't resist.

I'd righted wrongs, rescued the girl—even if she had been Old Nanny—and got paid. It felt good. I felt alive and capable of staying that way. For now. There was nothing more I could ask for.

I glanced back. Duane and Conrad watched me walk. Except ... it would be safer if I could stop falling in love.

Until Next Time...

Eva's story continues in Book 2, *A Thorne for a Crown*, available now.

Did you enjoy this book? Please take a moment to leave a review. What you say will determine whether someone else takes the plunge into Eva's world, so please ask them to dive headfirst. Thank you!

Join our mailing list at lorelclayton.com to get a free Eva Thorne novella, short stories, and other book deals.

# ABOUT THE AUTHORS

Lorel and Clayton were teen sweethearts, brought together by a fierce love of books (and hormones). Despite being married for 30 years, they are still madly in love and still writing. As writing partners, they meld logic, creativity, and genres. Fantasy, science-fiction, mystery, horror, steampunk, thrillers, the classics ...

they read them all, and if they can mix them, they will!

Still reading? Want to know more?

Lorel has a PhD in molecular biology and Once Upon a Time did cancer research before turning to the dark side (aka marketing), but she uses her powers for good, helping to raise funds for charity. She loves books, movies and animals, and would gladly spend all day with a cat on her lap and the wind in her hair (Conan reference there), while tapping out a story on her keyboard. Or maybe a movie script. With coffee of course. And lots of chocolate!

Clayton is an artist and has recently tackled digital painting, mostly because there's a hyperactive eight-year-old boy running around the house (their gorgeous son, in case you were wondering if that's normal). Clayton is severely dyslexic but loves books and story-telling. He adds vast imagination and a discerning ear for effective prose to their creative collaboration, not to mention the book cover art.

Born and raised in the western United States, they traveled to Sydney, Australia in 1997 and never left, finding the sunshine and beaches of "Oz" too irresistible. Look them up if ever you're Down Under.

• 407 •

## Connect with Lorel Clayton

Website: http://www.lorelclayton.com/
Twitter: https://twitter.com/lorelclayton
Facebook: www.facebook.com/AuthorLorelClayton/

www.ingramcontent.com/pod-product-compliance
Lightning Source LLC
Chambersburg PA
CBHW030648120726
47905CB00001B/110